AF472252

A Matter of Loyalty

Gail Logan

A MATTER OF LOYALTY

This is a work of fiction. All of the characters, names, incidents, organizations, and dialogue in this novel are either the products of the author's imagination or are used fictitiously.

iUniverse books may be ordered through booksellers or by contacting:

iUniverse
1663 Liberty Drive
Bloomington, IN 47403
www.iuniverse.com
1-800-Authors (1-800-288-4677)

ISBN: 978-1-4917-5094-0 (sc)
ISBN: 978-1-4917-5095-7 (e)

Library of Congress Control Number: 2014918970

Print information available on the last page.

iUniverse rev. date: 10/29/2014

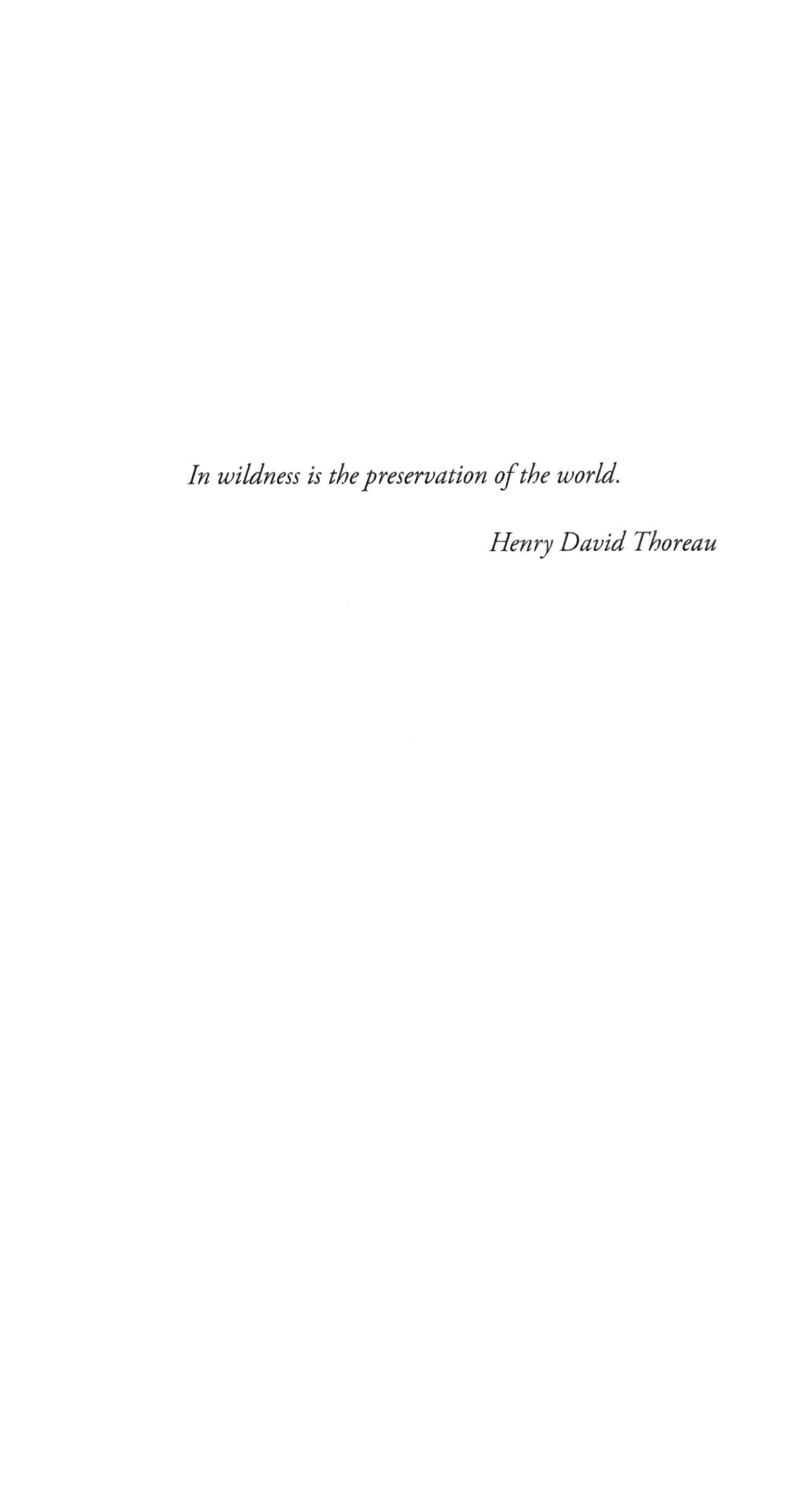

In wildness is the preservation of the world.

Henry David Thoreau

Chapter One

A rather thin, mysterious looking young man in his mid twenties pulled his cloak tightly to himself and shivered in the bitingly cold mid afternoon air. He dropped the hood from the cloak and quietly watched unseen as the women behind the fence took their daily walk in a garden. The Perm house where they'd been imprisoned since the summer of 1918 was in a rather remote location and not far from the Ural Mountains. It was now early December. The world believed them dead.

Count Carl Zurofsky, a descendant of the infamous Count Dracula, lacked his ancestor's thirst for blood. If he was a vampire, as some believed he was, he was a man accustomed to daylight. He quietly observed one of the women, a slender girl of 19 with honey blond hair and wide searching gray blue eyes. The girl cautiously moved towards the figure on the other side of the fence and recognized Carl to be a friend of her family, who prior to the revolution, sometimes had visited them. The count knew Anna, her mother and siblings, had not died with the Tsar in the cellar of the Ipatiev house in Ekaterinburg. He had learned through Intelligence reports that only the Tsar, a doctor and a few family servants had died in the Ipatiev house. What Carl now saw, confirmed the report's Truth.

Anna cautiously gazed at Carl before picking up the small terrier dog following her and holding him close. She was just a few feet from the closed gate where shadows blocked glaring daylight. Nobody seemed to notice her or the dog as a carriage approached the house, the gate swung open allowing a Bolshevik official to enter the premises, and Anna quickly slipped unseen through the gate.

Clothed entirely in black, his long cape matching his dark clothes, the count moved quickly towards the girl. If he wasn't a vampire, then he was a magician. He opened the cape hanging from his shoulders and concealed the young women still carrying the dog. The gesture was not just a chivalrous one. The cape like a coat of armor was sufficient to protect the girl and the count from others. Anna and her family had always believed Carl to be a man of supernatural powers. He proved the rumors true as gently he led the grand duchess forward and directed her away from the loathsome house.

"Hurry" he said. "There is a train awaiting us. It will take us across the Russian border to Romania." As they moved towards a waiting carriage appearing almost indiscernible in the sun's late afternoon glare, Anna glanced upward at Carl's piercing blue eyes. Then with the dog nestled in her arms, she nervously sat down in the carriage.

"My mother and sisters" she stammered. "What will become of them?" she asked as the carriage approached the train.

"Perhaps someday when you are Empress you will discover their fates" he replied helping the grand duchess board the waiting train. Anna quickly glanced over her shoulder, and tried to see if anyone had followed them as they made their way towards a comfortable private car.

She wasn't sure she wanted to go on living without her family. Tears filled her eyes. She was frightened and uncertain. Was the count really a friend? Was he taking her away so that like her father, she might be executed? The girl sobbed as she contemplated last seeing her father alive. After the Tsar's assassination the remaining family members had been moved from Ekaterinburg to Perm. So many sad things had happened since that tragic day. Anna thought of her younger brother too. When he was little, she and her older sisters had tried so hard to make him happy. He'd cried when he'd realized he couldn't have a bicycle to ride with his sisters. He had to be protected. The Tsarevich finally was free from his misery. He had died in Perm from the hemophilia he'd had since birth. Anna's face was somber as she thought about Alexei. She remembered a time he fell and bruised himself and that the doctors feared for his life. Only the holy man, a monk with strange healing power, had been able to stop the bleeding and save the boy's life. The holy man hadn't been there to save the Romanovs after the Tsar's family was imprisoned. Rasputin had been murdered. He had prophesied that upon his death the Romanov rule of Russia would end. That prophecy had proven to be true.

"You have a future" Carl said gazing at her pale melancholy face. Anna dismissed his comment as nothing more than a cruel joke and recoiled at the count's awkward effort to comfort her. She placed her little dog upon a seat before sitting next to him in the train's private car. She then gazed uncertainly at Carl as he took his cape from her before handing the girl one of her own. "Put it on. It will conceal you from your enemies. In a few days we'll arrive at the border crossing. Before we arrive there, the train will be searched." He didn't tell her that he worked with an underground network of spies that assisted members of the aristocracy to escape from imprisonment or flee assassination. "I assure you no one will recognize you".

Anna clutched the little dog tightly to her. She wasn't sure if any of the things Carl had told her were true. She wondered why in a time of revolution he traveled in a private railway car. As if reading her thoughts, he said, "In my capacity as Chief of the European Red Cross, I travel in a private car. I'm curtailing my mission to Russia. Now that I've rescued a grand duchess my mission has been accomplished."

After hearing what Carl had said to her Anna silently stared at the floor. Then with the dog in her arms, she got up from where she'd been seated in the moving train car but quickly sat down as the train rounded a curve. She wasn't sure if she was grateful to the count for rescuing her, and quietly said "take me back. Let me die with them". Carl knew Anna couldn't have meant what she'd said. He ignored her comment, and gazed out a window. When the train was stopped and searched and the missing grand duchess not found aboard it, she was grateful to him for concealing her.

"Live", he said as she buried her face in her hands and sobbed in relief. Carl tried to comfort Anna. He took one of her hands in his and held it.

"I have no place to go now", she said slumping back in the seat before succumbing to exhaustion. The count gently spread a blanket over her before watching her sleep with the small dog alongside her. The train's rhythm was soothing as Anna dreamed of the life she'd known before imprisonment. She could see herself and sisters running up and down the stairs at the Winter Palace or playing in the gardens behind the Alexander Palace at Pavlosk.

She remembered too the wonderful cruises the family took aboard her father's imperial yachts. She could still see the blue sky, the azure water, and almost taste the wonderful salt sea air. Dubbed the "imp" by her family, Anna was a child of practical jokes and mischief. In her dreams, she was still happy and carefree. Nobody could hold her captive in her dreams. Her mind soared in luxurious reverie as she dreamed of once was.

Although bright and intuitive, Anna never relished the intense schooling, especially in foreign languages, that she'd had to undergo. She considered school lessons to be a waste of time. The world outside her school room window seemed far more interesting than her classroom studies. She didn't know when she gazed afar at an unfamiliar distant world, that soon she would be abandoned to that world.

After days of traveling aboard the train, Carl rarely left the girl's side. "Your German is excellent" he said when she finally awoke from slumber and conversed with him first in German, then Russian and finally in English.

"A Knowledge of languages enables one to pretend to be whoever one wants to be and it will take a person anywhere in the world", she added wistfully as she gazed first at the count and then out a window at a world that seemed almost too large for her to take in.

The count offered her a warm drink as the train's whistle, sounded a shrill note, startling her. Anna spilled the cup of hot chocolate in her hand then laughed when he quickly wiped the sweet liquid from her tattered dress and jacket. "The chocolate might improve the dress's appearance" she said impishly as the train rounded a bend and prepared to go through a dark tunnel.

As the train swiftly continued towards its destination he said "You must conceal your identity right now but you always should remember to be you". Anna solemnly considered the count's advice to her. She gazed mysteriously at him as he avoided her eye contact. She found him to be kind and charming. When they had safely crossed the Romanian border and were nearing his castle estate, she said, "My father always admired your family. He said your family was able to avoid conflict by living apart from others and that you lived in a world few people knew."

"My world is rich in wonder", he said smiling at her before turning and gazing through a train window. He watched the deep forest landscape unfold before them like a huge green blanket. "I've always lived within the forest and among its inhabitants," he said without facing her. "Since my parents were afraid that I would be ridiculed for being descended from vampires, I was educated at home. I too have learned other languages besides my native tongue and Russian. I've studied at some of Europe's greatest universities. I've learned the languages of the forest too. I understand what the wolf, fox or bear is trying to communicate with their primeval calls. I understand the songs of birds and I know their calls of joy or grief.

"My castle home lies within this mountainous terrain", he said facing her. "It isn't inaccessible. There are some who are afraid to approach it though. Those who are good and brave like your father was, find that they are always welcome here."

Anna listened spellbound to the Count. She was fascinated to know that her father and Carl had hunted together in the forest. "Your father once wandered too close to the wolves' den. He thought they were ready to attack. I knew better. The wolves remembered me. I'd fed them one harsh winter season. They never would attack me or my friends. They quickly turned and ran away."

Anna started to weep again. "If only you had been with us when the human wolves attacked us, you might have been able to save my father from them."

Carl gently replied, "Humans are crueler than animals. I doubt if I could have made a difference when the Bolsheviks stormed the Winter Palace and took you and your family prisoners" he said before telling her that the train was approaching the village. When it finally slowed and came to a halt, Anna got up from where she sat and with the small dog in her arms stepped step down from the train. A troika was waiting to transport them to the count's castle situated on a mountainous hill overlooking the village.

It was dark when they sat in the sleigh pulled by two fine black horses. The evening air was cold and snow crunched beneath their hooves as the horses pulled the sleigh along the road. Anna snuggled next to the count beneath blankets and furs with her dog Micha beside them, and gazed ahead at the mysterious castle silhouetted against early evening darkness. A light snow fell around them and lighted lanterns welcoming the count's return lined the dark roadway. The sleigh stopped before the castle's entranceway and Anna took a deep breath. She knew she looked disheveled and unprepared for a visit to the count's home. Carl helped Anna step from the sleigh and noticed the uncertainty reflected in her face as Micha jumped from Anna's arms, barked then followed at their heels. He sympathetically led her toward the heavy carved wooden doorway to his home where a maid opened the door then curtsied to them. Carl smiled acknowledging the greeting and led the untidy looking young woman followed by her little dog through the entranceway. Anna nervously approached a sitting room where a door had been left ajar. In that room near the hearth, a very attractive middle-aged woman sat on a sofa. She had been busy crocheting but put her work aside when she saw her son with Anna enter the room. The count walked over to his mother, kissed her on the cheek and said "I've brought someone I'd like for you to see."

Although it had been years ago when Anna, still a child, remembered meeting Countess Marina, she appeared not to have aged at all. Slender and lithe in appearance, Marina smiled at the girl as she approached her. "It is so good to see you again, my dear" she said embracing Anna in welcome. Anna gratefully acknowledged her welcome then gazed at Countess Marina whose straight medium length light brown hair gracefully framed her beautiful still unlined face. Anna was relieved that despite her awkward appearance, the countess, who was impeccably groomed, had remembered her and had received her with such warmth.

"Your son saved my life", said Anna removing her cloak as the count took it from her shoulders and handed it to a servant.

"Your escape would have been impossible if you hadn't had the courage to walk past the gate and go with me".

Anna blushed to think that the count had recognized her bravery.

"Your escape has not gone unnoticed", said Marina glancing at the two of them. "European newspapers are speculating that you are still alive. They challenge rumors regarding your death last August in Ekaterinburg. The Bolsheviks are looking for you. Every train and means of transport is being halted and searched as people cross the border from Russia into other territories." Marina then reached out and took Anna's hand in her own before remarking, "You're trembling and your hand is cold. Come rest and sit before the fire. You may stop running now. You have nothing to fear. Our borders are safely guarded from hostile intruders. The Bolsheviks never would pursue you into our territory."

"How can you be sure?" she asked sitting down on a sofa and accepting a cup of tea from the countess before enjoying the food that was set before her. Marina evaded the question and instead watched amusedly as Anna's little terrier Micha, sat upon his hind legs and begged for more rewards as Anna talked amiably with her hosts. Finally Marina said, "It is getting late. You must be exhausted. My maid will show you to your room and bath. In the morning, after you've rested we will discuss how we might help you and your family." Anna wanted to trust Carl and his mother but she was still fearful. The girl slowly moved uncertainly towards her rooms upstairs but nervously glanced over her shoulder when she saw strange shadows jump upon walls as the sitting room's flickering hearth fire continued to burn and dwindle.

The count knew there were few who could offer the beleaguered grand duchess safety and refuge during times of such political turmoil. He knew too that she possibly was heir to the Russian throne. Anna's siblings might be dead.

"How did you learn that they might be dead?" asked Marina wearing a floor length black velvet gown, and nervously twisting the ropes of precious pearls wound around her neck.

"When we were stopped at the border, I left Anna only momentarily so that I could speak privately with a Bolshevik double agent. He informed me that when Anna was found missing, the rest of the family was moved to a more secure location. The Bolsheviks wanted to make certain the other women wouldn't escape. He thinks their refuge there is only temporary and that if they are not already dead they eventually will be shot."

"How shall we ever break the news to her if it is true?" she gasped. "Anna seems so fragile."

"We mustn't do so right now. She needs rest. She must prepare for what may lie ahead for her. To tell Anna that her mother and sisters may have been killed might be too much for her to bear right now."

Marina's eyes welled up with tears as her son heaped another log upon the fire in the hearth. She tried to ignore the impact of the tragic news, and froze in silence unable to accept what her son had told her. "It can't be true" she finally said before rising from where she had been seated. She poured herself a cup of tea then watched her son take a bottle from a corner bookshelf. Carl poured himself a glass of the liquid then gulped the vodka down as he silently watched flames in the fireplace leap upward.

Marina motioned for her son to sit opposite her in a chair. "Anna must never try to claim title to the Russian throne. She must never say she is the last Russian Tsar's only living daughter."

The count wasn't so sure. "We must wait for further developments. When the controversy dies down concerning Anna's escape, the situation might for the better change for her. Until Anna is ready to present herself to the world as the Tsar's daughter, she will assume a privileged existence with us sheltered within our isolated confines."

"People will recognize her", said Marina.

"People will see who they want to see and believe what they want to believe", he said getting up from the chair. "This year when we host the New Year's Eve ball we will present Anna to our friends."

Marina knew that photographs of the grand duchess had appeared in newspapers since the girl had been a young child. "She will never escape the scrutiny."

The count emphatically responded to his mother's comment by saying, "The girl must go on living the life to which she has become accustomed. To abandon her to anything less would be unthinkable." Carl's handsome face was distant, almost defiant. He understood what it was like to live alongside the enemy. He understood Anna's plight. He knew how hard it was to hide one's true feelings and loyalties. He knew that sometimes one's very life depended on hiding them well. "She mustn't openly speak to people. At all costs she must be protected. No one should be allowed to know what she is thinking."

Marina listened to her son's remark then calmly placed aside the teacup and saucer she had been holding in her hand. "Do you really think you know what the girl is thinking?"

Carl didn't answer his mother. Instead he turned and walked towards the huge finely carved mahogany staircase. "If she hasn't learned to do so already, Anna must learn to live like us. She must learn how to defeat those who would defeat her." Beside the staircase and gazing down from a wall, was a portrait of his ancestor, the notorious Count Dracula. Carl pointed to the portrait then turned to his mother and said, "Dracula may have been thoroughly evil. He became so through circumstances. Once he was just an ordinary man who wanted to live long enough so that he could defeat those who had defeated him. When conquest of his enemies became impossible for him he became one of the undead so he could return and do battle until the enemy was vanquished."

"Dracula's cursed shadow still touches our lives. It has taken our family many years to live down his terrible reputation" said Marina.

The count deferentially bowed to his mother before saying. "You have certainly down your part in dispelling the evil legacy concerning our dreaded ancestor. Your example as one who has helped the poor in time of need has made our family once again welcome in this mountain community. Our friends will help us shelter the beleaguered grand duchess."

Marina ignored her son's remark. She wasn't sure if their friends would help them protect Anna. "It's getting late. I think we both should have a good night's rest. If you'll excuse me, I'll retire to my rooms."

Chapter Two

After the maid had shown her to her rooms, Anna used the washtub and towels sitting outside the door to bathe Micha. Although the little dog had tried to extricate himself from the warm soapy water, eventually he allowed Anna to scrub him clean then dry him off with towels before she would allow him into her rooms. Anna then left Micha in her bedroom and went into an adjoining room where she luxuriated in a warm bath and was comforted by the welcoming fire in the hearth. When she'd returned to her bedroom, Anna was wearing the new nightclothes she'd discovered lying across her bed before she'd opened the closet and saw clothes befitting a princess including a lovely white beaded ball gown. The privileged life that once had been hers was returning in a strange sort of way. Tears filled Anna's eyes. She touched the gown and remembered attending balls at the Winter Palace and wearing dresses such as the one that now hung in the closet. As past memories flooded over her, Anna made a special effort to regain her composure. She knew she needed to rest. She also knew she must adjust to the new life granted her. Her world was becoming beautiful again.

She crossed to her bedroom's window and gazed at the evening sky. A half hidden moon emerged in pale ghostly splendor from behind a snow filled cloud. Anna sighed. Perhaps she had a future. It was hard to blot out the terrible past. She had to focus upon what good fortune might lie ahead for her. She felt strangely attracted to the count. He had risked his life to rescue her. She knew she was young and that youth often wasn't the best judge of character. She must be cautious when with him. Then she thought of her mother and sisters. She longed to see them again. She felt guilty that she alone had been spared the terrible tragedy that she feared might await them or had already befallen them. When Anna finally climbed into her warm soft bed,

Micha snuggled beside her just beneath a heavy fur blanket. Together they listened to the sounds of the night, the wind's whistling as it blew the swirling snow around the castle, the hooting of an owl, and the haunting distant howls of wolves as they cried beneath the moon. Anna also thought of Dracula, the count's notorious ancestor. Was his presence still to be felt somewhere within the castle's dark confines? When she finally fell asleep at dawn after thinking of that possibility, the haunting whistle of a distant train entered her dreams and she saw herself aboard that train surrounded by strange vampire images. Daylight gradually enveloped the room and Micha nuzzled the dreaming girl awake so that she might carry him to a window where together they could see and hear morning magic and mystery unfold before them. Anna gazed in fascination at the forest's primeval beauty before spotting a distant lone black wolf with nose pointed skyward, howl and greet in exultation the blood red sunrise.

Anna was so absorbed by what she saw from the window that she'd hardly heard a maid gently knock upon her door before entering the room. "Countess Marisa told me to tell you that breakfast is at 7:30 am. She and the count expect you to join them."

"Thank you for telling me" said Anna realizing she had to make haste so she wouldn't be late. She quickly washed and dressed after selecting an appropriate outfit from the many that were in the closet. Then, followed by Micha, Anna made her way downstairs but before he was allowed into the dining room a maid led the little dog outside for a morning romp. A few minutes later, after he'd been allowed back inside, Anna was relieved to discover her missing dog beneath the dining room table.

Anna apologized for her tardiness by saying. "I didn't realize how late it was until the maid knocked upon my door and told me that it was almost time for breakfast." She then smiled at the count and his mother before saying "Thank you for the lovely clothes. The ball gown is beautiful but when shall I ever have the occasion to wear such a gown?" she asked as a breakfast plate was set before her.

"You must be presented to our friends at the annual New Year's Eve ball. They must get to know you. It would be inappropriate for someone as distinguished as you to remain with us without introduction." said Marina glancing across the table at her son.

"My identity must remain secret" replied Anna.

"It will be for the time being" interrupted Carl. "We'll simply introduce you to everyone as our distant cousin. Even though there will be present at the ball those who would recognize you for who you really are, they will see the wisdom of adopting a new identity for you." Anna knew she had to go along with whatever the count and his mother decided in regard to her present situation. She was not only their guest. She was totally at their mercy. There was really no one else now with whom she could turn to or consult with in her time of need. Anna picked at the delicious breakfast set before her. Like a finicky child eager to get away from the table, she fed Micha a few scraps from her plate when the countess wasn't looking. She then smiled wanly across the table at the count. He seemed to know exactly what she was thinking.

Carl noticed that Anna was wearing a simple riding habit and realized his lovely guest might want to escape the confines of his luxurious castle. "The snow is not too deep this morning that we shouldn't enjoy a short morning ride. Afterwards I will show you through my home."

Anna agreed. She told Carl that she was looking forward to exploring the beautiful grounds surrounding his estate. "I had no idea how high up we were in the mountains until I gazed from my window this morning."

"We're not so high up in the mountains that you won't enjoy the pine scented air or glimpse the abundant wildlife and vegetation that thrive here even in the harshest winter months."

After breakfast, Anna walked with Carl along a short trail leading to a fence where two horses were tied but ready for them to ride.

Anna patted the gray horse before untying and mounting him. When she caught up with Carl, mounted upon the black stallion, they reined in their horses as he pointed out familiar landmarks to her. The distant mountain peaks, houses and train tracks in the valley below looked like toys or thin ribbon drawn across the landscape. The scene before Anna's eyes was as surreal as one of her dreams. Later when they descended toward the valley below they reined in the horses, and noticed people going about their daily business unaware that someone from afar watched them.

As they continued on their morning ride, the welcoming warmth of the late morning sun had made the air seem less chilly and the environment more pleasant. Anna's shoulder length hair streamed out behind her in the cool sunny breeze and enhanced her face with a look of healthy carefree beauty. When Carl quickly glanced at her he couldn't help but notice how lovely she looked as they slowly rode along together.

After they'd returned to the castle and dismounted their horses a groom began leading them away when Anna spotted Micha barking and sitting atop castle steps. He raced down the steps as Anna swept the little dog up in her arms. She then followed Carl through a castle entranceway before entering a sitting room, and joining the countess in a cup of warm cider. Marina couldn't help but notice how happy the couple seemed together. They laughed and joked as they sat and talked with her. Later, after Anna was rested, Carl found a small leather leash to attach to the dog's collar so Micha could accompany them on a tour of the castle. "Come", he said taking Anna by the hand, "I'll show you around my home."

Countess Marina silently stood in shadow and watched unseen as Carl led Anna down a corridor lined with armory and weapons of all sorts. If he wanted to impress her with all the beautifully crafted swords and spears on display in his home, Anna took it in stride. She knew he wanted her to know that violence had been part of his past too. "Our family has a notorious history tainted with blood and violence," he said pointing to a heavy suit of armor finely made and sitting upright against a wall. He then took Anna by the hand and gently pulled her and the little dog with her along the corridor before they entered another room. "Today I want to show you some other things that are part of our family's legacy."

Paintings by prominent 15th and 16th C. artists lined walls. Since Anna was accustomed to being surrounded by beautiful objects, she felt quite at home appreciating the beauty of priceless tapestries or tables and chests inlaid with lapis lazuli or covered in marble and semi precious stones.

When they stood in front of a painting, of a man astride a horse, Anna recognized the figure to be Peter the Great, her ancestor. She smiled at Carl and placed her hand on his shoulder when he mentioned that the painting had been a gift to his family from that Tsar. "He came here often to hunt. He found our forests to be a sanctuary both remote and beautiful in a way few places are. Nothing much has changed since he visited us, only now the castle has modern conveniences that it didn't have then" he said smiling and taking her hand in his as they moved along the corridor together. Anna visibly shivered when they came to stairs, turned a dark corner then stood in front of an intricately carved heavy wooden door. Opposite the door were windows covered by dark crimson drapes.

"The hallway here seems so forbidding" she said suggesting that they open the drapes and let the light shine through the windows. When she reached upward to pull the drapes apart, Carl quickly took her arm and prevented her from doing so.

"I'm afraid the window drapes, as well as the entrance to Dracula's apartments remain closed. Even though Dracula is gone no one ever pulls the drapes apart or enters his apartments." Anna stared at the door with its strange carved diabolical symbols.

She then gazed questionably at Carl before saying to him a little nervously, "I've always heard that Dracula's home was in Transylvania."

"You are right. Dracula lived in Transylvania but he also lived here part of the time. He felt safer in this inaccessible Romanian ancestral home than he did in his Transylvanian castle." Anna trembled to think that she had drawn so close to an apartment that once had been Dracula's

When the count showed the girl the secret passageway that was another of Dracula's mysterious haunts, Anna held Micha close to her before placing him on the floor where he nervously barked and strained menacingly at his leash. Shadows, created by several lamps lighting the way flickered as they stopped to study graffiti Dracula had scrawled upon the wall. "Hush" Micha said the girl again picking the little dog up in her arms so she could decipher the message. "The light of day surrounds us but night's darkness alone will prevent us from becoming light's slaves." Then stepping backwards, and turning to the count, she asked. "What was that? I thought I heard a noise like someone stumbling in the darkness."

"It was nothing. This dimly lighted passageway creates strange illusions. Like the rest of the building it's very old. I can assure you that what you heard were only a few loose rocks falling from crevices in the passageway's ceiling."

Anna was relieved when once again they were standing in a familiar sunny room where patterns from late afternoon light danced across an intricately woven Oriental carpet.

When Marina, entered the room and learned where Carl had taken Anna she admonished her son for showing the girl such a forbidding place as Dracula's secret passageway. "I assure you, my dear the memories of an ominous past are no longer part of our lives anymore." Anna nodded her head in polite acknowledgement of the comment.

Marina then motioned for Anna and her son to sit down opposite her as she began the conversation by saying, "You have a new life here Anna. You must make your way in the world and leave the past behind you now."

Anna thanked the countess for her advice but she couldn't fight back tears. "How am I to press forward in life not knowing if my mother and sisters are safe?" As if wanting to turn his back upon the awkward conversation, Carl got up from where he was sitting and poured himself a glass of vodka from a bottle atop a marble covered side table alongside a stack of books.

Micha curled up next to Anna on a brocade sofa. The girl sensed that the count's mother was about to tell her something she didn't want to hear. She stared silently at the floor and waited.

Marina began the conversation by saying, "We both feel you have a right to know the truth. We feel it would be wrong for us to keep what information we have concerning your family from you. A secret agent has informed my son that following your escape from the Administrative Excise House in Perm your mother and sisters were moved to an unknown location. There is a possibility that they may have been executed by the Bolsheviks."

"There is a possibility that the information is incorrect" interrupted the count. He walked over to her and stood by the sobbing girl before leaning forward and trying to comfort her. "The man is a double agent. What he has told me might be something the Bolsheviks wanted him to tell me."

Anna refrained from weeping. Instead she picked up Micha and began smoothing his wiry brindle colored coat before whispering, "We must wait for further developments." With the dog still in her arms, Anna then stood motionless. She gazed first at the count and then at his mother.

Carl could sense that Anna doubted their sincerity. He didn't want her to believe that they were trying to hurt her when he said, "You mustn't let your enemies defeat you by giving up hope".

Anna quietly nodded her head in agreement. She felt trapped like a small bird in a cage. She wanted to fly from her present comfortable circumstances but she knew she must accept the hospitality that was being extended to her by the count and his mother. She had no other place to go.

"I shall always be grateful to you for your kindness" she said quietly before walking toward the dark staircase that led to her room. The count and his mother gazed with concern after her. "Perhaps I should go to her", said Marina.

"No, she needs to be alone right now," he said.

Anna entered her room and noticed that the fire in the hearth still burned slowly with welcoming warmth. At least she was comfortable in her misery. She then threw herself across the bed and sobbed as Micha jumped upon the bed then nuzzled her gently before the two of them fell asleep before the hearth fire's warm glow.

When she awoke, Anna spoke to Micha as if he understood. "Somehow we've got to find mother. We've got to find our way back to the train station and board a train back to Russia." Then Anna remembered that the Bolsheviks were looking for her, and that her life might end abruptly if she were caught sneaking across the border without proper credentials.

Wisdom dictated that she remain where she was. There would be a time when she would be able to escape from the count's comfortable castle refuge and begin looking for her mother and sisters.

Anna crossed the room then gazed outward from a window and realized that late afternoon sunlight had given way to darkness. Then upon hearing a knock, she went and opened her room's door and saw that a maid had brought her dinner on a silver tray and some food for Micha as well. Placed upon the tray with her dinner was a note from the countess inviting Anna to help distribute Christmas presents to villagers in the morning.

Anna smiled through her tears. She felt guilty for even thinking of running away. Instead, in the morning she would visit the village with the countess. Life would go on.

Freshly fallen early morning snow covered the ground as Anna and Marina sat in a horse drawn sleigh loaded with children's Christmas presents, as well as food and clothing for their families. Anna began their conversation by saying, "I'm glad you told me about my mother and sisters. You are right. I needed to know what fate might have befallen my family now that I'm no longer with them. I feel sure that if your son is right, if there is a possibility that they are still alive, I shall eventually learn the truth about them."

The countess's eyes welled up with tears. "My dear, it is I who should apologize to you for burdening you with something that already may be too much for your young shoulders to bear. The Bolsheviks would want nothing better than to cause those who are still loyal to the Tsar and his family to give up hope now that he is dead. They would want the world to believe that you, your mother and sisters are dead as well."

Anna smiled grimly but abruptly ended the conversation by saying, "Perhaps you are right."

Once they had entered the village where friends of the countess already were busy distributing gifts to children and their families, Marina had the opportunity to introduce Anna to people cheerfully welcoming her into their midst. They seemed charmed by Countess Marina's cousin and smiled and laughed with her while passing out presents and toys to the children.

Still Anna couldn't help but overhear a friend of Marina's say to another woman, "there is something strangely familiar about her. I know I've seen her somewhere else. I can't quite place it."

Anna shuddered. Until she'd overheard that remark, she'd been joyfully interacting with everybody. Now she wanted to withdraw from their company. She was terrified that someone might realize she was the missing grand duchess and notify the Bolsheviks of her presence in Romania. Anna wanted to leave the assembled villagers but the countess gracefully took her arm in hers and whispered, "Be brave. Don't pay attention to gossip or comments."

Anna steeled herself against further remarks but she was relieved when the gifts had been given to recipients and it was time to return to the castle.

It was Christmas Eve. Anna and the countess removed their warm coats and joined Carl who sat in a comfortable chair before a hearth fire. Micha let go of playing with the glove Anna had dropped to the floor and followed her into the sitting room. He then sat upon his hind legs and begged as if expecting to be rewarded for his mischief. Carl glanced up from the intelligence reports he'd been studying and noticed how lovely Anna looked with her cheeks still flushed from the outside cold. The girl smiled at Carl and sat near him as she offered her little dog a delectable item from a small plate set before her. While Marina poured her a warm cup of tea, Anna conversed with her hosts and Micha entertained himself in a room corner by playing with crystal bulbs hanging from lower limbs of the family Christmas tree. When one bulb dropped to the floor, the little dog began rolling it along the smooth carpet until Anna took it from him and replaced the bulb on the tree's limb. Even though he'd found it hard to forget the grim reality of the world surrounding them, the count realized it was impossible to continue with the task at hand. He somberly put aside the intelligence reports. He found Micha's antics amusing and Anna's company a welcome interlude from cares that weighed upon him.

Anna realized a joyful holiday had been sadly overcast by world events seeming utterly out of control. She knew why the count seemed so subdued. How could either of them celebrate in earnest knowing how embroiled the world was in turmoil? She realized what Carl must be thinking and smiled sympathetically at him.

Until now, Carl's life and aristocratic world had seemed so secure. He was no fool. He knew he had to live with the new Communist rule. Secretly he had been an admirer of Carl Marx. He knew that the Communism Marx had advocated was not the Communism the Bolsheviks were adopting. Marx had written about the eventual accession to power of the bourgeoisie after a democratic revolution. But Lenin was declaring that the bourgeoisie had come to power in Russia as the result of a mistake on the part of the proletariat. Lenin had called for the immediate transition to a socialist revolution.

Marina pensively gazed at her son as if she knew what he was thinking then said to him, "Come help place a few decorations on the tree's highest branch."

Carl left the chair where he'd been sitting and watched his mother and Anna with Micha at their heels busily add more decorations to the family Christmas tree. Then taking a silver star in hand, he reached upward trying to place the star on the tree's highest branch. When he realized he couldn't do it, he felt almost disappointed as if he knew what he'd wanted to place atop the tree was more than mere decoration. Carl knew there were many in Russia who had hated the Tsar. There were also the disillusioned who had witnessed a culture disappear and disintegrate before their eyes. Jubilance over the fall of the Romanov dynasty had fast given way to fear. Like Anna, Carl knew he and his family were prisoners and outcasts of the times. He knew it would be hard for him to adjust to the Bolshevik rule now sweeping across Russia. The symbols of the life he'd always taken for granted were no more and so was that life. Anna recognized Carl's sudden change of mood, and watched him return to his chair and pick up the pile of papers he'd been studying.

Carl had secretly moved within the world of the Bolsheviks. He'd adopted other identities, clandestinely attended their meetings and met and talked with men like Lenin, Kerensky and Trotsky. He wasn't ignorant of the power struggle going on within the new regime. He understood the cruel game of power and deception. He'd learned how to protect himself and his interests, and the best way he'd learned how to do so was to become like the men he'd come to know.

Carl sometimes felt uncomfortable with them though. He'd witnessed enough intrigue and cruelty ever to become one of them. There was only one man among them whom he admired above the rest. He didn't stand for the same things the count stood for but he was a brilliant man and an astute politician. The man's name was "Koba". To those who knew him well, he was Stalin.

Unlike the other men Carl had known, Joseph Stalin was a man who played the game of power with frightening reserve. Carl knew Stalin sometimes had participated in terrorist activities and that during the revolution he had been a Tsarist police informant who'd betrayed those with whom he conspired against the government. Before the revolution when Lenin was running from authority, Stalin helped Lenin hide but he was loyal to none. Stalin played a careful game of deception and distant detachment. He'd often disappear when there was violence and trouble. Now that the Bolsheviks were in power, Stalin's tactics hadn't changed.

Carl's face was pale and distant as he contemplated the dirty game of political espionage with which he'd become involved. He didn't want to emulate Stalin's tactics. Yet he felt too trapped by the fear and terror surrounding revolutionary Russia not to emulate them.

Anna stared at the count. She wanted to get to know him. Inwardly Anna realized he was a man who wasn't close to anyone. She felt a chill when she gazed at his solemn handsome face.

As if sensing that Anna had been scrutinizing him, Carl looked at her and smiled. It was late in the day. The tree had been trimmed. Countess Marina looked at them both. She suggested that they follow her into the dining room where dinner was being served. Micha had managed to find another fallen crystal Christmas tree ornament but stopped rolling the ball across the smooth oriental carpet. He quickly followed at Anna's heels and found a place beneath the dining room table near her feet.

The countess, who was fond of dogs, laughed amusedly when she'd seen what he'd done. "He may sit at your feet. I assure you that a good meal awaits Micha after we've finished ours."

The dining room, like the sitting room where the family had been for most of the day, was filled with the aroma from incense burning candles. And the Christmas tree, brought from the forest so that it might decorate the adjoining sitting room and drawing room, added to the beauty of rooms that were already beautiful regardless of the season.

Anna began the dinner conversation by saying, "You've been so generous to me. How shall I ever repay you for what you've done for me?"

The countess gently smiled at Anna. "To see you regain a spirit of happiness is the greatest reward we might have," she replied.

Marina knew that Anna was beginning to realize that their lives were unlike those of other noble families. She'd suspected that Anna probably knew that Carl's connections with espionage and revolutionists were more than superficial.

Anna quietly glanced across the table at the count. He smiled at her. She wondered how he'd managed to discover where in Perm she, her mother and sisters had been imprisoned. She wondered too how the count had dared rescue her.

Anna ate the delicious roast goose. She tasted the plum pudding with the brandied hard sauce and all the other delicacies that were plentiful at the count's table. Then she remembered the deprivation and suffering her family had undergone at the hands of the Bolsheviks. After the Tsar had been assassinated, Anna's mother had been so brave. Her children had emulated their mother's courage. They'd been able to go on in the midst of misery.

Anna felt guilty for her good fortune. She also wondered how long that good fortune would last. She tried to place the pieces of the puzzle together. She trembled to think that the count might be using her as a pawn in a secretive power struggle. Micha softly growled and nuzzled Anna's foot as she contemplated that thought. Anna then reached under the table where the little dog waited for a handout and gave him one. She then gazed across the table and discreetly smiled at the count. He returned her smile by picking up his wine glass, and seeming just a bit tipsy proposed a toast to her. "Here we are on the merriest of occasions isolated and securely hidden from a world that is ready to self-destruct. May the beauty you embody live on without interruption", he said, bowing his head slightly before imbibing the liquid in the glass. He then set down the empty wineglass on the table as Anna blushed slightly at the extravagant compliment. She was about to interject a comment regarding the holidays but dinner conversation was interrupted when a maid entered the room and told the count that there was a gathering of people waiting at the door and wanting to extend holiday greetings to him and his family. Followed by his mother and Anna, Carl quickly rose from the table and made his way towards the castle's main entrance where he greeted the assembled carolers and invited them inside his home. As her hosts spoke with members of the assembled group, Anna's gaze fell on one man in particular. She wondered why he had come.

For a short while, Anna, and her hosts could enjoy the beauty and festivity of a special holiday. Only Anna found the music almost unbearable and hard to listen to. She remembered her mother playing carols on the piano during Christmas Eves past while friends and family gathered beside her and sang to the musical accompaniment. Tears of joy and sadness came to Anna's eyes as she listened to the carolers and recalled those happier times. When the carolers finished singing, the count invited them to stay for refreshment. Warm mulled wine was served along with delicious pasties.

Anna's anxious gaze again fell on the grave young man talking with the count. Since he was obviously ignoring her, she pretended she didn't know the man's name. She pretended she'd never even been introduced to him. She'd immediately recognized him. She knew him well. He was the Bolshevik official who was in the carriage the day she'd walked through the opened fortress gate in Perm.

Anna continued to avoid the young Bolshevik but then curiosity got the better of her. Her heart pounded as she started to approach him. The countess quickly took her arm and started to introduce her instead to some of the carolers. Anna politely conversed with them but she desperately wanted instead to speak with him. "Come away from the door" said Marina noticing that Anna was wearing neither shawl nor sweater. Anna shivered and gazed behind as Marina took her arm and led her away from where the young man and the count stood talking.

When the carolers had left for the evening and Anna was alone with her hosts, she asked Carl about the man with whom he'd been talking. "He was at the gate that day in Perm", she stammered. Carl was trying to protect Anna. He found her to be beautiful and vulnerable. She was also intelligent and wise beyond her years. He wanted to protect her from the worry and fear that was gnawing at his soul. He wanted to tell her that he was falling in love with her but he had to continue to play a game of caution.

"Why was he here?" she asked looking directly at Carl and expecting him to answer her truthfully. Countess Marina left Anna alone with her son.

"He is a friend of mine. He is a high official within the Bolshevik regime. There are many things I'd like to tell you right now but you wouldn't understand. You might become afraid if I tried to tell you too much. You must trust me. Don't waver in your opinion of me."

"Does the man know what happened to my mother and sisters?" she asked.

"That's why he was here tonight. I told him I needed to see him and that I needed to know the truth about whether or not your mother and sisters are still alive. He came to tell me that recent intelligence reports received today indicate that White Regime sources, loyal to the Tsar, have overtaken Perm, and that following your escape, your sister Tatiana tried to escape too but was captured. She is feared dead. After her attempted escape, it is believed that your mother and remaining sisters were moved first to a convent and then to another location."

Anna gasped. "Why wouldn't you let me talk with him then? Shouldn't I have been allowed to speak with him?"

"No", he replied. "You must wait. Allow events to take their course. The man with whom I spoke with tonight answers to those more powerful than he. They watch his every move. He easily could be executed or imprisoned if he fails to act in accord with the wishes of higher authority. If he is seen talking with you, those who trust him and me might begin to doubt his loyalty."

Intuitively Anna knew what the count was telling her was true. Inwardly she rebelled against that part of her that was compelled to go along with a game of cruel deception. She knew that trust and loyalty played little or no role within the revolutionary regime that had murdered her father. She thought that the men with whom the count was involved would murder him and his friends as easily as they had murdered her father.

Anna's face was pale as she gazed into the count's eyes. She knew he had told her the truth and wasn't trying to deceive her. He took her hands in his and kissed her upon the forehead. He then turned her hands over and kissed them. "It is getting late. The world we once knew has ended."

"Why?" whispered Anna who was still too young to grasp all the political complexities that had caused the revolution. "I won't let you leave me tonight until you explain to me why."

On Christmas Eve the count tried to tell the girl why her father had been defeated. "He acted to preserve his power but in the wrong way. When the events of the First Revolution began, the Tsar must have understood he was weak. A new center needed to be established." Although not deeply religious, Carl knew how politically persuasive religion could be: "The church should have become a rallying point. Only a strong church might have kept Russia from eventual catastrophe. The Tsar had not heeded the sign. People starved. The church and government hadn't alleviated their suffering. Instead of inviting the opposition to openly participate in forming a different sort of government, one that might have leaned towards socialistic principles, the Tsar's government condemned anyone who leaned towards the principles of Communist rule. Revolution, the Russo-Japanese War, World War I and civil war had brought Russia to its knees."

"The Tsar and church authority have been replaced by men who are terrorists and murderers. The state is their god. The strongest man among them is their dictator" said Anna defiantly.

"Not entirely" he replied.

Anna shuddered at the count's words. In her short life she had learned that death and revolution had been her family's legacy. Her great-grandfather,

Tsar Alexander II, was one of Russia's greatest reformers and in 1881 had been preparing to give Russia its long awaited constitution. If he had done so, he would have brought an end to despotism and Russia would have entered into the ranks of other civilized nations. He didn't live to bring about the reform. The bomb designed by young revolutionaries killed him.

A Tsar's murder had given birth to more bloodshed and misery. During his short reign, Alexander III unwittingly avenged his father's assassination. He'd persecuted groups of people or individuals he thought responsible for revolution and for his father's terrible death. Thousands were driven into the Pale of Settlement and encouraged to emigrate. After Nicholas II succeeded his father, Alexander III, he continued following a path that foreshadowed his own dark legacy. Nicholas II wasn't at the Winter Palace on Bloody Sunday, part of the first unsuccessful revolution of 1905, a day when thousands of people, incited by revolutionary fervor, stormed the palace. Over 1000 victims died on the palace square and nearly 3000 were wounded. As the poet Osip Mandelstam wrote: "Any child's cap or mitten, or woman's scarf pitifully abandoned that day in the Petersburg snows became a reminder of the fact that the Tsar must die, the Tsar would die." Anna's father continued a legacy that was to end in blood and in his own death.

The count held Anna, weeping in his arms before releasing her and watching her ascend the dark castle staircase as if she were walking towards a haunting destiny. She knew she was in love with him and he was with her. In such loveless times to declare one's affection for another seemed almost forbidden. When she reached her room and retired for the evening, Micha jumped upon the bed and tried to comfort Anna. He thrust his cold little nose into the palm of her hand and licked it.

Anna struggled to rest but sleep wouldn't come. Exhausted and half asleep her thoughts kept shifting until her thinking almost turned to dreaming. She could still see the count talking with the young man in the black overcoat and cap. She knew he had noticed her. She knew he hadn't forgotten her. He'd told her that they must forever remain strangers to one another. Anna knew better. She knew they could never forget one another. Did Koba want her back? Perhaps the Bolsheviks wanted her back or were planning to kidnap her and return her to Russia where she might be executed. And then Anna thought of her sister Tatiana. Was Koba right? Had Tatiana really been captured and possibly killed after she'd tried to escape imprisonment? Anna would always insist that until there was definite proof regarding her mother and sisters' fates, she would believe them to be alive.

The wind outside howled and Anna got up from where she lay in bed before crossing to a room's window, so she could look outside. Utter darkness surrounded her and the outside window was encased in ice. The room was growing cold and flames in the fireplace were dying. A coal heater was available to her but instead of using it she threw another log on the hearth fire so her room would remain warm. Once the log burned down to embers, coals from the fire would provide comforting light and warmth until morning. Anna then climbed back into bed and slept as Micha nestled beside her.

Chapter Three

Christmas morning came and went in joyous sunny splendor. The previous night's discussion between Carl and Anna seemed to have been forgotten. A sleigh ride through newly fallen snow was followed by an early lunch attended by a few friends and distant neighbors who'd come to extend holiday wishes. They had heard the mysterious rumors surrounding Anna, and had dropped by in part to see her. Anna shyly tried to evade their questions and was grateful to the count and his mother for steering the conversation away from her. Later in the day, after their guests had left the family, Carl and Anna took Micha for a walk through the snow. The air surrounding them was cold and brisk but the mid afternoon sky above was brilliant, sunny and clear. Micha ran just ahead of them and jumped over small drifts of snow before taking off in another direction and treeing a small squirrel. After gazing downward and seeing wolf tracks, Anna quickly went and gathered the little dog in her arms.

"There are human tracks as well" said Carl cautiously glancing around them before pulling his parka's warm hood up over his head and ears. "There must be hunters in the area", he said realizing the wisdom of not straying too far alone on foot. Then turning to Anna who huddled and shivered in the hooded wool parka she wore, he said "you must be feeling a little fatigued. It will be dusk soon. We'll turn around and go home."

Even though Anna enjoyed being alone with the count, she knew they had been gone too long. She was relieved when finally they reached the castle's comfortable surroundings but blushed when the countess met them, and scolded her son for taking Anna for such a long walk on such a cold day.

"Micha was ready to pursue the wolves into the forest. I caught him just in time" said Anna laughing after she and Carl had removed their coats and, with Micha at their heels followed Marina into the family sitting room where they made themselves comfortable before the hearth.

"Did anyone call while we were on our walk?" asked Carl nervously waiting for his mother to answer the question.

"Yes, that young man with whom you spent so much time talking with last night came for a visit. I told him that you had gone for a walk. I didn't know how long you'd be gone. He left this book for you to read. He said that if you peruse the book's pages you'll discover a plan that must be implemented."

Carl picked up the book. He casually glanced at the book's pages. "Koba has only left more party propaganda for me to read. He's a fool if he expects me to implement any sort of plan of action from this" he said casually throwing the book aside.

Anna glanced down at the untitled book lying in front of her and wondered what was contained within it. She picked up the book that the count had discarded so casually. Then flipping through its pages, before setting the book aside, she smiled a secretive smile.

* * * *

New Year's Eve came early as Anna gazed from her window and looked outside. The world was brilliantly sunny and cold. Icicles hanging from trees shimmered as the sunlight glanced through them before dancing and playing with shadows in early morning sunshine. Inside the castle the mood was one of joyful expectation as the ballroom was being prepared for the evening's event. Sparking chandeliers had been polished and huge oriental carpets usually covering floors had been rolled back for the occasion. Exotic flowers grown in the Castle estate's greenhouses gave off a delicate aroma as servants placed huge containers of the flowers around the room.

As evening approached and Anna nervously prepared for the ball, she gazed into a mirror but turned when she heard a knock on her door. Countess Marina, elegantly dressed in a soft pink brocade gown entered the room and greeted Anna before fastening a lovely jeweled necklace around her neck. She then placed a small sparkling tiara upon Anna's soft dark blonde hair, and said, "You must wear the proper jewels to go with such a beautiful dress."

Anna thanked the countess for her generosity. She then slipped on the white kid gloves she was to wear for the occasion and accompanied the countess to the top of the huge winding dark staircase before uncertainly following her down the stairs. When they reached the sitting room where he waited for them looking handsome in a formal dark suit, Carl made a bow to his mother and Anna. Anna shyly smiled then curtsied. The beautiful white beaded ball gown she wore fitted her perfectly. Never had the count seen her look so lovely.

With his mother on one arm and Anna on the other, they then entered the adjoining room where guests had been awaiting their arrival. Since the ball was also a costume ball, some guests had chosen to wear masks and a costume. They wondered who the mystery guest dressed as a real princess was.

Anna needed no mask. She was too involved in another masquerade not to play her real self now. As people bobbed and curtsied before the princess on the arm of the handsome count, Anna smiled graciously or complimented those who greeted her on their choice of costume.

"Who is she?" whispered one woman before lowering her feathered mask so she could get a better look at the mystery guest. Anna smiled a look of satisfaction. So far nobody dared recognize her.

As the orchestra played a romantic waltz, Carl gazed into Anna's sad gray blue eyes. For a moment the couple seemed lost in each other's company. Anna felt as if she were floating. They held each other tightly as if they were clinging to something that soon would melt before their eyes. Anna epitomized grace and beauty, everything Carl had ever loved. He could never imagine losing her. Yet Anna felt they were only playing a game with one another. She was sure the music would stop suddenly and there would be just a glass slipper left to remind her of the evening's wonderful dream.

The couple continued to move together in their own world and when the music finally stopped, there was no glass slipper to be found. Instead everyone in the room was looking at them. The count quickly took Anna's arm in his so they could move throughout the room and chat and mingle with guests.

When the music started again, nobody seemed to notice a medium sized man wearing a dark coat and worker's cap. Covering the man's face was a mask so people wouldn't recognize him. He watched Anna and Carl dance together and when the music finally stopped, he chatted amiably with them before asking Anna if he could have the next dance. Anna quickly glanced at the count as if hesitating to accept the invitation. Carl nodded, encouraging her to dance with the masked man who was a stranger to everyone in the room except to them. Carl watched silently as Koba and Anna slowly danced to the haunting musical accompaniment of a strange waltz. As they moved to the music, the mood in the room seemed to change. Anna was drawn to the young man wearing the mask. She let him hold her tightly and her heart pounded feeling his control and calm assurance as he led her around the dance floor.

"I came here only to see you" he said. Anna felt weak as he continued to hold her in his arms. She knew what he wanted could never be for them. Yet something inside her told her that she might someday become part of his world. "I came to tell you. When I rule Russia, you will be my wife. Russia will have an Empress once more."

"No, Koba", said Anna. "The old woman--- the prophetess told my mother that my sisters and I would be wed to death. I could never accept your proposal of marriage."

"If you marry the count you will be wed to death as well," said Koba suddenly leaving an astonished Anna standing alone in the middle of the floor. Anna felt remorseful. She'd said the wrong thing. She was reacting. She was harboring the anger she felt towards Russia's new rulers. Koba wasn't responsible for her father's death yet he was one of them. She would never forgive the Bolsheviks for her father's assassination. Koba quickly left the castle ballroom.

The count could see that Anna was not looking well and immediately was at her side. He tried to make it seem as if everything was perfectly normal and that nothing out of the ordinary had occurred to upset her. He took her in his arms and they danced to a smooth Viennese waltz and when the orchestra struck up something even livelier, he whispered in Anna's ear, "smile".

Anna leaned on Carl as if she were trying to regain her composure. "Don't let them see you like this" he said. "People are watching your every move. They know who you are."

"Do they know with whom I was just dancing too?" she asked with tears beginning to well up in her eyes. "He said he would someday rule Russia."

"Koba is Lenin's right hand man. If Koba ever rules Russia it will be over Lenin's dead body".

"Will it be over your dead body too?" she asked with a strange quizzical expression on her face.

"Perhaps not quite yet" said Carl who seemed a little taken aback by what Anna had just said to him. "I've got to live long enough so I can marry you," he said as if trying to make light of what she'd just she'd said to him.

Anna pretended not to hear what Carl had said. She went on talking as if what she was telling him was more important than what he'd just proposed.

"Koba must be a thoroughly evil man she continued nervously. I've heard that he was behind that terrible 1907 bombing in Erevan Square in Tiflis. He masterminded the theft of all that bank gold."

"Hush", said the count smiling. "You can't be sure of that". Anna solemnly gazed up at Carl. She reined in her emotions before saying quietly, "You're right I'm not sure of that."

Carl hesitated before finally asking her again, "Will you marry me?" Anna realized Koba had just proposed to her too. She understood the importance of power. Koba represented the new power. "Of course, you must know I am in love with you" she said with tears welling up in her eyes—"but when?"

"Your twentieth birthday is at the end of January. We'll be married on your birthday." The music had stopped and the count led Anna to a darkened corner of the ballroom. From a distance Marina discreetly watched them from behind her fan. She knew her son already had asked the important question. She'd seen him place a diamond engagement ring upon Anna's finger before taking her in his arms. "The wedding will be a private one held here in the chapel. Just a few close friends will be invited to it" he'd said smiling, "Perhaps someday, after you're Empress, I will help you rule Russian."

Anna's face became sad. "My eldest sister Olga should be Empress if she is alive. Mother always said my younger brother was too ill to reign, that Olga should succeed my father as ruler." The Tsar knew the boy might never live to rule. He'd been training his eldest daughter to rule and would find a suitable husband for her: A man who would love and protect her and Russia's interests. "My father's ministers reminded us all that Paul I's Law of Succession, made it impossible for a woman to become Empress."

"We live in extraordinary times. A Law of Succession created so long ago should have no bearing on today's world", he replied.

"I don't know why we're even talking about the Law of Succession. I will never be Russia's empress ",she said softly but almost defiantly.

"Will you be happy sharing your life with me anyway?" he asked? Anna knew in her heart she could never say no to that question. "Yes" she said gazing up at Carl before lovingly leaning against him.

The count then kissed Anna's hand. "The subject is closed", he said before taking her in his arms.

For the time being Anna had found refuge from life's turbulence. She felt safe and warm in Carl's arms yet she knew he must be deeply involved with spies and espionage. She was a survivor though. Even though her life with him might prove to be a precarious, dangerous existence, Anna was drawn to Carl. He had offered her the love and security that the young man who had stunned her, and who had unknowingly swept her off her feet, hadn't promised.

After the ball, Anna lay in bed in her room with Micha curled up beside her. She remembered the time the count had told her that Koba was loyal to the cause. Anna wasn't sure which cause her future husband meant. Koba's quiet rather reserved self-assurance indicated something else. She was sure that Koba was loyal to only one cause, the cause of furthering his interests within the Communist hierarchy. Was that where her future husband's true loyalty lay too? She knew the count admired Marx, and that he didn't approve of Lenin's new Communist philosophy that made the proletariat the chief player in the developing Communist regime.

Anna also knew that people within the aristocracy married for convenience. The count must love her. For him to marry her right now was not to make a marriage of convenience. Surely his alliance with her would strain his relationship with those within the Communist hierarchy. Anna also knew that without proper identification, she could hardly prove to the world that she was Nicholas II's last surviving daughter. Perhaps she was safe.

Chapter Four

On her 20th birthday Anna prepared to take the vows of matrimony. She knew she had made the only decision for a grand duchess the world presumed to be no longer alive. She was marrying for love and convenience.

About 30 people gathered in the castle's small chapel and watched Anna, looking lovely in her white silk gown, walk down the aisle to the musical accompaniment of a stringed ensemble. In her hands she carried a small bouquet of white roses and a wreath of white miniature roses adorned her dark blond hair as she smiled at Carl and joined him at the altar. As they waited for the service to begin, she nervously put aside the bouquet she'd carried, and remembered her mother telling her about her wedding day. It had come soon after Alexander III's death and her husband's ascent to the throne. Anna knew her mother had walked down the aisle in the shadow of mourning. Now Anna walked down the aisle in the knowledge that she was perhaps the sole survivor of her immediate family.

She lovingly gazed into Carl's eyes as he slipped the wedding ring on her finger making them husband and wife. If there ever had been any doubts as to their affection for one another, they were gone. Anna knew she loved him. She would love Carl until death parted them as it had parted her from so many other people she'd loved in her short life.

Marina pensively watched her son kiss Anna during the reception then mingle with close friends and neighbors who'd come to celebrate with them. If any of them questioned the count's wisdom in marrying the mysterious young woman who'd suddenly come into his life, they were silent. They only wished the couple well, and showered them with rose petals when following the reception, Carl carried Anna away to a romantic undisclosed location.

The count dared not take Anna too far from the secure confines of their castle refuge. She didn't mind that arrangement at all. There really was no honeymoon. She was content just to be with her new husband in their secure and beautiful surroundings. For a while he would stay with her. He wanted them to get to know one another. Intuitively Anna felt he soon would leave her though. She would stay alone with his mother as he once more stepped back into his other world.

The months of February and March were especially happy ones for Anna. Carl had tenderly loved her in a way she needed to be loved. She felt the pain of separation though when at the end of March he told her he was returning alone to Moscow. Anna was correct in assuming that her husband was going to Moscow in hope of discovering final corroboration regarding her mother and sisters' fate. She didn't know that her husband's secretive friends and mistress were there. Anna had to trust Carl. She rebelled against his separation from her though. She needed her husband's attention especially now since she knew she was pregnant.

At first Anna received no news at all from the count. Instead he sent her letters telling her how much he loved her but that he still had work to do in Moscow.

The group of young intellectuals he knew in Moscow, like Carl, espoused beliefs in a Communist ideology other than the Communism adopted by Lenin. They were involved in an ongoing but quiet rebellion against the present regime. One man in the group had been in Perm following Anna's disappearance. He had proof and information regarding the fates of Anna's mother and sisters. He was a spy and had obtained a copy of a report from another spy, an official who'd been present the day White Regime sources invaded Perm. According to the report, the Romanov women had been moved by train from Perm to Glazov. From there, it was believed that they'd been moved to Moscow, and now were possibly dead.

Carl had told Anna that he would remain in Moscow indefinitely. He'd changed his plans. He had a copy of the official report in hand. He would return home immediately and show it to her himself.

Even though he had a mistress in Moscow, she was not the focus of his affection now. Anna was. She'd made him a married man. In the dangerous world in which he moved, a mistress was sometimes a liability. Carl knew he would have to end his relationship with her.

Anna was surprised and relieved when Carl returned home sooner than anticipated. As if sensing that her son had something important to tell Anna, Marina left the couple alone after she'd welcomed him home. Carl hesitantly began their conversation by saying, "I know you were hoping for good news. I wish I could give it to you. I'm afraid that I can't though."

Carl sat next to Anna on a sitting room sofa and handed her the report contained within an envelope. After reading it she handed the report back to Carl and burst into tears. "I can't believe this is true" she sobbed as he held her in his arms but "somehow I must get on with my life."

Carl knew he couldn't leave his young wife and return to Moscow. Under the circumstances, he would stay with her. He had been doing some research on the writings of Marx. He would compile a report on Marx's writings while he worked at home. With the recent revelation of the final sad news regarding the Romanov women wisdom dictated that he stay with Anna.

Several months passed. The baby was due in October. For the time being, Anna had accepted the sad news regarding her mother and sisters, and even though she felt insecure regarding her circumstances in life she was somewhat relieved. The count still was at her side. While he worked alone in his study, Anna and Marina prepared a nursery for the anticipated new family member. To pass the time, Marina showed Anna how to crochet. They took great joy in lovingly making baby blankets, little sweaters and other such necessary items. Anna enjoyed her friendship with Countess Marina. Since she missed the companionship and advice of her own mother, she found Marina to be a woman with whom she could easily converse. Yet Anna suspected that Marina had her secrets and would not easily divulge them to others.

Anna wondered why a woman as beautiful in middle age as Marina should not have remarried after her husband's death. The countess rarely confided in others. The isolated castle environment had left her reluctant to reach out to the rest of the world and talk. "My son's father was much older than I when we were married", she confided. "I was only eighteen. He was in his late thirties. My marriage to Count Zurofsky was arranged and offered security and wealth. I didn't love him at first. I was in love with a younger man closer to my own age. His family wasn't wealthy. He was struggling to make his way in the world. My father said "no" to him when he asked for my hand in marriage. After my marriage to the count I tried very hard to forget the other man and to become a good wife to my husband. He was good and kind to me and after several years my son was born. When my husband died, Carl was only 21 when he inherited his late father's estate. He wanted me to remain here as I always have. I've never felt free to travel or to go many places but when the man I once loved suddenly contacted me several years ago, I went to see him. Now I go to Budapest several times a year to be with him. His wife is dead. Neither of us wants to be remarried. We are comfortable with our lives the way they are. He makes me feel alive and very special. I suppose that is what keeps me young." Anna listened with sympathy to Marina's story. She knew life for women was restricted in the late 19th C. and early 20th C. As a grand duchess, Anna's life had been restricted too. She had grown up in an environment where she'd never had to pay her own bills, do shopping or freely mingle in the real world. Now all that had changed. She hadn't been prepared for what lay ahead for her after the revolution. She wondered how she'd been able to find the courage to pass through the gate and enter the real world that fateful day in Perm. Anna had left the horror and restrictions of imprisonment for an environment offering her enormous possibilities. The countess had never lived as dangerously as Anna had but she had found the courage to move on in the face of a woman's restrictive world. Countess Marina put down her crocheting momentarily. She reached for a teapot, poured a cup of tea for Anna and then one for herself.

Anna was grateful for her new life. She didn't mind her quiet existence at all. She was especially happy when Carl would take breaks from his work and they would take short walks together. Micha would follow eagerly at their heels before he spotted a ground squirrel or some other small creature and take off after it. The count almost had forgotten how wonderful life could be. The smell of the pines during any season throughout the year had made him forget the political environment in which he'd moved. The forest Carl gazed upon was something that had been there for centuries and he couldn't imagine it not being there always. The warm wind rippling the waters of a pond or the leaves of a tree made him reflect on how important it is to preserve the natural world. He was convinced that the preservation of nature ultimately would save the world. When Anna got a little tired during their walks together, the couple would sit down on a bench so they could appreciate the natural environment in which they moved. Sometimes during those walks they thought the baby would come early. Yet he was born on schedule in October.

Anna had already selected his name. Ivan was named after one of Russia's most notorious Tsars, a true tyrant. As she gazed at her little son bundled next to her in bed, she'd only wished her father had been tougher. Her father had been "the peacemaker" who'd admired I.Bloch, a philosopher who'd written about the consequences of waging a limited war in Europe. Unfortunately nobody had listened to either Bloch or her father. Anna was young. She was also astute. She realized her father's efforts to keep Russia on a path away from war had been ignored. She'd sometimes eavesdropped on quiet conversations: "The Tsar needed to be stronger." Anna knew her dear father had been criticized unmercifully. He hadn't wanted to be Tsar. He hadn't wanted anyone killed yet Russia had slowly slipped from under her father's control. The consequences had been severe. Anna knew it would take a strong ruler, perhaps another tyrant to lead Russia out of its difficulties. When Carl realized Anna had already selected a name for their son, he was curious as to her choice. "If only father had been more of a tyrant like Ivan the Terrible", she said. The count didn't argue with his wife about the choice of his child's name. He was elated. Anna had given him an heir. Ivan would be the name.

Carl was so proud of his new son that he decided he would remain at home for awhile. At first he'd ignored invitations to return to Moscow to be among the circle of intellectuals he knew. He didn't miss any of them at all. Since his last visit to Moscow, he felt strangely uneasy about being with them. The atmosphere surrounding them had become one of fear. Although Lenin was in declining health, he and his supporters still wielded power. They didn't want anyone challenging the kind of Communism they advocated. The count's circle of friends had done just that.

Like her mother, Anna made every effort to make her husband's time at home comfortable. Nicholas hated to be away from his wife and children for any length of time "A husband should be happiest when he is at home" she'd remembered her mother telling her. "Look how fast Ivan is growing" Anna would say dangling the baby in front of Carl in an obvious attempt at keeping her husband at her side.

Anna's reasons for keeping Carl at home and with his family were more than superficial. She'd noticed men sometimes hiding behind trees near their home. No longer did she take the baby in his stroller followed by Micha for long walks around the castle. She stayed closer to home. "Who are those men? Don't you know who they are?" she'd ask Carl.

"No" he'd replied nervously. He'd leave the castle and disappear for hours when she asked him the question again. It was nearly dark one night when he finally showed up late for dinner before announcing to his wife and mother that he would be leaving for Moscow next week. Anna was shocked at the news and began to cry so did the baby. Countess Marina picked Ivan up and tried to comfort him but Anna had left the room. When Carl went looking for Anna and finally found her, he saw that she was looking at intelligence reports lying atop his office desk. She'd suspected he was under surveillance. There in front of her atop the desk was the proof.

"Is this the reason you're going back to Moscow", she asked, her face pale and tense as she stood holding the papers in front of him. "Your name is on this list. You are under surveillance. Moscow is probably one of the worst places you could be right now."

The count ignored his wife's comments. He was furious with her for delving into his affairs. For the first time in their marriage he began to think that he'd made a mistake in marrying Anna. He wanted to get away from her and sort things out alone. He started going through drawers until he found something. It was a revolver. "Here," he said handing it to her. "I'm going to teach you how to use it tomorrow. You'll feel more protected while I'm gone.

"I want to return to Moscow so I can discover the reason why my name is on that list". Anna was no fool. She thought her husband might be fed up with being tied to home. She didn't realize that he was trying to protect her and his family by drawing attention away from them. In doing so, he hoped that by returning to his friends in Moscow and by living the life he'd been leading before she'd interrupted it he'd be protecting them.

Anna couldn't tell her husband what to do. He had dual citizenship. He was free to enter Russia whenever he chose to go there. She wanted him to remain at her side though. "Please, don't leave me" she said meekly. "You don't know what sort of situation you might be facing in Moscow".

"Darling, I'm going because I don't want either of us to feel hemmed in. We need a little breathing space. You'll get on fine while I'm gone. I'll be back before you know it."

Anna wasn't so sure. She'd lived through enough uncertainty lately. She didn't want to add any more terror filled chapters to a life that had already known too many of them. She began giving Carl a tangled array of reasons for him to stay at home with her. "I believe you can sort things out quite nicely if you'll just take a few precautionary measures. When my sisters and I realized our family would be imprisoned, we burned our diaries. Our most private thoughts were written there. The Bolsheviks wanted to know what we were thinking. I believe the reason they are outside our home sometimes is that they know you are writing something they'd like to find. They are looking for some kind of proof regarding your disloyalty to the new Communist regime. I'm not suggesting that you burn everything but you should be cautious regarding where you place things. Hide your work. Don't show anyone what you've written. Please don't return to Moscow. You don't know who among your friends is really loyal to you. You are a man of influence. You know people in high places. You are watched when you associate with men who are espousing ideas that don't conform to Lenin's Communism. Please don't leave me."

The count listened to his young wife's wisdom. He knew that in Anna's short lifetime, she'd been through more terror then most people could even imagine. He would remain at home. He would watch those who were having him watched. He would put on a façade and he wouldn't react to being scrutinized. Carl knew he was being unrealistic, perhaps even reckless by thinking he might somehow be able to get his name and his friends' names removed from the dread surveillance list. Yet he still wanted desperately to return to Russia and try. He knew he had to find just the right time to do so.

Anna took her husband's arm in hers before saying, "I've had the cook make something very special for you to eat tonight. The food may be better in Moscow but here it's especially prepared just for you. That's something you won't find on every Moscow menu."

Ivan was already asleep in the little cradle that had been placed in the sitting room. Countess Marina was sitting next to Ivan's crib when Anna and Carl joined her.

"I apologize for leaving you so abruptly. Carl and I had to discuss something in private. I see that Ivan is asleep and not behaving too terribly right now. Thank you for rocking him."

Anna was relieved. Carl had promised her that as a family they would stay together and remain alert. He would hide his papers and he would be cautious regarding where he placed things. He knew it was wisdom to keep the baby with them even when they ate their meals. Ivan was Nicholas II's only grandson. If under the Law of Succession, Anna couldn't succeed to the throne, perhaps Ivan could. The count carried his little son's cradle from the dining room where he had placed it while they ate dinner. Micha peered from under the table where he'd hid during the dinner hour then followed the family from the room. He too knew how to be alert in his surroundings. Baby Ivan was well protected.

The next morning Carl gave Anna and Marina each a revolver. "Keep it with you at all times" he'd said showing them how to use a gun and watching them target practice. Later in the day, he watched from a distance as Anna, packing a pistol, took the baby on his daily airing followed by Micha ready to bark loudly if anyone approached them. Nobody dared.

Several months passed. To Anna's relief, Carl broke off working on some of his most controversial writings and burned them. The plan he had implemented was working. The people watching him were losing interest. Time was fleeting so was Carl's idea about returning to his friends in Moscow.

Chapter Five

It was now 1924. Ivan was four years old. For Anna, life thankfully was uneventful and deliciously boring. She had managed to keep her husband at home by making him believe that life outside their little world might culminate in collapse if he suddenly left her side. She didn't know their world was about to cave in when Carl learned that life for his Moscow friends had become something akin to catastrophic. He had to know if the dreadful rumors were true. He had to see if there wasn't something he could do to help his friends. Only yesterday, through an independent source with intelligence connections the count had been told that his former mistress had become the lover of another man in the circle of intellectuals where he'd once moved. The affair had ended. Disappointed in love, the unfortunate woman tragically had gone to the police. She had hoped that an investigation would lead to arrests. The awful plan had worked. Her lover had been arrested and later released but only after he'd provided evidence against his comrades of disloyalty to the current Communist regime. Before the police could pick him up again, the man shot his former mistress and then himself. The damage had been done. Everyone in the circle of intellectuals to which Carl once had belonged had been arrested -- everyone, that is except the count.

Carl wouldn't tell Anna or his mother the reason he was leaving for Moscow. He didn't think he could face that scenario. Instead he told Anna that he'd be gone only a short time. She pleaded with him not to go to Moscow. She felt uneasy when he wasn't home. Although she hadn't seen people hanging around their home trying to observe her family lately, she was sure they hadn't given up watching from afar.

Anna was uneasy when she learned that Countess Marina would be leaving her as well. "I'll only be in Budapest for a short visit" said Marina, who'd never let Anna know, that she blamed her for Carl's unexplained irritability shown towards them lately. "I always enjoy my time in Budapest. I couldn't possibly turn down an invitation to visit there", she said.

Anna's face clouded with disappointment as she wondered if the count and his mother weren't conspiring against her.

"Please my dear" said Marina, suspecting that Carl and Anna must be having unsolved marital problems neither of them had told her about. "You mustn't feel as if I'm deserting you or Ivan. I promise I'll bring back something special for you both upon my return home."

Unlike his mother, Carl hadn't promised to bring Anna something special from Moscow. His plans for returning home were so vague that Anna wondered if Carl planned on returning home at all.

The day the count prepared to leave for Moscow he promised Anna that he would be in touch with her as soon as he arrived there. "Please darling, don't go" she said watching him throw clothes in a suitcase. She wanted to accompany him to Moscow. She still had no proper identification. The authorities would question her for not having any identification. She had to remain where she was. Anna hadn't dared ask her husband if he could obtain identification for her. She felt it would only upset him more if she demanded that he take her with him. In the murky world where Carl moved obtaining identification was no problem for him. He'd changed his identity whenever it was convenient for him to do so. She wondered why he hadn't obtained any identification for her. She was frightened.

"It was a balmy unseasonably warm early January morning when she walked alongside Carl down winding castle steps towards a waiting car. "How long will you be gone?" she asked.

"I'll be gone for just a short time, perhaps only a few weeks. Don't worry about me darling. I have some business contacts I need to make. I'll be in touch with you soon" he said giving her a quick kiss on the lips before stepping into a waiting car.

Anna had her doubts. The January snow had melted but the fear that for years had held her prisoner hadn't. She stood on steps and watched the car disappear carrying her husband to the train depot. She then entered a nearby castle entranceway and ran into Ivan's nanny. When she realized she was about to take the child on a morning walk, Anna quickly glanced up at the sky and said "I think it's going to rain, I'll take Ivan for a walk later."

The nanny followed Anna back indoors while Ivan tugged on his mother's arm and tried to get her attention. Anna stooped and quickly hugged him before picking him up and saying to his nanny, "There are some toys and games I've placed for him in his playroom. Use his free time from lessons that way. I'll send for some juice from the kitchen so he can have a break."

She then quickly handed Ivan back to his nanny before turning and leaving them and hurrying upstairs toward her husband's office so she could make sure the count had put away all his important papers. The room mustn't invite intruders, she thought as she carefully replaced papers that had been lying atop the desk or strewn around the room. She then found the desk drawer key, locked the drawers and placed the key in her pocket. Finally satisfied that nothing in the room was out of place, Anna went to her own office where she unlocked a desk drawer and found the revolver her husband had given her. For a moment she stared at the revolver in her hand and tried to analyze the feeling of terror gripping her. Her life slowly was becoming a nightmare and she again was falling into the dark tunnel of despair that she thought she'd managed to escape. Anna sat down at her desk and tried to get a grip on her emotions before placing the revolver in a belt worn beneath the sweater she wore. Her heart pounded as she glanced at the clock. She was determined that her terror would not interfere with her daily routine. It was getting late. Ivan had been confined to the indoors too long. The nanny could take a break. Anna had a gun for protection. She and her little son would take a short walk.

Several days passed. Anna was certain that Carl had arrived in Moscow. Still she'd had no news from him. She was feeling alone and vulnerable and was beginning to give into despair when a maid showed an unexpected visitor into her midst. "Koba", she said her face brightening in demeanor. Anna started to reach out to him but stopped. Stalin's face was grave. He didn't return the enthusiastic greeting.

"Where is your husband?" he asked in a nervous tone of voice that would suggest that he already had the answer to the question.

"Why he's in Moscow", said Anna seeming frightened and puzzled at Stalin's obvious concern. "Why do you ask?"

"I was on my way back from party headquarters in Berlin. I thought I should pay you a call and tell you that your husband may be in danger if he remains in Moscow. He needs to return home immediately."

Anna was distraught and frightened. She started to ask Koba a question but wisdom dictated she remain silent. She would let him do the talking.

"I'll get word to him. Can you tell me, what the nature of the danger confronting him is?" she finally ventured, expecting an honest answer.

"No", he replied. "Just promise me that you'll contact him immediately."

"You know I will do so." Anna was trembling. She sensed something must be terribly wrong in regard to her husband.

"By the way, why aren't you with him?" asked Stalin.

"I have no identification papers. I lost everything when my family was imprisoned. You should know that."

"I'll see that you receive identification papers," he said leaving. "Please tell Comrade Zurofsky I said hello when you see him?"

"You know I will do so Comrade Stalin. I'm sure my husband will be disappointed to have missed seeing you. Your visits to us have become so rare lately." Stalin turned and nodded his head in farewell but said nothing in reply to the remark. He quickly left her home.

Anna was stunned but not entirely shocked to learn that Carl might be in danger. She had hoped for better news. Her intuition had told her that something might be wrong. He'd left no address of any sort telling her how to contact him. Then she remembered the name of a Moscow hotel where he'd sometimes stayed. She would contact the hotel and leave a message for him saying that there was a family emergency. He needed to return home immediately. Nearly a week passed. Anna still had no news from Carl. In fact her message to him had never even been received by him.

Stalin's warning had come too late. When she tried calling the hotel again she seemed unable to speak with anyone connected with it. Instead an unknown source cut in informing her that her husband had been arrested by the secret police. "Why?" she asked as she heard a click. There was no one on the line. He had hung up.

Anna gasped then placed the phone receiver down. She knew she must contact Stalin immediately. Surely he would be in a position to help Carl. Only yesterday the news had appeared in a morning newspaper headline that "Lenin was dead". In days following, it would become apparent and later official that Stalin, following Lenin's recent death, would succeed him in power.

Anna quickly began writing a letter to Stalin. She needed information regarding Carl's circumstances. Then she received a strange phone call from an unknown source informing her that her husband would remain in prison awaiting execution. Anna gasped. The caller again hung up.

Anna burst into tears. She knew that under the circumstances Stalin was the only person who could help her husband. Whatever it cost, the letter she was writing must reach Stalin as soon as possible. She paid a large sum of money to have a government courier deliver her letter to Russia's new leader in the Kremlin.

When he received the letter and realized it was from Anna, Stalin's reply was short and terse. "I need to see you" he'd written giving her the name of the city, the date and address where the meeting was to take place. Enclosed along with his short reply were the identification documents she would need to enter Russia. Her true identification: Anastasia Nikolaevna, daughter of Nicholas, had been enclosed along with a false one. Enclosed with the identification papers were copies of her marriage certificate and her baby's birth certificate.

There could be no doubt in the eyes of the world that she was Carl's wife and that her child was his. At first Anna thought she should use the false identity on which to travel. She quickly changed her mind. Stalin had indicated in his short note to her that she would be traveling by train first to Moscow and then to Leningrad with prominent government officials. If Stalin knew who she was, they possibly would know who she was as well. Anna would use her real identification document for her journey.

She knew she had to hide Stalin's reply to her and the documents in a secure place. In his absence, Carl had given Anna the key to unlocking the passageway's door. She quickly made her way toward the drawing room and slipped behind the drawing room's wall tapestry before pushing against the heavy passageway door and unlocking it. Anna's heart pounded as she nervously entered the passageway alone. The atmosphere surrounding her was forbidding and the door creaked upon its hinges before slowly closing behind her but still remaining slightly ajar. With flashlight in hand, Anna hid Stalin's letter and the documents behind a loose stone in the wall. She then quickly tried to exit the passageway but tripped on the unevenly paved stone floor and fell. For a moment, Anna seemed stunned and unable to move. Finally she found the strength to crawl slowly towards the exit but noticed that the passageway's door had closed behind her, and the flashlight's bulb had become so dim that she could hardly see to move forward. When Anna finally reached the door she stood up trying to unlock the door but discovered it wouldn't open. She now was feeling so weak that she collapsed while pushing against the door and trying to force the door open. When she realized she was trapped, she wanted to cry out for help but she didn't dare. Carl had told her that the passageway was a family secret. Anna gasped for breath. The atmosphere surrounding her had become so intolerable that she almost fainted before the door gradually opened wide for her and she slowly crawled from the passageway. For a few moments, she lay exhausted in front of the tapestry before crawling away from it and making her way across the drawing room floor then staring. Across the room was a shadowy, almost indiscernible figure who quickly left the room and disappeared. "I must be hallucinating" she thought slowly getting up from the floor. Anna then staggered forward and managed to leave the drawing room before closing its heavy door behind her. When she finally reached the staircase leading to her room upstairs, she sat down pale, trembling and out of breath on a lower step, until a passing maid saw her and asked her if she was all right "May I bring you some tea or something to eat?" she asked, seeming obviously concerned.

"Yes, please do. I haven't had anything to eat today. In fact I think I'll sit right here and enjoy some tea if you'll please bring me a tray."

"Of course" replied the girl who quickly returned with the tea.

After eating and drinking, Anna left the tea tray on a lower step of the stairs before slowly crawling up the stairs toward her room, and collapsing on the bed. She then fell into a deep hypnotic sleep and dreamed of howling wolves and the strange sounding whistle of a distant train that shrieked in unison with the wolves' primeval calls that caused her to restlessly toss and turn until she suddenly awoke to morning daylight.

Chapter Six

Several days had passed. Countess Marina hadn't yet returned from Budapest. Anna was relieved. She didn't have to be the one to break the news to her mother-in-law about her son's desperate circumstances.

She began packing her bag in preparation for her journey but Anna still felt weak and disoriented from the strain she'd been under lately. She knew she needed to relax but her inability to do so was getting the better of her.

In the morning a car would pick her up and deliver her to the train depot. From there she would join others aboard the private rail car bound for Moscow. Anna hastily scribbled a note for Countess Marina telling her she'd be gone for a few days but soon would be home. She refrained from instructing her mother-in-law not to worry. She'd wanted to tell her that if she and Carl hadn't returned home within a few days that she should get in touch with the authorities but Anna hesitated. She knew it would be futile to advise Marina to do that. There was really nobody other than Stalin who could help her and Carl. Anna also left instructions for the nanny to keep a close watch on her little son while she was gone, and to restrict all outside recreation: "Let Ivan ride his tricycle up and down the armory room's corridor."

When morning arrived and it was only a scant hour before she was to leave on her journey, Anna was terrified of having to enter the forbidden passageway to retrieve her documents. She was stunned and stared with disbelief when she realized she wouldn't have to do so. In her desk drawer and next to the flashlight, were the documents she'd hidden in the passageway. She was sure she hadn't placed the documents there, and then she remembered the strange shadowy figure she'd earlier seen. Had he placed the documents in the drawer for her to find? She wouldn't speculate. With suitcase and documents in hand, she left the castle and stepped into a waiting car delivering her to the depot where she boarded an official train bound for Moscow.

Once aboard the train, Anna was shown to a seat where she sat alone and nervously glanced at people seated across from her. She hoped nobody would ask the nature of her visit to Moscow. She was afraid of saying or doing something that might jeopardize her husband's precarious and dangerous situation. Surely nobody knows that Carl is in prison she tried to tell herself. Anna knew better. She silently gazed out a window at the landscape of early melting snow and patchy green scenery or she buried her nose in a book as the train rapidly made headway. When someone offered her a cup of tea, Anna smiled and relaxed. "Thank you comrade" she said grateful for the kindness she so sorely needed right now. Later another kind attendant showed her to a private compartment where she could be alone. A couple of days passed. The train finally arrived in Moscow, and a car picked her up at the station and delivered her to the Kremlin where an attendant showed her to a private room where she could rest and prepare for the next day's journey to Leningrad. Anna assumed Stalin was in Leningrad and not at the Kremlin. Her meeting with him was to take place in Leningrad. She then sat down in a comfortable chair before getting up from it so she could cross the room and gaze at her reflection in a mirror. There were huge circles under her lovely blue eyes. In despair she buried her face in her hands but refrained from weeping. She knew she needed rest. She was too nervous and frightened to get a good night's sleep. She was grateful that her meals were delivered to her room without her having to ask for the warm tea and scrambled eggs she especially liked. Anna appreciated her quiet surroundings. She sank again into the comfortable chair and observed a wall clock methodically ticking away the hours as if time was of little consequence.

But time was of great consequence. She wondered how much time her husband had. Why was everyone trying to make her comfortable yet at the same time trying to avoid having a conversation with her? Why wouldn't anybody open up and give her just a hint as to where her husband was being held prisoner? Someone must know where Carl was. Anna climbed into bed, and bawled into her pillow.

The following day, she boarded a train en route to Leningrad. Comforts aboard that official train afforded luxuries that weren't available to ordinary comrades. Extra pillows and blankets even chocolate and spirits were available to her but Anna refrained from indulging in any of them. When an attendant showed her to a private compartment, she felt relieved to be alone. She slumped down on the small bed then listened to the train's easy even rhythm as night hours diminished and early morning daylight brought her closer to her destination.

Once called St. Petersburg, Leningrad was a city she'd remembered well as a child. Anna pressed her hand against a window as if she were trying to reach out to the past and somehow retrieve the lost years. It was emotionally wrenching to see beautiful buildings and palaces she hadn't seen for so long. She wanted to step into that long ago world once more but she knew she couldn't. Instead, she was shown to a room in a comfortable but modest hotel where she tried to rest but found she couldn't sleep. She kept tossing and turning after waking from terrible nightmares. Anna tried not to think of how desperate her husband's situation was. She also felt remorse because her family's regime during the revolution hanged Lenin's brother. Stalin was in charge now. Anna knew that during the revolution he'd sometimes been an informer to the Tsarist police and that his loyalties had vacillated. She hoped that Stalin's loyalty towards her husband rather than to a cruel system would win out in the end. Surely Stalin would help Carl and see that his friend was justly treated. Anna slowly drifted off to sleep.

The following morning Anna heard a knock and opened the door so she could receive the breakfast tray that had been delivered to her room. "Thank you comrade" she said before placing the tray aside. She was unable to think about food right now. Instead she brushed her hair and quickly started dressing. She chose a black dress for her meeting with Stalin. It would go well with her simple beige coat and black shoes. Black was an appropriate color to wear. Her husband might die. She tried putting on mascara. Her eyes were too red and swollen from crying. She couldn't do it. A little lipstick and a hint of makeup would have to do. Anna then looked at herself in the mirror. She was ready to meet Stalin. Finally she heard a knock upon the door before a maid entered the room and informed her that a government car was waiting for her. Anna quickly took the lift downstairs where a driver met her then led her to the waiting car. After she'd gotten into it and the car was making its way through traffic, the world around her seemed a blur. Anna was feeling nauseous and dizzy but she knew she couldn't collapse now.

When she arrived at the Winter Palace just before 10:00 AM Anna felt almost numb as she stepped from the car and made her way upstairs to Stalin's office. It was precisely 10:00 AM when a guard opened Comrade Stalin's office door and Anna gazed across the room at where he stood. He was looking out a window with his back to her when he heard her say to him, "Koba I need your help." She didn't need to tell him. Comrade Stalin knew why she was there. He seemed quite isolated and terribly alone as he slowly turned around and faced her.

"Your father was a good man. I am saving your husband's life because you are Nicholas II's daughter." Stalin again turned from her and gazed out the window. Anna slowly approached him. For the first time ever, she realized how powerful Stalin had become. Anna knew that power isolated those who possessed it. It could destroy the one who lost it. Power had destroyed her father. She knew power made one vulnerable to those who wanted power too. Stalin was not allowing power to slip from him. He would use whatever means necessary to hold on to it. He would crush anyone who would try to take it from him.

Anna wanted to understand this man who'd suddenly become so powerful. He turned around so she could search his face. Anna gazed into Stalin's eyes. Was this the man she'd come to love? Stalin gently placed his hands on Anna's shoulders."I am saving your husband's life because he is a good man and because I love you." Anna started to sob. He held her in his arms as if he were holding a child before gently pushing her away from him. "Go" he said, "He is waiting for you." Anna thanked Stalin and immediately left him. She was eager to see Carl. She felt enormous relief and gratitude when she'd left Stalin's office. She knew what he'd done for her was almost unprecedented. Yet she felt overcome by sadness as she approached the Fortress where her husband waited for her. She shuddered when realizing Stalin had chosen this place over any other for her to be reunited with him. She knew those who entered this particular prison never came out of it. Anna was certain that Stalin hadn't had her husband and friends arrested. Lenin's regime had. She presumed that everyone except Carl now was dead. When she saw the condition he was in though she wanted to vomit. When she went to embrace him she held the ghost of the man who had been her husband.

Carl hadn't deserved the misery he'd endured. He hadn't seen any of his political friends in over four years. Yet she'd had to come begging to Stalin to save Carl's life. Anna felt confused and resentful. At least she had her identity back. That was something Stalin had given her. She never would have obtained her marriage certificate, her baby's birth certificate or her own ID if it hadn't have been for Stalin's insistence that she come to visit him.

Despite the cold damp day, Anna was tempted to ask the driver to let her out of the car. She felt frightened and upset. She had to clear her mind and get a grip on a clouded situation. She wanted to walk back to the hotel, gather her belongings, and take the next available train to Moscow alone. Perhaps she was overreacting.

Her husband looked so pitiful. Anna knew she'd played the fool. She'd played along with the whole outrageous cruel charade and won. She was furious with them. If Carl and his friend hadn't had the same mistress who'd turned informer, his friends would still be alive and holding their clandestine political meetings. She felt ashamed of herself for what she was thinking. He'd looked so pathetic standing there waiting for her to get him out of hell's way. "Poor darling, He'd really been roughed up" she thought before affectionately holding him in her arms as he silently wept in them. His ordeal must have been far worse than anything she'd imagined. He'd had to lean on her as she'd helped him into the car taking them back to the hotel. He only had the clothes on his back. His other clothes and suitcase had been taken from him. Now he was the one without id. How was she to get her husband out of Russia without his papers?

Suddenly Anna felt empathy towards her husband regarding his trying ordeal. She hadn't realized that what Carl found to be even more unbearable than his horrific imprisonment was the thought that he and his friends had been betrayed by revolutionists they'd once supported and helped put in power. In his heart Carl was burdened by the morbid thought that he should have died with his friends. Anna didn't know what Carl was thinking as she tried without success to comfort him. She only knew she'd been determined to save his life regardless of the cost. Anna also knew she had to get him home to Romania.

But first she again would play the meek little wife. She would contact Stalin and ask him for the return of her husband's papers, id and personal belongings. Surely Stalin would see that Carl was returned everything--perhaps even the suitcase. Right now Carl needed a doctor. Anna asked the driver to wait while she helped her husband out of the car, into the hotel and into an elevator. She quickly escorted him to her hotel room before leaving him there and asking a passing maid if she please could bring her husband breakfast. The maid knew who Anna was. She was the guest of an unnamed government official. "Of course, comrade", she replied

Anna got into the elevator delivering her to the small hotel's lobby, and hurried out to the waiting car. She then instructed the driver to take her to the Winter Palace. The man seemed reluctant to do that. His instructions had been to return Anna and her husband to the hotel. He knew that she was a friend of an important government official. On second thought, He decided he would take Anna where she wanted to go. The car entered the gates surrounding the Winter Palace and swept past guards before stopping in front of the building. Anna quickly left the car, entered the palace and made her way to Stalin's office. A guard was standing outside his opened office door when Stalin looked up from what he was doing, and told the guard to allow Anna to enter the room.

Anna visibly trembled and fought back tears, before approaching Stalin. "Carl's identification papers, suitcase, clothes and all personal belongings need to be returned to him. He also needs a doctor", she sobbed. Stalin gently showed Anna to a chair so she could listen to what he had to say.

"When Carl entered prison, it was assumed that he wouldn't need identification papers or personal belongings anymore. Now that he has been released and not marked for execution, I'll see that new identification papers and travel documents are delivered to him today." Stalin picked up a piece of paper and scribbled an address on it. Then handing the paper to Anna he said, "Here, go to this address. Select whatever clothes you think your husband might need. The bill will be sent to the Kremlin. As for the doctor you've requested, I've already had one sent to the hotel. He's with your husband now."

Anna got up to leave but hesitated. She turned to him then calmly said "Thank you Comrade Stalin". Stalin quietly showed Anna to the door and opened it for her. He watched from a window as she got into the car carrying her away. Anna gripped the car's armrest before bursting into tears. She understood the risk Stalin had taken in helping her. She knew Stalin's position within the Bolshevik regime was a precarious one. Lenin was dead but there was a power struggle going on even now within the Communist party. The struggle was bloody and cruel. Stalin was winning and would continue to win but he wouldn't seize complete control of the party until 1929.

The official car pulled up beside the hotel and Anna quickly entered the hotel, and found the room where Carl was sleeping. The doctor had attended to his injuries and had given him a sedative so that he could rest. Anna sympathetically gazed down at him. He was terribly thin. She only could imagine the ordeal he'd been through.

The clothes she'd selected for him to wear on their journey home soon were delivered to the hotel. Along with them were their travel documents and her husband's identification papers. Anna sighed with relief when she received the items and signed for them. She glanced at her sleeping husband before taking a look at the travel documents. They would leave tomorrow evening on an overnight train bound for Moscow. That train would connect with another that would take them across the border to Romania. She placed the documents back in the envelope but she didn't put them aside. Anna was exhausted. She removed a few of her clothes and with the documents in hand she slipped into bed next to her husband. At last he was beside her. She was taking him home alive.

Chapter Seven

For the time being, Anna wasn't looking back. Stalin had released her and she had won her husband's freedom. Anna was also aware that Carl was dazed and slightly in shock after they'd boarded the train and silently sat together in it. Yet even though he appeared uncommunicative, Carl was acutely aware of what Anna had done for him. He knew she'd taken a risk in approaching Stalin. Carl suspected that Stalin was in love with Anna. In saving his life, Stalin had done it for Anna as much as for him.

When the train finally made its stop at the village station, a car awaited the couple to take them home. Anna was so relieved when they set foot in the car that she burst into tears but quickly regained her composure when the car delivered them to their front door. Micha was already at the door barking when Anna walked through the doorway and swept him up in her arms. He'd heard the sound of the car's engine even before the vehicle drove up the steep castle driveway."Dear Micha" she said cuddling him as Ivan who'd heard the car pull up too, came running to greet his parents. The count was still quite weak and he didn't try to pick his son up in his arms as he usually did when he ran to them. Ivan hadn't noticed his father's weakened condition. He'd only noticed that the father he loved was finally home. The count stooped down and let his son place his arms around his neck as Anna stooped and greeted the child with a hug and kiss.

Marina had only yesterday returned home from Budapest. She was unaware of her son's recent ordeal or of what Anna had had to do to bring him home. Anna wanted to keep all that a secret from her mother-in-law. She also knew that her husband needed rest and time to recuperate. Marina had noticed her son's condition and immediately was concerned. "It's so good to see you again mother" said Carl quickly greeting his mother but clearly evading any questions she might ask regarding his health or recent absence. Anna quickly took Carl's arm in hers and followed by Micha led her husband upstairs. In the morning, she would consult another doctor but today Anna wanted to give Carl the emotional support he needed. She also wanted to shield him from household scrutiny and she asked the servants to bring all meals for them to his room. For the rest of the day they would remain alone sequestered together.

Anna sat on the edge of the bed where Carl lay appearing still somewhat dazed. She then picked up Micha and cuddled him in her arms before placing him on the floor so she could reach for the small tote she'd carried with her into the bedroom. She rummaged through the tote and found the sedatives the doctor had prescribed for Carl and gave him one before again cuddling Micha in her arms. When Carl finally fell asleep, Anna could only imagine the horrors of his nightmares. She hoped that the medication she'd given him would block the trauma he'd been through. She hoped too that soon she would have him back, and that he would be the man he'd been before he'd left her to go to Moscow.

After replacing the medicine in the bag and removing the documents from it, Anna wondered if she dared again hide the documents in Dracula's passageway. Even though she was apprehensive, she wanted to test her vulnerability. Her intuition told her that it would be safe for her to do so. With flashlight and documents in hand, Anna bravely made her way downstairs and slipped behind the drawing room tapestry before unlocking the passageway door. Upon entering the passageway, she shivered and trembled with astonishment to see a lantern slowly illuminate her dark forbidding surroundings. For a moment, Anna just stared in disbelief at the lantern, before hiding the documents behind a loose stone in the wall. After hiding them, she turned to leave and shivered seeing the lantern light dim behind her as she closed the passageway door. When she returned to the upstairs bedroom, Anna again cuddled Micha and watched Carl sleep. He appeared to be so peaceful she couldn't resist gently leaning forward and kissing his forehead. The welcome calm of her surroundings prompted her to reflect too on her recent passageway visit. Anna wondered who had placed the lantern on the floor allowing her to maneuver so easily through the passageway's deep darkness. She was sure that whoever had done so must have been friend and not foe.

Anna left Carl's bedside only when a maid knocked on the door and announced that Countess Marina was having tea. She was flushed and embarrassed. "Of course", she would join her mother-in-law for tea she said leaving the room as Micha followed at her heels.

Ivan was crying because the parents he loved had disappeared so abruptly. Marina had tried to comfort the child. "Your Mommy needs to be with your Daddy right now. You'll have a visit with him later." Ivan left his grandmother's lap and ran to Anna when he saw her enter the room. He then leaned against his mother, now sitting in a chair as his grandmother poured tea for Anna and herself.

"I'm so sorry to have been rude. Carl hasn't been well. I needed to see that he followed doctor's orders and get some rest." Marina knew her son looked as if he'd been through a terrible ordeal. Wisdom dictated she refrain from asking questions regarding Anna's recent absence from home. Although she was concerned about her son's condition, Marina would wait for her daughter-in-law to broach the subject.

"My dear, you look exhausted", she said handing Anna a cup of tea. Ivan reached for one of the delicious iced buns sitting on a silver plate before either his mother or grandmother could stop him.

"He eats entirely too many sweets" said Anna taking the roll covered with thick icing from the child's hand as he started to cry. Anna hugged her son then wiped his sticky little hands with a napkin and gazed sadly at Marina. She wanted to tell the older woman everything. It was all too shocking and unbelievable. She had to get a handle on her emotions.

"Whatever you have to tell me, will wait until you want to talk about it."

Anna was grateful to Marina for her calm assurance. She was relieved that she hadn't had to burden the older woman. Anna then sighed and gazed at the room's familiar surroundings. She was beginning to feel safe. Ivan climbed into his mother's lap and Anna broke off a piece of the bun and gave it to the child. She then wiped his sticky little face with a napkin and continued her conversation with her mother-in-law. As they talked, Marina noticed the tears welling up in Anna's eyes but she said nothing. She knew Anna wanted to hide the pain concerning an almost intolerable experience.

Anna gazed across the room at a window. It was still winter but the snow outside was almost gone and lately the days seemed more like spring than early February. Anna was still reluctant for her son's nanny to take the boy outdoors. When she appeared, and Anna had the opportunity to do so she asked her if she would let the child have his nap. "I'll take him for a short walk later."

"I miss you Mommy" said Ivan as the Nanny started to lead the child away from his mother. Anna felt guilty. She hadn't been a good mother lately. She'd left her little son too long. She knew he was feeling neglected. Marina silently thought so too. Micha lay down on the floor near the chair where Marina sat, as Anna called to her son, "Mommy will take you for a walk later."

"It was late in the afternoon. Anna knew she probably wouldn't take her son for a walk today. It soon would be dark. Anna hated darkness. She'd moved in too much of it lately. She'd lived through a nightmare. She hoped it was over now. Something inside of her told her that it was just beginning.

Tears again welled up in Anna's eyes and she suddenly broke off the conversation she was having with her mother-in-law. "Excuse me", she said before placing aside the teacup and saucer. "I need to check on him again." Marina concernedly watched Anna quickly make her way towards the stairs leading to the bedroom where she found Carl dressed and standing at the edge of the bed. From the expression on his face, Anna knew their marriage was in trouble. She wanted him to hold her. She wanted him to understand that she'd only gone to Stalin because she was so desperate that he shouldn't die.

"What did Stalin ask from you in return for my life?" he asked quietly.

"The count slowly placed his hands around her neck but he didn't try to hurt her. Instead he pushed her down upon the bed where she lay sobbing. "Nothing, nothing" she continued sobbing.

"Do you love that monster?" he asked. Anna stopped sobbing then sat upright on the edge of the bed. She knew she didn't love Stalin in the way her husband thought she did.

"They were going to execute you. I went to Stalin. I asked for your life. He gave it to you" she said getting up. "I don't know why you were hurt the way you were. I only know that Stalin said you weren't supposed to come out of prison. Your clothes, identification, suitcase, everything had been confiscated because you weren't supposed to be freed. You were supposed to die with the others! Yes, I love Stalin for saving your life."

Anna gently took Carl's hand in hers before placing her arms around him and sobbing. He held her close before slowly pushing her away from him so he could search her face for the truth. Could there be any trust or sincerity between them anymore? He knew Stalin had proposed to her too. He knew he'd promised to make her Empress of Russia. And then he remembered the day he saw her in Perm--- a bedraggled waif with a little dog in her arms. Carl knew his wife had looked to anyone even Stalin, who would love her. Carl realized that he owed his life to Stalin as well as to Anna. He knew he was being a fool for his sorry behavior in holding resentment toward the people who'd won his freedom. Yet circumstances had nearly destroyed him. His friends-- some of the people who'd meant the most to him in the world had been executed. That wasn't Anna's fault. In his heart Carl knew it wasn't Stalin's fault either. Anna had only wanted to save the one person in the world who was protecting her. He knew he was that person. He also knew that Anna, in her innocence had thought she could align herself with Stalin. "Tell me you'll never go to him again", he said.

Anna knew that Stalin in his way loved her. She couldn't say that Stalin would never find her again. She knew that while the count was alive she would never go to him.

"I won't go to Stalin again", she said. Anna loved Carl. She could never betray him, and she hoped he understood that. Yet she didn't know that her husband hadn't looked to her or anyone for help or rescue.

Anna was just beginning to understand her husband's emotions when he asked her, "Why didn't you let me die with them?"

"You have to go on living so you somehow can avenge the wrong done to your friends" she answered yet seeming shocked by what he'd just asked her.

Carl knew Anna was right. He knew everything he and his friends had been fighting for had been demeaned by a powerful regime that couldn't be challenged. Like Anna, he was a lone survivor, and his life could only have meaning if he had the courage and strength to go on living and searching for the freedom for which he and his friends had been fighting.

Carl placed his arms around Anna. Somehow they had to find each other again. There was too much pain between them to talk anymore. They searched for each other the only way they knew how right now.

Chapter Eight

Several months had passed. Life had returned to normal. The count had regained his former strength and Anna was busy being a good wife and mother. The atmosphere surrounding the family had become less fearful. Countess Marina hadn't asked either Anna or Carl any questions regarding their recent absence from home. Neither of them wanted to bring the subject up with anyone. It was a closed chapter in their lives. Anna and Carl alone would hold the remembrance of that difficult journey. Yet Anna was eager to learn if Stalin was maintaining his power within Russia. There was no question about it. She shuddered when she thought of the power struggle going on within the Bolshevik regime. Ivan sat at her side and Micha at her feet as each morning Anna read the daily paper. She scanned the front page with nervous anticipation before reading less important news contained within its pages.

The count knew he couldn't remain at home indefinitely. He knew eventually he would have to become part of the dangerous landscape unfolding before his eyes. And yet for the time being, he knew wisdom dictated that he remain sequestered with his family. Stalin was testing not only his authority within the party but society's intellectual climate as well. In days ahead, Stalin's relentless persecution of anyone who wrote or said anything he considered detrimental to his policies focused on the poet Osip Mandelstam who had predicted Nicholas II's destruction after Bloody Sunday.

> "We don't live, we just tiptoe through life
> At ten paces words are mere silence
> And if an occasion for converse occurs
> We remember the man from the Highlands

In the Kremlin with chicken-necked chieftains all around
The rabble he mocks and relies on . . ."

Mandelstam was arrested and banished. Mandelstam's wife pleaded with Stalin on behalf of her husband. At first Stalin appeared to be accommodating with people like the writer Pasternak and others who rallied to Mandelstam's cause. The damage had been done. Other people within the intellectual community slowly were arrested.

Anna shuddered. Something within her rebelled against what was happening to the intelligentsia. Anna and Carl knew that Stalin's arrest of people he saw as a challenge to him was one way he tried to maintain power within the party. He would intimidate others if doing so enabled him to hold onto power. Anna was a survivor. She understood how cruel the game of power could be. Her father was dead and her family destroyed because the Tsar had forgotten how to be ruthless. Although she would never admit it to Carl, Anna looked to Stalin as a protector for her family. Russia had been brought to its knees with revolution, civil war and World War I. Stalin would take any measures necessary to bring about stabilization within Russian society even if that meant silencing the voices of opposition.

For the time being, Anna would play the gentle role of wife and mother. She was pregnant again. She would wait until after her baby was born. She wasn't content to sit on the sidelines and watch the power struggle unfold. She felt destined to become part of it. Through her husband, Anna would be part of it. The count was a man who was loyal to none. Yet Anna sensed that her husband would work with Stalin. He would befriend him again if doing so meant protecting himself and his family. Carl was still a spy. He'd not forgotten how to move within a dangerous world and survive in it. Yet that world was becoming increasingly treacherous. The individual rights of men had been absorbed by the will of the powerful. Carl was a realist. He knew that for the time being at least his will had to be Stalin's.

Anna had named her first son for her favorite Tsar, Ivan the Terrible. Her second child was named for her husband and her late father, Carl Nicholas.

The count gazed down at the boy who lay in his mother's arms. Anna looked up from cradling her new baby and said "Why is it that I'm able to have healthy sons? My mother could only have healthy daughters?" The count didn't answer his wife. Anna knew how much the Romanovs had wanted a healthy male heir. Her face grew sad as she contemplated their disappointment.

"Rest, darling" he said kissing her before leaving her so she could sleep. As Anna rested, her sleep was uneasy. She kept waking up and gazing down at the little bundle next to her. She didn't want anyone to take him from her. When finally Anna was able to rest, her sleep was disturbed by nightmares. The sound of a distant train whistle interfered with her slumber. Half awake and still in the throes of a nightmare, Anna suddenly awoke. At first she thought that she was still aboard the train that was taking her family away. When she gazed around the room and realized where she really was her fear subsided. A fire still burned in the hearth. She half expected to see her mother standing nearby. She wanted to show her new baby to her but her mother wasn't there. Anna's eyes glazed over. Her mother would have been so pleased for her. Anna always would believe her mother and sisters were somehow alive. She must never give up hope. Yet Anna knew what hope she had for the survival of her family now lay asleep and wrapped in a small blanket next to her on the bed. She felt almost guilty for her good fortune, and new found joy.

Chapter Nine

Time was passing quickly. Anna loved her husband and family. She and Carl had spent the recent passing years watching their young sons grow. Anna wanted to hold onto those precious memories. Those years were an important part of her life. But so was the time when she'd first come to live at her husband's mountainous castle retreat. On early morning walks alone or with Micha on his leash, she remembered that time years ago when she'd stood at a window, watched the sunrise and heard a lone black wolf cry and greet in exultation the blood red sunrise. During those walks, Anna sometimes thought she'd again glimpsed that wolf of long ago but he'd suddenly disappeared in shadow as if the image of him had been only a mirage. Anna realized her world of wilderness and isolation was unlike that of other people. She wondered if some the things she saw around her weren't simply illusion. Yet the image of the wolf seemed to be too wild and beautiful to be illusion. When Anna finally discovered the trail where she thought she'd last glimpsed the magnificent creature, she went looking for his tracks so she might prove to herself that he was real and not a figment of her imagination. Instead she felt herself slipping backward in time as if she were reliving the past. As she moved in that other world, she was astounded to realize her past life remained unmarred and happy. Her lucid dream was so real that Anna was comforted by the thought that no shadow of death had ever touched her family's life. Yet even if the painful memory of her father's death and the unknown fate of her mother and sisters, contradicted the one of her lucid dream, Anna knew she had to move forward in life. Her world of wilderness and beauty compensated for all the cruelty she'd ever endured or witnessed. Anna had the courage to face her waking dream because she had found enough love within herself to take hold of her new life and live it. Despite the trauma and insecurity she'd sometimes felt in her marriage, and the realization that Countess Marina was still the matriarch of her husband's household, Anna was grateful to them. They had introduced her to a new life. They had given her a second chance but then so had Stalin.

Anna was almost wistful as she went about her daily routine fulfilling her role as wife and mother. She wasn't sure if she deserved the peace and security she felt in life. She then thought about Stalin and remembered that he too was an integral part of her life's complicated web. She had found her way forward in life partly because he had opened the gate for her. She told herself that she was no longer in love with him but she was curious about his life, and she wondered if he was happy in his marriage.

Nadezhda (Nadia) was beautiful and Stalin loved her yet she was at times melancholy and her melancholy had put a strain upon their marriage. Nadezhda had seen how ruthlessly her husband had wielded his way to power. His ruthlessness frightened her and she was also jealous if Stalin paid attention to other beautiful women.

Stalin was too cautious to become seriously involved with any of them but he liked to flirt with women especially those who were attractive and who could laugh with him when he told a joke. Nadezhda and Stalin had a little daughter Svetlana and a young son Vasily. From all outward appearances Stalin was enjoying a happy family life.

The couple often relaxed by entertaining other comrades within the party. Since the political climate within the party was often changing, beneath the conviviality there was often an undercurrent of fear and uncertainty at such gatherings. Nadezhda was sensitive to the changing political climate. She knew there was dangerous intrigue surrounding her husband. She'd looked especially lovely one night at a party celebration. She'd wanted her husband to notice her. She'd worn a beautiful silk print dress that evening. In her hair was one perfect rose. She'd observed Stalin flirting with another woman. It was nothing serious but Nadezhda, suddenly left the gathering of friends. She went home alone and shot herself with a revolver.

Outwardly Stalin continued with his life as if nothing tragic had happened. He showered attention on his children. He continued to flirt with the pretty women but Stalin had become a lonely man. Mention of Nadezhda's name brought tears to his eyes.

Several months passed following Nadezhda's death. There were too many people close to him who had their own theories about what happened the night she died. For the time being Stalin ignored the gossip and treachery. Instead he concentrated on reforming the party. Old colleagues in arms, men who had served Lenin gradually were replaced. The ex-leaders, the united Trotskyist, Zinovievite center: Kamenev and Smirnov were sentenced to death by shooting. While he was destroying some party leftists, Stalin also was getting rid of a few party rightists. Prominent men like Ryutin and Yagoda, who had been in charge of the Moscow Volga Canal construction where starving and overworked workers died by the thousands, were shot too.

Anna knew her husband still had contacts within the world of espionage. Carl knew that Stalin had destroyed prominent members of his party and others less prominent. Carl also was aware of the cruelty and tensions existing elsewhere in Europe. The count didn't want his family to become involved in Russian or European political intrigue. Carl knew he was being unrealistic in thinking he could leave his comfortable castle retreat and take his family elsewhere to live. He felt bound to his ancestral home. Yet the world was becoming increasingly dangerous. The situation in Nazi Germany and in other European countries was like some ominous threatening cloud ready to explode. Stalin had spared his life but at what cost? The Communist regime had nearly destroyed him and his wife. Carl also realized that eventually he would have to declare his loyalty either to the Nazis or to Stalin. He would choose the lesser evil. If self-preservation dictated that he become part of Stalin's world again he would do so. Anna was too naïve to understand the darkness and tension growing throughout Europe. The count would protect Anna. He knew he was stronger than the dictator. He was the one who had rescued the Romanov grand duchess that day. One can only imagine what would have happened to Anna if she hadn't slipped through the gate and gone with him to Romania. Carl felt guilty for telling himself that Stalin hadn't played a major part in Anna's rescue. He knew he was jealous of Stalin. He couldn't afford to be disloyal or jealous of a man who'd saved his life yet a sense of insecurity haunted him and Carl sometimes allowed himself to indulge in petty emotions regarding his old comrade Koba. Carl knew Stalin needed men who would be loyal to him. He sensed that Stalin thought he was one of the loyal few and that he soon would pay him and his wife a visit.

Anna had believed that the world in which Stalin moved might become theirs again. Yet she didn't want again to be drawn into a system that had destroyed her parents and siblings. Anna understood power. She also understood cruelty and she condemned it. She knew Carl would want her to welcome the dictator if he approached them. What other choice did either of them have?

When Stalin finally contacted Anna it was an awkward meeting. Had he come to test her loyalty? Anna was an intelligent woman. The years of trauma and turmoil during revolution and war had given her political savvy. She was also a realist. Anna knew that she and Carl had to befriend Stalin if only in the interest of self-preservation. Anna also realized a man as proud as Carl must be the one to extend the hand of friendship to the dictator.

It was a rainy late afternoon when a maid led Stalin into Anna's presence. Her husband stood just outside the room and eavesdropped on their conversation. It was a conversation that would draw Anna and Carl even closer together as husband and wife. Upon arrival, Stalin had given Anna a box. When she opened it she saw that it contained items that once had belonged to her late father. The beautiful Faberge egg the late Tsar had placed on his desk contained portraits of his wife and children. And then there was the letter her mother had written: "forgive them for they know not what they do." Did Stalin realize what the Bolsheviks had done to her family? Stalin's words fell on deaf ears when he told her that the men who'd carried out her father's assassination had been executed. Anna knew the man who had ordered his death was still alive. She didn't know he wouldn't be executed until 1942. She was polite to Stalin but behind the façade was a woman who harbored resentment toward a regime she couldn't forgive. Never once did she invite the dictator to take a chair so they could talk.

The count hadn't entered the room. Instead he'd continued to eavesdrop on the conversation his wife was having with Stalin. He was pleased. Anna was behaving as he'd hoped she'd behave.

It was a cordial meeting. Stalin hardly realized how cordial everything had been until he left the count's home. Finally Carl entered the room and found Anna standing alone.

"I'm afraid Stalin has just left", she said when Carl asked her where he had gone.

Carl ignored her comment and quickly found a lantern before running outside in search of Stalin. He held the lantern up and in that light he saw in the near distance a shadowy figure making his way down the steep driveway. "We need to talk" he called out to him." Upon hearing Carl's voice, Stalin turned and approached his friend.

"Forgive me for intruding upon you and your family so suddenly. I came to talk with you. I assumed you weren't at home when you didn't join your wife and me in the conversation we were having."

"I apologize for my absence. I insist that you join me and Anna for dinner. There isn't another train back to Moscow until tomorrow morning. You must remain here with us tonight. You are an important man. It isn't safe for you to stay unguarded in a village inn."

From a distance and in the dim lantern light, Anna was relieved to see her husband and Stalin confronting one another. She knew Carl remained the dictator's friend. The political climate demanded it yet Anna had her own personal reasons for wanting the count to remain friends with Stalin. The darkness, the death struggle within her soul drew Anna to Stalin. Yet Anna loved her husband. She'd never loved anyone as much as she loved the count. She knew the dictator needed her husband's loyalty and help in the dark struggle that lay ahead for Russia. She also knew that her husband held little allegiance to anyone. Anna shuddered as flames from the fireplace created a false sense of warmth and security after Anna met Carl and Stalin and they sat together in a nearby sitting room. It was the mid 1930's. The American and European depression had dealt a devastating blow to the world economies. The count had predicted that in light of the dismal economic conditions, another European war was inevitable. If there was another war Anna knew where her husband's loyalty must lie. It had to be with Russia. Stalin was Russia.

It was a cordial family dinner. Countess Marina joined the couple and their guest in the dining room. Marina was a good conversationalist and an experienced hostess. She knew how to make the visitor feel at home. She also knew how to unburden her daughter-in-law who was feeling shaken by Stalin's visit. Anna hadn't wanted to give that impression to Marina. She didn't have to do so. Neither woman said anything when they'd observed Carl and Stalin get up from the table so they could talk privately. The older woman understood when following dinner Anna said "Excuse me".

Marina simply said," I've visited with the children and I've read a good night story with Carl Nicholas." Anna thanked her mother-in-law for her thoughtfulness before leaving her and turning to go upstairs. Both understood the other's need to be alone.

Carl knew what Stalin wanted from him even before asking as he invited the dictator to sit down in a comfortable sitting room chair.

"I want you to handle all security involving me" he said.

The count hesitated. He was a man of independent wealth and he wanted to be perceived as such. He wanted Stalin to think that he didn't need to do anything in life that might jeopardize him or his family's wellbeing.

"I'm not asking that you live entirely in Moscow. You have your home here in Romania. You and your wife will be given a comfortable apartment in the Kremlin. Your official title will be Social Advisor to me. You and Anna will be invited to important party functions. Your chief duty though will be to guard my interests. If there is anyone who needs to be eliminated within the party, I know your skilled tactics and experience within the world of espionage will enable you to carry out your mission and mine to our mutual satisfaction."

Carl was silent. He knew he had to make an immediate decision. Stalin would perceive any hesitation on his part to be weakness, perhaps even disloyalty. He couldn't say no to the man who'd saved his life. Yet he knew if he accepted Stalin's offer to work for him that he again would be entering a dangerous world of intrigue.

He didn't want to consult Anna regarding the decision. He thought he knew what she would say. He also knew that Anna was not in a position to advise him regarding the matter.

When Carl slipped into bed next to his wife she was asleep and he didn't want to wake her. He didn't want to tell her he was working for Stalin.

* * * *

If Carl thought Stalin had paid his family a visit unnoticed, he was mistaken. The following morning, Stalin had just finished breakfast with Carl and his family when a maid appeared. She told Carl that a car was waiting to take Stalin to the train depot.

Carl accompanied Stalin to the door and watched as two agents met the dictator before leading him to a waiting car chauffeuring him away and quickly disappearing along the narrow driveway leading from the estate.

Anna hadn't joined her husband standing at the door and somberly watching Stalin's departure. She knew Carl had something important to tell her. He wouldn't tell her anything about his meeting with Stalin just now. When she saw him quickly turn and go upstairs to his office, Anna understood Carl well enough to know she shouldn't follow him just now. He needed to be alone.

Whatever concern she had about her husband would wait. She wanted to be a good mother as well as a good wife. Yet she was struggling with her personal priorities. Marina could see the tears in her eyes when they met at the foot of the stairs and Anna left her mother-in-law so she could spend an hour or so with her children.

She then took a walk by herself. It would be a walk of darkness and uncertainty. Anna knew she had to remain positive. She had to believe that her husband was making the right decision for himself and his family. She almost burst into tears when following her walk, Carl Nicholas greeted her. He'd seen the look of anxiety on his mother's face. "Mommy, what's wrong?" he'd asked. He placed his hand in her hand and squeezed it. Anna hugged her son. In his childlike way she thought he was trying to tell her everything was all right. He couldn't promise his mother that though. Nobody could.

When Anna finally confronted Carl about his recent meeting with Stalin, she said quietly, "You're going to work for him aren't you?" At first Carl seemed evasive in answering that question.

"Yes", he finally answered. They knew Stalin was a cruel man. They knew about the gulags and they'd heard about the Kulaks, farmers forced to leave their lands so collective farming within the Communist regime could expand. Stalin's purges would affect men within the military establishment and other groups too. Yet Carl would work for Stalin "How could I say no to him?" Anna shuddered when Carl told his wife some of the things Stalin had told him:

Stalin's agonizing struggle within the party; his brigand years and the years he'd lived carrying out revolutionary work while hiding within the oil fields, making sure the money he gained from such efforts went straight to Lenin: Those were the things Stalin had told Carl. "You must help me hide my past" he'd said. The count had listened to the dictator but he was thinking of the drawbacks that might accompany working for him. Carl would work to protect Stalin's interests but only to a degree. He'd already speculated what Stalin hadn't mentioned. Many of Stalin's comrades in revolution had been shot or would be shot or end up in Stalin's camps. He didn't want to end up as one of Stalin's statistics. When he told Anna about the interview he'd had with Stalin her advice, even though it was unrealistic was adamant.

"I know it can be done. We both know it can be done. When I walked through the gate in Perm, when I saw you standing on the other side of it, I knew I was walking toward freedom and a new life. I was afraid but I kept walking. I didn't look back. Don't let Stalin close the gate behind you. You can refuse to work for him. Keep moving. We have each other. We have the children and we've a life together. Nobody is going to take that from us."

Carl ignored what Anna said to him. Instead he said, "I know Stalin expects you to accompany me to the Kremlin too but there is danger there. I want you to remain here with the children."

Anna seemed almost stunned by what he had said to her. "No" she quietly said. "I want to be with you. If you think that I can stand being separated from you knowing that you are possibly in danger you're wrong. We don't need to be in Moscow all the time. We'll stay here in Romania just as we have always." Carl wanted Anna with him yet he felt guilty for including her in a venture that might prove to be too dangerous for them. He wondered if he'd given in too easily by accepting Stalin's offer to work for him. He knew Anna had walked through a gate he'd never had to walk through. She'd left one life and crossed the threshold toward another. He knew it would be difficult for them both to walk back through that gate again and face the injustice, intrigue and turmoil once more. Yet Carl was certain too that in their loyalty to one another as husband and wife, nobody not even Stalin could block their access to freedom.

A month had passed. Stalin hadn't yet made final arrangements for them to go to the Kremlin. Anna was pleased. She had managed to keep her husband at her side. She was being the good wife and mother. Her children needed their father. They needed to understand his goodness and decency. Right now her sons needed to grow up. They needed to become like him, their father, the man she loved. They needed to have a sense of self-worth. They didn't need to know about her family's tragic past.

The years were passing quickly. Ivan was almost thirteen and Carl Nicholas soon would be ten. At 34, Anna was beautiful and elegant. She was no longer the frightened waif her husband had rescued that day in Perm. She was Count Zurofsky's wife. She was also a grand duchess. Tears came to Anna's eyes as she contemplated the count's goodness to her. He had helped push the darkness from her. She didn't want again to be drawn into the web of fear that had entangled millions of people since Lenin and now Stalin had assumed power in Russia. Anna understood fear and oppression. She'd rebelled against it. When she'd visited Moscow and Leningrad, she'd seen how lost people seemed to be in the face of relentless dictatorship. Anna had been too engrossed in her own personal challenge to grasp the full terror of others. Yet even during her desperate ordeal to save her husband's life, Anna had sensed the pain and fear of others. She'd seen the shadow of hopelessness reflected on the faces of nameless people she'd passed on the street. Where was freedom? Where had it gone? Would the people of her generation ever find it? Perhaps it would take another generation to know freedom. Perhaps her sons would know freedom someday.

Anna knew that for her sons to know freedom they must know their father. They would learn to emulate this man for his courage and persistence in times of personal trial.

Anna only hoped her sons would understand that the family separation would just be temporary and before long she and Carl would be home again. If the children questioned their parents' need to go to Moscow they said little regarding it but Ivan gently placed an arm around a tearful Carl Nicholas. Anna felt uncomfortable and fought back tears too when she couldn't explain to her sons why she and their father were going to live in Moscow. She didn't know what to do to comfort them other than to say, "You'll get on fine without us. Grandmother will be here in our absence. Please don't worry about us." She tried to comfort herself with the thought that once they returned from their time in Moscow, she and Carl would make their sons feel as if they'd never been absent from them.

Anna was standing at the door and next to Carl one day when he received a letter delivered by a Moscow courier: Stalin demanded his services. He was to report immediately to the Kremlin.

When the day came for them to leave for Moscow, Carl vacillated regarding his decision to have Anna accompany him to the Kremlin. "I'll send for you when I'm certain it's safe for you to be with me".

Anna shook her head. "The last time you left for Moscow, I had to come looking for you. It's never safe in Moscow these days. We both know that." The count was pleased with what Anna had said to him. He knew he'd been testing his wife's loyalty by telling her she must remain behind. Anna knew that too. She knew she must do what was necessary to keep up appearances and accompany Carl to the Kremlin. Carl conceded to his wife's wishes and said, "Darling, I can't imagine being without you".

"I've explained to your mother and the children that our absence from home only would be temporary," she said before turning to go upstairs and finish packing for their journey to Moscow.

The count wasn't so sure that their absence from home would be temporary. He didn't want to get into a discussion with Anna regarding the matter.

When the day came and the car arrived that was to take them to the train station the couple was surprised to discover that they'd been assigned bodyguards. They assumed but weren't sure if Stalin had arranged for the escort. Like it or not they accepted the security as their due. It wouldn't be until they arrived at the Kremlin that Carl would have a chance to ask Stalin in private why the bodyguards were necessary.

Stalin was evasive in answering the question. He didn't want to tell Carl the reason for the extra security. He would leave it up to him to decide. Instead Stalin would make it clear to his friend why he had hired him to work for him. "I'm being followed by unwanted security agents. I want you to find out why they are following me, and I want to know who is doing it."

Carl found it hard to imagine that someone who seemed as much in control as Stalin shouldn't know the reason why he was being followed or who was behind it. Carl knew how to move within the dark circles of espionage. He knew that it would be only a matter of time before he found out. He already had an idea who was following Stalin. He needed proof. Yet the count also knew he could never employ the sort of interrogation methods that Lenin's regime and now Stalin's used to extract information from others. "I'll get to the bottom of everything," he said leaving Stalin's office and walking down a darkened hallway as if he were embarking upon a journey along a terrible and unknown labyrinth of fear.

* * * *

Now that the couple was settled in the Kremlin, Stalin made sure that Carl and his wife accompanied him socially and that their Kremlin residence provided them with the same luxury Anna had known while living there as a child. He wanted her to think that under his regime nothing had changed. Stalin knew Anna loved the ballet and decided that one evening they would visit the Bolshoi Theater. The theater was crowded with party officials and their wives the night Anna sat in a box with Carl on one side of her and the dictator on the other during a performance of Tchaikovsky's "Swan Lake".

Yet Carl's focus wasn't on the performance any more than Stalin's was. Both men cautiously, sometimes nervously observed people sitting in the audience. Both knew tonight's performance was an occasion to be seen and move socially within the dark political circles of the Communist regime.

During intermission, Carl rose from his seat and followed prominent members of Stalin's party who'd also left their seats. He was doing precisely what Stalin had hired him to do. He watched them drink vodka or sip champagne. He observed familiar party faces and he became familiar with the ongoing intrigue by eavesdropping on gossip and conversations.

During the intermission, Carl hadn't noticed Stalin's beautiful mistress Zhenya seated with her husband in the audience but Anna had. Zhenya quickly glanced up at Anna sitting alone in the box next to Stalin.

Carl gazed around the theatre. There was a crowd of people standing just a short distance from Stalin's box. Where was Stalin's security? His agents seemed to have momentarily disappeared. Anna felt uncomfortable sitting alone beside the dictator. People in the audience below were scrutinizing her. She wanted the count to return to her at once.

Stalin knew there was disloyalty surrounding him in the audience. He wished he could have escaped from the intrigue and danger by retreating into the brigand days when he was just a young revolutionary. He hadn't been the focus of a power struggle then. He was just trying to survive as best he could. And then there was the time before those years, before he'd traded the vocation of a life committed to God for one of relentless revolution and repression. Stalin tried to ignore the guilt and pangs of regret that inwardly haunted him after he'd deserted the seminary. He'd lost the inner spirit that might have made him whole and that might have brought solace into his tormented life. He'd achieved his worldly dreams, rising within a ruthless and cruel regime that had elevated him to its highest level. Yet the price he was paying for being part of such a regime or for elevation within it seemed almost too high.

Stalin wasn't thinking of his spectacular rise to power as he gazed down at the audience. He was thinking instead of all the things that had come before he was dictator. He thought of his first wife Ekaterina. She was beautiful and he loved her but he'd been terribly poor then and unable to care for her in illness. He'd had to take her and his young son Yakov to live with her parents. After his first wife died, he didn't have much contact with his son until after he became dictator. Stalin didn't know that Yakov tragically would die in a Nazi prisoner of war camp during World War II. He didn't know that Russia would even be drawn into conflict with Germany. Stalin stopped thinking of his first wife and their son Yakov. Instead he gazed at the audience sitting in the Bolshoi Theatre. He knew the intrigue there easily could tear the power he held from him.

So many things had been taken away from him or would be taken from him. His second wife Nadezhda had been taken from him. And then he thought of Anna. Her love and goodness had brought light into his dark world. Theirs had been a secret love affair. He'd come to her when she was held prisoner at the Perm house. She had welcomed his kindness amidst the misery. Stalin knew his affair with her had to end. He couldn't bear to lose her yet he couldn't bear to think that something terrible might happen to her if she remained a Bolshevik prisoner. Count Zurofsky was a spy. He would carry Anna to safety in Romania. The world would never know of Stalin's affair with Anna. They would outwardly behave as if they'd never known one another.

Anna gazed down at the audience. She looked especially lovely wearing a red burgundy velvet gown and ropes of precious pearls wound about her slender neck. The intermission was ending. Her husband still hadn't returned to his seat. Anna was anxious about him. Then just as the lights were beginning to dim for the final act of the ballet's performance, Carl sat down beside her and took her hand in his. Anna was reassured. He'd come back to her.

Following the performance, Carl had ordered that security surrounding the dictator be increased. Yet he didn't trust that security. He'd sensed its laxity was due to something ominous and unseen. Although he hadn't had the opportunity to discuss the matter with Stalin, he was sure that the underlying reason for the lack of security surrounding the dictator had to do with an ongoing power struggle within the party. Stalin had allowed party men like Kirov to carry out work for him that Stalin knew only could become unpopular after the work was completed: Thousands of laborers had died building the White Sea Baltic Canal.

Yet Stalin had other reasons for seeing Kirov as a problem. His power and influence had become almost as great as Stalin's. In 1934, after the Seventeenth Congress, it was rumored in the party that Kirov was to be transferred to Moscow where as a member of the Politburo and a secretary of the Central Committee, he would occupy the second place in the party hierarchy.

Carl knew that Kirov was in a position to challenge Stalin's power. He knew the power struggle entailed the matter of kill or be killed. No one could overshadow the dictator. Carl knew where the threat to Stalin's life lay. Kirov and the men surrounding him would be the focus of his investigation. He wouldn't tell Stalin anything regarding his suspicion of Kirov's betrayal until he had proof of that betrayal. Yet Carl as well as Stalin had an uncomfortable sense of the inevitable.

Carl's face was pale and grave after he and Anna left the theater and stepped into an official car that was to return them to the Kremlin. Stalin wouldn't let the count know. He'd already marked Kirov for assassination. Anna could sense her husband's lack of ease. She silently gazed from the car's window at the dim streetlights. She could feel the emotional heaviness surrounding them. Her heart pounded when Carl opened the car's door. She didn't want him to leave her even for a few minutes. Her distraught look told Carl how uncomfortable she was feeling. Although Stalin's bodyguards met them, she wasn't sure who among them was loyal to the dictator or if there weren't men hiding in shadow ready to carry out not just Stalin's assassination but Carl's as well. After he'd left the official car so he could accompany Stalin to his apartments Anna anxiously awaited Carl's return. It seemed like an interminably long time before he opened the car's door and allowed the frosty cold night air to penetrate the car's warm interior. "Sorry to have left you so long darling" he said kissing Anna who trembled and shivered in fear inside her warm fur coat. Although she said nothing to him, Carl could sense Anna's distinct discomfort with having been left alone in a car without any protection.

After they were finally home in their own Kremlin apartment Carl drew Anna close to him and asked, "Are you sure that you did the right thing in accompanying me to Moscow?" Anna was hesitant before whispering, "Yes there is much unexplained intrigue surrounding Stalin. I feel safe in this environment only when I'm with you. If you'd left me at home as you wanted to do, I don't think I would have understood what you were going through." Anna then asked Carl, "Did you happen to notice that man who left his seat during intermission? He didn't return to it?"

"Yes, he's Kirov"

"When Kirov didn't return to his seat after intermission, Stalin appeared a little nervous. I couldn't help but notice his reaction to the absence. Did you see Kirov leave the theatre?"

"Yes, I started to follow him. I wanted to see if he met anyone else. My prolonged absence from the theatre following intermission might have been misconstrued if I'd left you alone with Stalin." Anna's face was pale at his remark. She'd remembered Carl's suspicions in regard to her past relationship with the dictator.

Anna knew her husband was a spy. She knew it was unwise of her to ask him too many questions. He might perceive her inquisitiveness to be some form of disloyalty. She must remain within her husband's life. Yet she knew she could never step beyond a certain perimeter surrounding it.

She gazed at him as if she longed for him to tell her what she wanted to hear. "Are you glad I'm here?" she whispered.

The count was a man who could be distant. He didn't want to tell her that he was pleased that she was with him. He didn't want to tell her that he couldn't bear to be without her. He opened the door to the bedroom where she followed him. She waited for his answer to her question but it didn't come. He looked at her as if he was still questioning her loyalty to him. Anna wanted him to know that she could never betray him.

When they slipped into bed together Anna knew why he'd wanted her with him. He'd answered her question. In return for his answer, she wanted him to know that she loved him.

The following morning, Carl met Stalin in the dictator's Kremlin office. The count suspected but couldn't confirm Stalin's suspicions of Kirov's disloyalty. During his interview with him, he realized that Stalin had seen Kirov as someone who'd become increasing disloyal to him. Stalin had wanted people to know about the role he'd played as a leading Bolshevik after the Civil War in Georgia and Azerbaijan. Kirov hadn't delivered that message. The men had quarreled over farm collectivization too. Stalin wanted it increased in Kirov's area. Stalin knew the count couldn't do what Stalin planned to do. Stalin ordered the interrogation of men he suspected were involved in a conspiracy to overthrow him and have him replaced with Kirov as dictator. Once he'd gotten confessions from them, he'd have them shot. Plans to assassinate Kirov could be carried out unhindered.

Carl held Anna's arm as they accompanied Stalin to Brother Kirov's funeral in the Hall of Columns of the House of Unions on December 5, 1934. Anna shuddered. She and Carl watched Stalin approach Kirov's coffin, bend and kiss his forehead. Stalin told his friends how much he felt Kirov's loss. "After Nadezhda's death Kirov had taken care of me like a child." For many onlookers though Stalin's words fell on hollow ears.

After the funeral Stalin knew he had to face the darkness of what he'd done. It was overwhelming. Even the bottle of vodka he'd reached for hadn't quelled the guilt he felt. When the effects from the alcohol wore off, Stalin wanted another drink. He knew he had to remain sober. He had to face what he'd done. He had to face friends and foes alike. Regardless of how he'd tried to justify his actions it was difficult. He tried to convince himself that in having Kirov assassinated he had just acted out of self preservation. Stalin felt so empty and dismal over what he'd done to Kirov that he found himself reaching out to the God he'd known but had abandoned. Stalin was still alone in his pain. He had achieved his life's goals. He'd obtained power far beyond anything he'd imagined yet peace eluded him. Where was Koba the idealist who'd wanted to change things for the better? He was trapped in his personal hell.

Now that the funeral hall had emptied, Anna had seen Stalin standing by himself. He seemed almost unapproachable. She went to him anyway. As if sensing his pain and knowing that Stalin wanted only a few moments alone with the woman they both loved, the count left his wife with the dictator. Anna gently brushed Stalin's face with her hand. Stalin wanted her to know that he'd only been fighting for political survival within a treacherous party. Stalin knew Kirov would have done the same thing to him if he'd been in a position to do so. Anna knew what Stalin was thinking.

Stalin had given her back her life that day in Perm when he let her leave the hell in which he moved. Now he needed Anna's understanding and pity. He needed her softness in face of his agonizing world. Tears streamed down the dictator's face, and Anna brushed them away with a handkerchief. Stalin knew Anna soon would leave him. The bright light that had come to him in darkness would be extinguished. He couldn't bear to lose the goodness and gentleness that she embodied. Instinctively he knew he'd driven her away, that he'd never be able to get her back. Yet she was the one person on earth who understood him better than anyone else. He would come to her again. Circumstances somehow would draw them together.

The count had turned and walked away from his wife's encounter with the dictator. Carl knew that Anna was his. Stalin could never have her. He let them be alone together if only for a few minutes.

"I understand", she whispered almost inaudibly. Anna didn't tell Stalin that she couldn't forgive the dictator's cruelty. She didn't tell him that she still loved him despite of what he'd done. She wanted him to know that. She gazed into Stalin's eyes. "Come back to me" she said leaning forward and embracing him. It was a farewell embrace. The moment was difficult for them both. Could she ever understand the pain and treachery he'd endured? Could she ever know the fear with which he lived almost on a daily basis? Anna continued gazing into Stalin's eyes. She was searching for the man she knew and loved. She wanted him to leave his loveless world. She wanted him to find safe haven again in the God he'd known in the seminary.

Stalin gazed into Anna's soft gentle eyes. What he saw was a woman with great compassion for others. He gently drew her to him It was a farewell embrace and kiss. The count's back was still turned as he walked away from them. For a moment, Anna was alone. The two men she'd loved had left her. Stalin had walked away. He had disappeared along an empty hallway that led to the outside world. It was a long walk for Stalin. He didn't want to face that world. He knew he had to though. He had to face the silent criticism that engulfed him.

Words had been silenced. Members of the intelligentsia were afraid to speak out against him. Even the composer Shostakovich, would become the focus of Stalin's wrath. In succeeding years when the 5th Symphony was debuted in 1937 those who understood the music perceived the message. People had sat in their seats and wept. There was hardly anyone in the audience who didn't know of someone in one of Stalin's miserable gulags. Stalin didn't want to face the outside world. He didn't want to look upon the faces of those who wept. Stalin's legs felt heavy, almost as if they would buckle beneath him. He didn't look back in Anna's direction. He couldn't bear to look back at what he was leaving behind. Anna now stood by herself in the empty Hall. It was as if she was being forced to make a choice between the two men who'd become so important in her life.

Anna knew where her love and obligations must be focused. She was a wife and mother first. She had to find her husband. She would go with him wherever he led her. Her face was sad when she met him. He gazed questioningly into her eyes before he took her arm in his and led her from the dreaded empty hallway. Neither of them spoke. For the moment, neither knew what to say to the other. Her husband could only be satisfied that Anna had made the right decision in rejoining him. Anna was his and would be his.

Even after they'd left the Hall, the count instinctively knew that he and his wife would again be drawn into other power struggles involving the dictator. Stalin's struggle would be not just a personal struggle but a struggle that would encompass civilization. The forces of good and evil that would clash one against the other at times would become blurred and almost indistinguishable. Yet the dictator would be an ally to the forces of good within the world. The count knew that he and Anna would stand by this man who ruled Russia at a time when Russia nearly would be brought to its knees. Yet neither the count nor his wife dared discuss with one another what they thought the future held in store for them or the world as they silently walked along together.

Later Anna buried her face in her husband's shoulder. "How could he do that to a friend?" she sobbed as if not wanting to admit to herself that they both already had the answer to the question. The world they'd known was changing. Stalin had been betrayed by political opponents and even men who'd once supported him because of the changing political climate. Yet Stalin was to face an even greater threat. He knew he needed to confront the foreign rival that soon was to wreak havoc on Europe. The count didn't want to wait for that political threat to surface. He knew that he and Anna had to leave the Kremlin immediately and return to their home in Romania.

* * * *

Carl and Anna's journey to the home they'd left behind was one of light and hopefulness. They embraced their sons and spent precious time with them as a family within their castle sanctuary. Yet Anna would agree with Carl when he decided that it was time to leave their home and go to England. Already there were unwanted changes taking place around them. Some of the servants had left the family's employment because the political atmosphere in Romania was becoming such that they no longer felt comfortable there.

The count wouldn't find replacements for the servants who'd left his employment. Instead he and his sons would hide as many of the family art treasures as possible and place them in Dracula's secret passageway. The passageway then could be sealed up and the family would prepare to leave. With his many connections within the world of espionage, Carl was able to obtain documentation for his entire family. He'd already purchased a large home in the English countryside. The family could live in England until the political climate in Romania hopefully stabilized.

Anna sighed. It was so good to be home again. She didn't want to leave the home where she and Carl had been married and where their children had been born. Their castle had been more than a home. It had been a refuge from forces that had destroyed the rest of her family. Yet Anna would follow her husband wherever he decided to take them. They would be a family regardless of where they lived.

Anna looked for all the things that had become familiar to her. Her dear little dog Micha was now fourteen years old. He was blind in one eye and he had slowed down considerably. Anna had half expected that Micha might not be there at all when she and Carl had arrived home from Moscow but he was there. The children who loved the little dog too had assured their mother that Micha knew she was coming home because he kept barking just as the car carrying their parents drove up to the castle entranceway. "Dear Micha" Anna whispered. "I don't want to go anywhere on another journey if I have to leave you behind again" she said cuddling the terrier in her arms.

Even though he'd hired a couple to maintain his home while he was gone, Carl wanted his family's departure to remain secret. He knew his children didn't want to leave home. They loved the outdoor freedom where they could play and appreciate the wondrous magic of the mountains and wilderness surrounding them. Carl knew political circumstances were driving him and his family from the home they loved. He still held a dim hope that he might be able to work something out enabling them to remain at home for it was the one place where they all had felt free.

During the afternoon ride that was to be one of the last they would take as a family, the couple watched their children freely move within the forest landscape. The trees the boys had climbed the games they'd played and the horses they'd loved were significant parts of their lives. Anna's face appeared rather sad as she reflected on the many times she'd watched her sons joyfully ride their horses along the mountain trail. She wanted to tell Carl that they mustn't leave their home hidden within precious landscape and dense wilderness. She felt that if they left it, circumstances might prevent them from ever returning to it. Carl didn't know what Anna was thinking. He thought she was just feeling melancholy when he said to her,

"Darling, you must remember you are loved. Be yourself. You are beautiful. People who know you can only love you." Anna knew that the love she was looking for extended beyond the personal and human domain. The forest and the creatures she and Carl had taught their children to love were her family too. She couldn't bear to leave them behind.

The fear and emptiness Anna once had known had diminished when she had drawn close to the wilderness and realized that the love she gave to her family must extend to the earth and its forest inhabitants. Anna had drawn strength from this non-human world and the magnificent creation surrounding her. In return, she wanted the abundant unimaginable beauty of the forest landscape and its creatures to know her goodness and compassion too. She wanted to extend love and protection to this non-human world for in doing so she was giving back to the magnificent creation from which she felt inseparable. Stalin had felt Anna's compassion for him because she'd drawn him into the circle of harmony and peace she'd known in the healing forest environment. Carl knew that peace too. He had introduced Anna to it. Yet in her heart, Anna realized that what Carl had shown her was something she inherently always had carried within her consciousness. That peace and beauty never could be taken from her for its source was eternal and came from a higher sense of peace and love that couldn't be diminished.

For the time being, Anna was relieved that Stalin couldn't reach out and take her from the forest and the creatures that loved and needed her too. She wasn't yet ready to leave that world.

Unbeknown to him, the documents the Count thought he had obtained for his family to travel upon had been shown to Stalin. The spy who'd obtained them for him worked for the dictator. Stalin smiled a look of satisfaction when he realized how easy it had been for him to discover where the count planned to take his family. It would be only a matter of time before Anna returned to Russia and Carl was working for him once more.

* * * *

Stalin paced back and forth within his Kremlin Office. Old political party rivalry had for the time being been put aside. Quite frankly there was nobody around to rival the dictator. Stalin wanted to make sure the atmosphere remained that way. He couldn't have too many spies or too many loyal people working for him in the Kremlin. Yet he always had the fear that people working for him could be disloyal.

Stalin got up from his desk, locked a few office drawers, pulled the shades behind his desk and left the room. He would test his vulnerability by venturing outside the Kremlin and slipping unseen past Kremlin walls.

It was late in the day-- nearly dusk. The shadows of day would hide his identity. Stalin wanted to look upon the faces of all the nameless people he would never know but who knew him. As he walked slowly along by himself he seemed to blend in with the crowd. At last Stalin felt almost at peace. He was living life as it should be lived, with anonymity and a certain air of personal independence.

It seemed so easy to continue living this way and to run from fears and responsibilities by simply assuming a new identity and becoming someone else. His enemies could never find him then. But then Stalin thought how complicated and cruel life could be. His enemies would discover a way to find him. They would attack him for running from responsibility. They would tell the rest of the world that Stalin was running from all the terrible things he'd done over the course of the years. They would demand that Stalin make amends for what he'd done. Stalin had to stay around and maintain his identity because that was the only way he could foil his enemies.

It was now nearly dark when he stood outside a shabby café and gazed through the window and thought of slipping unseen into the café as he'd done before during his days as a young revolutionary. And yet he knew he couldn't return to the past. He hesitated before pushing open the café's door and finding the corner table he used to sit at years ago when he'd found escape from informants and the police. Stalin remembered the nights he'd fallen asleep sitting at that table and waiting for daylight before he moved on with his revolutionary activities. Now he was dictator. Stalin's fortune hadn't changed much. He was still running.

He was running from the fear and danger of being trapped. Political success had trapped Stalin. He had no place to run now except back to the Kremlin where he was in charge.

Stalin left the café unnoticed and crossed a street. His long walk had taken him far from the Kremlin, and he knew he had to return to it. After he crossed the street, he noticed bodyguards following him. An official car pulled up behind him and Stalin tried to ignore the interruption to his evening stroll but couldn't. Comrade Stalin must be protected from his enemies. He would be chauffeured back to the Kremlin. He would resume his daily routine as if he'd never left his Kremlin office then later that evening Stalin would send for his mistress Zhenya. For a few hours she would help him face his loneliness. She would ease his pain and bring him temporary solace.

Chapter Ten

The count's face was drawn and sad the day he and his family prepared to leave the home of his ancestors. Since he didn't want anyone to know why they were leaving their secure surroundings for another country, he decided they'd travel with few belongings so it would seem to others as if their absence from home would be only temporary.

The children weren't fooled when their father announced that the family absence from home only would be temporary. They'd recognized the look of desperation reflected in his face. Carl didn't want his children to see his sadness. He didn't want to explain to them why they were leaving home. They were too young to understand the reasons. He excused himself from his family and wandered alone throughout the home he loved. He gazed longingly at the familiar objects scattered throughout his surroundings. One in particular caught Carl's attention. Before he hid it in a secure place, Carl quietly studied Dracula's portrait, and wondered if Dracula would consider him cowardly for running from the fear trapping him. Carl wanted to stand his ground. He wanted to protect his family and preserve its legacy. Carl wanted to emulate Dracula but not his evil ways. Dracula had been adept at knowing how to evade those who would pursue and destroy him. Carl wanted to evade the enemy too. He knew that if he left his ancestral home, he might never again return to it. Carl seemed lost in thought studying Dracula's portrait when Anna walked into the room and gently touched his elbow. He turned and took her hand in his as together they stood before the portrait.

The journey Carl and Anna thought they soon were to embark upon though would be replaced by another adventure when the unforeseen occurred. Anton Bockev, Countess Marina's Hungarian lover, was determined to see her before she left Romania. He was determined that if she were to leave the country it would be with him and not with her son. Unbeknown to Bockev, Stalin had found out through various intelligence sources of Bockev's long lasting affair with the count's mother. Stalin's spies had made it easy for Bockev to obtain documentation that would enable him to take Marina and the count's sons with them to England. Once there, Bockev and Marina would be married.

Carl had never met Anton Bockev. After his father's death he had suspected that his mother had been seeing another man. He had long thought that when Marina journeyed to Budapest for weeks at a time it was to see the suspected lover.

At last the man who'd loved the count's mother met her son. Anton seemed quite forthright when he assured Carl that they both had been faithful to their spouses. "I never tried to see your mother after she was married until your father died and my wife had died too. Your mother has always refused my proposals of marriage. Perhaps it was because she wanted permission from the son she loved to marry me. Now that we've met, I ask your permission to marry your mother."

Carl was touched that the older man, whose fortune had changed for the better, was prepared to care for his mother in a manner she'd always known. A middle aged partially gray haired man, Beckov was impeccably groomed. He was also wealthy.

Bockev moved within the same circles of espionage as did the count but not to the same extent. Bockev's ties and loyalty to Stalin didn't run as deeply as did Carl's. Bockev knew that Stalin wanted the count to remain at his castle estate and during their conversation Carl learned from Bockev what Stalin expected.

Anna was intelligent and charming, the perfect hostess. The count and his lovely wife could entertain high ranking Nazi officials. Stalin hoped the couple would learn from them what Stalin needed to know so that he could be kept informed of Nazi planned penetration within the Baltic and Balkan States.

"You must remain in Romania at least for the time being until Stalin decides your services to him are unnecessary." If Carl thought that comment was strange he said nothing. He listened as Bockev continued to talk. "Allow me to marry your mother so I may take her and your sons to England where they will be out of danger."

The count politely tried to hide his distinct dissatisfaction with such an arrangement. He would allow Bockev to marry his mother and take her to live in England where he and Anna had planned to live. He quickly changed his mind. England was too far from Romania. Bockev and Marina could live in Hungary. "You must be married here first but I think Anna and I would prefer that our sons remain with us."

Bockev seemed a little subdued but bowed deferentially to the count's wishes. He knew he hadn't gotten his way but he respected the count's toughness. Even though it had been a partial one, Bockev pretended to have won a complete victory. He affectionately embraced Marina and was grateful that Carl had not outwardly displayed any objection to his marrying Marina. Anna gazed at Carl. The look of desperation had disappeared from his face. She knew he would stand firm regarding the best choices available to them.

Anna knew it would have been difficult for them to be separated from their children. She was relieved, and grateful to Carl for having the wisdom to insist that their sons remain with them. If Stalin was protecting them, their sons should remain with them. Yet Carl felt uneasy with the information Bockev had given him. He wondered if any of the things Bockev had been telling him were true. Did Stalin really want him and Anna to remain in Romania? Sooner or later Carl was determined to find out whether or not Bockev was lying to him.

The count decided when Bockev could marry Marina. The family wedding would be held in the castle's chapel where Carl had married Anna. Yet Carl had something more important to think about than a family wedding. He had to see Stalin.

Carl had suspected that Bockev was a double agent. Carl knew many double agents in the world in which he moved. Some were good friends of his. The game of espionage was a dirty one but it had to be played with openness as well as care. There was no room in that game for mistakes. Carl felt self-satisfied yet at the same time a little guilty for thinking that he might be able to use Bockev if the opportunity arose. He knew he could never trust a man whose loyalties were questionable. Yet Bockev was marrying his mother.

When he had a chance to corner Bockev and pull him aside, Carl wanted to pump Bockev concerning the recent meeting he'd presumably had with Stalin. He needed more information from him regarding it.

Later in the day, while Marina and Anna were busy talking in a sitting room, Carl suggested to Bockev that they talk privately with one another. He directed him to a comfortable chair in his upstairs office. Bockev was vague. Knowing the dictator as he did, Bockev didn't want to misquote Stalin or misrepresent any of the things Stalin expected from the count.

Carl was uneasy. He knew that whatever he learned from the Nazis they'd want something in return for it. Was he being asked to become a double agent like Bockev? Stalin also was a man of contradictions. He would betray others in an effort to remain in favor with Hitler. Perhaps the only way to survive during such uncertain times was to hide one's loyalty or to be loyal to none. The count knew he was in a difficult position. He had to remain loyal to Stalin. He couldn't be drawn into the nightmare of becoming a political pawn. Yet the Nazis would want his loyalty too. The count knew he could never give it to them.

Now that Anna knew they wouldn't be leaving home, she told the servants to unpack the family's belongings. Later she and Carl along with their sons would find the hidden art treasures and place them throughout the count's home.

At Anna's insistence, Carl invited Bockev to lunch. He was staying at a village Inn. For the time being, until after the wedding at least, the count's hospitality wouldn't extend beyond invitations to lunch and dinner with his family.

Following lunch, Carl had an opportunity to take Anna aside. "I need to see Stalin. I must find out from him if what Bockev is telling me is true. As soon as Bockev and my mother are married, I'm leaving for the Kremlin. You can remain here with the children until I return"

Although reluctant to have him go to Moscow without her, Anna saw the wisdom of her husband approaching Stalin alone. "I don't want my visit to be a social call. Stalin must tell me himself that he wants me to spy for him." Anna wanted to cry.

"It's all right darling. It won't be like the last time I went to Moscow alone. I won't be gone long." Anna nodded her head seeming to agree with what he'd told her. They knew they had to move on. Anna also knew that she and Carl must use the utmost caution when dealing with the dictator. In the turbulent world in which she and Carl moved, Anna realized they had to have influential friends. Stalin was their most powerful ally. Carl would continue to befriend the dictator, and play the game of intrigue and hope that the cards he held in his hand were the winning ones.

Chapter Eleven

Bockev was a likeable man, intelligent, charming and obviously in love with Marina yet Carl was uneasy. He had misgivings. His mother was marrying a man he hardly knew. Although neither Marina nor Bockev had been unfaithful to their spouses, the count was resentful. Bockev had lived in the shadow of his mother's life for years. Carl had loved his father. He knew that his mother had been loved and well taken care of by his father. The count was sad to think that his mother could love another man as much as his late father. It hadn't been easy for him to give his mother permission to marry Bockev. Had he been disloyal to his father's memory? Carl struggled with his emotions. Bockev was a wealthy man but with questionable ties and loyalties. By allowing Bockev to marry his mother, the count was ignoring loyalty. Where was loyalty during times of political doubt and turmoil? Even family ties were being strained and broken. Suddenly the full impact of what his mother was doing dawned upon him. Surely his mother hadn't realized what she'd done to him. Carl knew he had to find the wisdom and understanding to forgive his mother. It would be difficult for him to do so though. She knew he moved in a dangerous world of espionage. She knew how easily he could be betrayed by those more powerful than he. Stalin was more powerful than he. Bockev knew that Stalin wanted the count to remain at his castle estate so Carl could befriend the Nazis and spy for him. Where was loyalty? Shouldn't Stalin have told him rather than Bockev that he needed him? The atmosphere surrounding Bockev's marriage to Marina was strained. Carl was amiable and charming but the mother he loved had unknowingly broken his heart.

Marina was no fool. She'd sensed her son's disappointment with her decision to marry Bockev. She didn't know he was a double agent. The count would never tell his mother what he knew. It would be too dangerous for him to let her in on that secret. Marina's only concern was that the son she loved should try to understand her reasons for marrying Bockev. "I loved your father", she'd said to him. "He was a wonderful man. I was proud to be his wife. Please understand that in marrying Anton my love for you and your children remains as strong as ever."

Anna had listened to Marina as she spoke those comforting words to him. Anna knew her husband had to accept what his mother was doing in marrying Bockev as gracefully as he could.

When they had a chance to be alone together, she told Carl that his mother had always been there for them. "It's time she made a life for herself."Carl grudgingly agreed. He still felt betrayed.

* * * *

The day following Marina's wedding to Bockev, Carl left for Moscow. He'd learned from several of his Kremlin contacts that Stalin would be there for the next couple of weeks. Carl knew Stalin's schedule was well planned in advance. Still he was determined that Stalin would grant him a Kremlin interview.

The count should have known that Stalin hadn't been pleased with his sudden departure for Romania after Kirov's funeral. Stalin wasn't an easy man to placate. Yet Carl was determined that Stalin still would regard him as a friend.

It was nearly a week before Carl was finally granted an interview with the dictator. Stalin wouldn't tell the count that he was furious with him for his recent actions. Carl and Anna's rapid departure so soon after Kirov's funeral had raised eyebrows. Stalin had been embarrassed. Carl's face looked a little distraught as the dictator tried not to appear too livid in his conversation with him. He had used the word insincerity in his conversation with the count. He wanted to say disloyalty but Stalin knew he needed him. The word disloyalty would have meant that the count had tried to betray him. Stalin had to leave the door open. He would observe Carl's behavior over a period of time. It would be awhile before either man would feel comfortable with the other though.

Stalin rose from where he'd been sitting behind his desk. He paced uneasily around the room. "How is Anna?" he asked. Stalin was always sincere in his concern for her. "Why didn't she accompany you to Moscow?" he asked as if Anna's absence from the Kremlin was again something akin to disloyalty on the count's part.

Carl's face was grave. He tried not to stammer as he nervously replied, "She hasn't had a chance to be with the children in a long time. They are at a difficult age and need parental guidance. She's also been busy planning a family wedding. After a long courtship, my mother married Anton Beckov several weeks ago at my home.

"Although Bockev approached me because he wanted my permission to marry my mother, I feel his main reason for approaching me was to tell me that you wanted me to remain in Romania."

Stalin's face was serious. He wondered if he could trust the count enough to do what he wanted him to do. "Did Stalin tell you I want you to spy for me?"

"Yes, he did so. I needed confirmation from you regarding the matter".

Stalin thoughtfully gazed at his friend before saying, "The Nazis will soon overwhelm the Baltic States and Europe for that matter. For the time being Russia must appear to be allied with Germany. Russia isn't prepared for war. We must work with Nazi Germany. Our survival may depend upon it. I want you and Anna to befriend representatives of the Nazi High Command in your area. I want you to entertain them and learn as much as you can from them."

"Of course" said Carl. He wouldn't tell the dictator that he had his loyalty. He knew Stalin would perceive such a remark, coming as it was, so soon after his departure from Moscow as being pretentious. "I'll spy for you. You'll be kept well informed."

Stalin's face was drawn and sad. The count should have brought Anna with him. He viewed Anna's absence from her husband's visit to Moscow as unacceptable.

After shaking hands with him, Stalin led Carl across the room and opened the door for him. He then watched as a guard escorted Carl down the corridor to an elevator. Stalin wasn't surprised when intelligence sources later told him that following the interview, Carl immediately returned home to Romania.

When Anna greeted her husband upon his return home, Carl told her that Stalin was disappointed that she hadn't accompanied him to Moscow. "I think my meeting with him might have been easier had you been there." Anna's demeanor was calm. Inwardly she didn't feel as controlled. She felt her husband might be alluding to the affair that was over with that she'd had with Stalin years earlier. Her heart pounded as she turned from Carl so he wouldn't perceive her emotion.

Later Anna again asked Carl about his meeting with Stalin. She wanted to be sure if what Bockev had told him was true. "Does Stalin really want you to spy for him?"

"Yes" he said. "He also wants us to entertain the Nazis so we can learn as much about their plans as possible."

"Now that we know what Stalin wants from us, what do you suppose our other options are? We can't leave Romania," she said.

"We have none", he replied." We must wait and let events unfold. If we befriend the Nazis they may ask us to become agents for them".

Anna shuddered. "You know you won't be able to do that".

The count was no fool. He knew that the Nazis would know of his close association with Stalin. He knew that Stalin had placed him and his wife in the precarious position of having to draw close to people they could never trust. He also knew in doing so, Stalin was testing the count's loyalty. Carl knew he'd be loyal to Stalin but he wondered if Stalin would return the favor.

Anna could sense that Carl felt his relationship with the dictator might be taking a turn for the worst. She could see the doubt reflected in Carl's eyes. She felt a chill and a strange sense of guilt too. Did Stalin want her back? Would he sacrifice her husband in a bid to win her back? Anna didn't want to face that scenario. She only hoped that her husband knew how much she loved him and that she never could betray him.

Carl embraced Anna. She felt warm and comfortable in his arms. She was safe and at home with her children and all the things that she loved and that were familiar to her. She wanted her life to stay that way. She didn't want it to become complicated.

Anna didn't want Carl to let her go. It had been awhile since they'd had any time alone together. It was late in the afternoon when they found that time. Later Anna asked Carl how much information Stalin had divulged to him regarding Bockev's ties to the Nazis. "Very little" he replied uneasily. He then spoke slowly and thoughtfully. "Whatever information Stalin has in that regard must be sufficient enough to make friendship with Bockev important." Anna shivered. The count held her close. She knew he couldn't have rejected Stalin's request that they spy for him by entertaining the Nazis. She wondered where Bockev fit into the picture. She shuddered when she thought of the new close family association with Bockev.

* * * *

Now that Carl had visited him in the Kremlin, Stalin decided he would pay him a visit. He knew Anna might be frightened by having to befriend the Nazis. She must be assured that he would protect her and her family from any danger arising from such a close association. Carl must also be aware that Hitler would pay a high price to make territorial and political modifications to Baltic and Balkan territories.

Stalin was thinking ahead to the secret clause of the Ribbentrop Molotov Pact. He needed assurance from the count that when Hitler's Reich minister Ribbentrop visited Romania, Carl and Anna would entertain him. He wanted to insure that the clause would be there when the German Soviet Non Aggression Pact with Hitler was formed: As Stalin's unofficial representative in Romania, Carl subtly would mention Stalin's desire that the Soviet Union's interests in Bessarabia be observed. Later when Stalin with Molotov at his side entertained Ribbentrop in the Kremlin, Stalin's interest in Bessarabia might be clearly understood by the German High Command.

Stalin's visit to Carl's home was low key but not without the necessary security accompanying it. Two bodyguards preceded the dictator before he entered the count's stunning residence. Even though the road had been sealed off leading to Carl's residence curious onlookers noticed the quiet visit.

It was in the middle of the day when Carl and Stalin had a chance finally to talk about Bessarabia. Carl told Stalin that he wasn't sure if Stalin was really being realistic by having him confront Ribbentrop over the Bessarabia issue. Stalin assured Carl that Bessarabia must be mentioned at least once by someone other than himself so the Nazis would know that his plans for Bessarabia had political supporters.

Carl still felt uncomfortable. He knew he couldn't tell Stalin that he didn't think he should be the one to place the cards on the table for Ribbentrop to see regarding Bessarabia. Nonetheless the count knew he had to intercede on Stalin's behalf or risk Stalin's disfavor.

Stalin knew the count's role as spy might be dangerous. He knew that circumstances had bound Carl to him. He trusted few people, almost none. Yet he believed in the count. They'd taken risks together and won. Stalin had confided in Carl and both men understood the treachery of others. They'd experienced it on too many occasions and Carl knew that Stalin's response to treachery had been swift and cruel. Yet Stalin would trust Carl. He would forgive him for leaving so soon following Kirov's assassination and funeral.

Later in the day when they had a chance to talk within a relaxed family setting, Anna was grateful. The strain she'd sometimes sensed between her husband and Stalin had disappeared, and at no other time during the day was that more apparent than before dinner when they enjoyed a cocktail together: vodka for Stalin and her husband, a glass of burgundy for Anna. It matched the color of the dress she'd worn that evening when she'd sat next to Stalin alone in the box at the Bolshoi theatre. Anna had on a blue dress today. It matched the color of her gray blue eyes. The governess brought the children into the sitting room so that Stalin could meet Anna's sons. Ivan bore a striking resemblance to the count whereas Carl Nicholas seemed to take after Anna's side of the family. Stalin could tell how proud Anna was of her sons. He talked about his little daughter. She was the joy and comfort in his life and her childlike ways had helped him forget his wife's sad death. Stalin relaxed in the comfort of his friends' home and momentarily forgot the personal burdens he carried. He'd shut them out and genuinely felt the warmth of the people surrounding him. When it was time for dinner, the children followed their governess from the room. It had been an honor to meet Comrade Stalin. They would realize too how fortunate their parents were to be friends with the Soviet dictator.

Following dinner, Anna remained behind closed doors when Carl and Stalin withdrew to a comfortable sitting room. The discussion between them concerning friends and foes within the Soviet regime would go on for hours. Stalin placed his pipe in his jacket pocket and stared at the carpet lying at his feet. He hesitated to bring up the subject yet he had to tell the count what was on his mind. He knew loyalty among comrades had fluctuated. Stalin told Carl he had to have consistency concerning friendships. Yet he wasn't sure who his friends and enemies really were.

Carl shifted uneasily in his chair as Stalin continued the discussion concerning the subject of friendship. He knew the resentment he held towards the dictator needed to go. Yet how could he ever forget the horrifying ordeal he'd suffered in Leningrad so many years earlier. Despite the obvious tension between the two men, the meeting between them went well. Even Stalin's resentment over his friend's abrupt departure from the Kremlin following Kirov's funeral seemed to have temporarily disappeared. Stalin realized that the count had lifted a huge burden of guilt from his shoulders by providing him with the confirmation of Kirov's disloyalty. Yet Stalin felt strangely alienated from the count for doing so. Stalin wouldn't tell Carl that he was haunted, sometimes on a daily basis by Kirov's death.

The count sensed that Stalin still was distraught about Kirov's death. Stalin was distraught because Kirov had become almost as powerful as he had. At times during their long evening discussion, there was an uncomfortable silence between them. Stalin reached into his jacket pocket for his pipe before nervously putting the pipe aside He'd been smoking too much lately. He wouldn't light it. He then gazed at the floor before reminding his friend that he must be cautious when dealing with the Nazis. "Ribbentrop must suspect nothing. He must perceive your curiosity as mere enthusiasm regarding Hitler's regime,"

Enthusiasm was out of the question. The count told Stalin he wasn't so sure he could mask his distaste for the Nazi regime. Stalin ignored his friend's remarks and continued to talk. "Anna's German is as good as yours. She knows how to charm friends and foes alike. Let her lead you in the game of espionage. When you have Ribbentrop's trust and confidence you may begin asking him the hard questions. I need to know the answers. Hitler isn't showing his hand to anyone. He is playing a game of deception but then so am I" he said thoughtfully gazing across the room at the fire in the hearth. "Russia must be given sufficient time to arm and prepare for war with Nazi Germany. Hitler's war machine is ready, cruel and efficient" he said slowly breaking off the conversation as if wishing to say no more on the subject. Stalin knew he could match that machine's cruelty. He knew he couldn't match the machine's efficiency.

The count knew that Stalin was heaping a huge responsibility upon him. He also knew there was little he or anyone else could do to slow or stop eventual Nazi aggression. Yet Carl understood his friend. He knew he couldn't fail Stalin or the people of Russia. He would stand with the Soviet dictator. He would help him foil Hitler's plans for the Soviet Union.

It was getting late. Stalin would remain at the count's estate until morning. Before they ended their discussion Stalin told Carl that he wanted Anna to join them.

Anna had remained in an adjoining room. She thought eventually Stalin would include her in the discussion he was having with her husband. She was reading a book but put it aside when Carl opened the door, entered the room and approached her. "We'd like for you to join us," he said as she got up from where she was sitting.

After she followed Carl into the other room, Anna saw Stalin huddled next to the hearth where he watched burning embers dance a final and fatal dance before their light diminished almost entirely. The count placed another log on the fire before sitting down in a chair next to his wife. Anna smiled cautiously at the dictator and wondered how Stalin planned to use her in the political intrigue game he played with the Nazis. Carl glanced at his wife as if he knew what she was thinking. He then quickly glanced as Stalin and wondered if the hearth's dwindling fire hadn't made Stalin feel uncomfortable in more ways than one. Stalin knew the options before him were few and time was fast dwindling. He needed more intelligence information before he could make informed decisions regarding actions he needed to take to prevent war. Russia needed to mend. It had already suffered one war and revolution and civil war had nearly torn the country apart. Anna waited patiently for Stalin to tell her how he wanted her to help him stem the tide of eventual Nazi aggression.

Through her father's political dealings with Germany prior to World War I, Anna had become familiar with people who were still members of the German High Command. She knew her father's attempt prior to World War I to call for peace among nations had failed.

"You mustn't be frightened if they recognize you", Stalin had told her. It wasn't that she was frightened. Anna thought delivering a message that already had been given might again be ignored. Yet Anna would do what she had been called upon to do even if she failed.

She didn't need anyone to tell her that maintaining peace in Europe entailed ending persecution. Anna was a realist. Like her late father, she believed that war and persecution would continue as long as a struggle for power among nations persisted. "There must be a call for peace, an appeal to the rulers if war is to be prevented," she'd remembered her father saying.

Anna couldn't condone Hitler's actions in persecuting others. Stalin was hard and cruel too yet Anna knew another side of Stalin that others who didn't know him well hadn't seen. Anna and Carl had gained their freedom from imprisonment because Stalin had put aside politics and cruelty.

Now Stalin wanted Anna to intervene for him. He wanted her to make Hitler's representatives realize that a message of peace always has relevance, and that victory won in war only could be maintained when the victor showed mercy towards the vanquished. War won in any other way only would be wasteful, cruel and destructive; bringing no final resolution to tensions or problems.

When Stalin started to speak to her, he spoke quietly. "They will remember you Anna. You must convince them how important your father's Appeal is." Stalin was a hard and unyielding man yet he hoped that the softness of one unlike himself, someone like Anna might stop the eventual flood of war and terror that soon would sweep across Europe.

Anna knew Stalin's past had been tormented. She knew that during the revolution he'd been rumored to be a provocateur. He'd turned on others before they could inform on him. He'd suffered betrayal and exile and his time in exile had been harsh. Stalin had not forgotten the cruelty. Yet Anna believed that at least for the time being that Stalin was using his power in a positive way by allowing her to carry forth her late father's message.

Stalin would pretend, at least temporarily to put aside the negative things that his spies had told him about Hitler and he would hope for peace. He would play a game of friendship with the Nazi dictator and he would hope that it wouldn't be perceived as pretense. Yet Stalin was no fool. Games had to end. Sooner or later Hitler would know that the game he played with Stalin was no longer a game. Stalin only hoped the game would last long enough for Russia to be fully prepared for war.

Anna sat in the armchair across from where her husband and Stalin sat opposite her. She shivered watching flames leap up in the fireplace. The room now was warm. Her discomfort was not brought on by the room's temperature. Anna was trembling in thinking about the past. She could still see her father's haggard face after war with Germany had been declared.

Anna felt frozen in silent resignation yet she knew there was no other alternative than to do what she was being called upon to do. She had to try to prevent the death and suffering brought on by war. She could still see her mother and sisters visiting the Russian war wounded lying in hospital beds. They'd sat with them, talked with them, read to them and wrote letters to their wives and mothers. Anna didn't want to see more war wounded. She'd lived through enough sadness in her life. She, her mother and sisters had been angels of mercy. Anna thought the sacrifice and suffering of the men lying in hospital beds was too great. Even angels have their breaking point. Anna would go home and cry after she'd spent hours comforting the war wounded. She knew Stalin already had sacrificed many lives for political reasons. He had few qualms in doing so. Yet Anna admired Stalin. Now he wanted to save lives. She would do what he had asked her to do.

She would make friends with the Nazis but only in an effort to help prevent the outbreak of war. She and her husband never would become political pawns.

Anna quickly glanced at Carl and then at Stalin. There was so much she wanted to say to them. Yet Anna believed in reticence and discretion. Under the circumstances she knew words were inadequate. She feared for her children's safety and for her husband's life. She knew the count took risks. She knew he wasn't afraid to participate in dangerous situations. Stalin wanted men like her husband working for him. The count would spy for Russia. Stalin was Russia. Inherently Anna knew her husband would sacrifice his safety and security if it meant protecting Russia. She shuddered with fear and uncertainty.

Stalin observed Anna's body language and outward emotions. He wondered what she was thinking. Anna turned her gaze from him. The fire in the hearth again was dying. It was late. Events were moving too fast. She wondered if she and Carl had too easily accepted Stalin's invitation to work for him.

Suddenly Stalin got up from the chair where he sat and said, "I must be leaving early tomorrow". The couple watched Stalin move towards the sitting room door and open it. He hesitated before turning and smiling at them before saying, "It has been a long evening. Difficult times await us. We must rest while we can."

Chapter Twelve

The following morning, Stalin agents advised the dictator that it wasn't safe for him to leave the count's estate. There were too many people who had learned of his travel schedule.

"You must remain with us until it is safe for you to leave" agreed the count.

Stalin decided that he would remain at Carl's estate for another day. The extra time would give them more opportunity to talk.

Yet Stalin hadn't expected to be present when Matilde Kschessinskaya, the famed Russian ballerina, visited Carl and his wife. Matilde had fled Russia during the revolution and now she and her husband lived in the South of France. Her husband had briefly met Anna after she'd fled imprisonment. The two had talked after Carl arranged for the meeting. The Tsar's younger brother had recognized his niece and later wrote her a letter confirming his belief in her. "Hold your head up high. You know who you are". Now Matilde wanted to meet her husband's mysterious niece. Since she had business to conduct with Moscow's Bolshoi ballet, she would visit Romania first so she could meet Anna.

Anna waited quietly as a maid led Matilde into a sitting room so they could meet. Although no longer young, Matilde was still beautiful and very slender in appearance. Anna smiled and invited her to be seated in a chair opposite hers. Matilde gracefully sat down in the chair, folded her hands in her lap and gazed across the room. She felt at home in her surroundings. A fire burned in the fireplace and gave the room an aura of warmth and welcome as Matilde glanced at a magnificent Renaissance painting hanging upon a wall.

At first both women seemed a little awkward with the other. Anna was silent as she gracefully reached for a tea tray a maid had brought to her.

She placed the tray on a small table in front of her. Then she slowly poured Matilde a cup of tea from a silver teapot before smiling and offering her the tea along with the milk and the sugar. After pouring herself a cup of tea and sipping it slowly, Anna placed the cup and saucer aside. She'd heard how much Nicholas had loved Matilde. She was determined that the older woman should feel welcome in her home. "I'm so glad you came" she said before cordially offering her a tea sandwich from the silver plate.

Matilde looked at Anna. "I now realize the rumors are true. My husband and others who believe in you are right. You are so like your late father. You have his gaze and his gray blue eyes. No one who looked into his eyes could ever forget."

Anna reached out and clasped Matilde's hand in friendship. Words were inadequate to express what she felt.

"Thank God, you managed to escape", said Matilde. Anna nodded her head as tears streamed down her cheeks.

She wanted to tell Matilde about her miraculous escape from imprisonment. Her husband had rescued her but Stalin had helped too. There was so much Anna wanted to tell Matilde but discretion dictated reticence.

Matilde quietly observed Anna. She was hesitant to ask her what the final days were like. "He was brave until the end", she said as if sensing what Matilde wanted to know. "When we were in Ekaterinburg, he never gave up hope that we might be rescued. When rescue didn't come, he didn't waver in his courage or love for us. I want to believe that other members of my family somehow survived but I think they are gone too. After father's assassination the Bolsheviks took us to Perm. My brother died of his illness there. Only I managed to slip past guards and escape to Romania", she said sadly gazing at the floor.

Matilde realized Anna felt guilty to be the lone survivor. "You must never feel guilty for having survived such a terrible ordeal" she said as Anna fought back tears.

Matilde reached for a watch she'd brought with her before handing the watch to her and saying, "This once belonged to your father. He left it with me one time. He never returned for it. He later became engaged to your mother. I never saw him after that."

Anna received the gold watch from Matilde's hands.' She ran her fingers over the intricately designed surface before opening the watch and finding the hands frozen. "The watch stopped working after he left me and I've never had it repaired" said Matilde.

Anna placed the watch aside, then reaching out to Matilde, the two women embraced. "Thank you for the watch" she said with tears streaming down her face.

"If ever you and your husband visit the South of France you must visit us" said Matilde getting up to leave.

Anna started to invite her guest for dinner but hesitated. The meeting had been an emotional one. The memories were painful for them both. "Good by my dear" said Matilde turning to leave. Anna showed her guest to a heavily carved wooden door, but hesitated to open it. Instead she turned and stood in front of the door.

"Please. You mustn't leave now. My husband would insist that you stay for dinner and so I must insist too."

Matilde hesitated. "Very well, I'd be honored to join you for dinner." Curiosity had brought her to Anna. The past had haunted her. In meeting Anna, Matilde had gained a feeling of closure. She had lived through extraordinary times. She'd known extraordinary people. The years and terrible events had passed so quickly that they'd hardly seemed real at all. Yet they had been real. The personal triumphs, the tragedy of revolution had touched Matilde's privileged life. Anna represented the past. In meeting Anna, Matilde had confronted her past.

Anna knew why Matilde had to contact her. She had to know. She had to be certain. Was Anna genuine? Was Anna the daughter of the man she'd once loved? There could be no doubt.

Anna had her maid show Matilde to a room where she could rest and wait for dinner. Having expected that she might be invited to stay for the evening or even overnight, Matilde had brought a few personal items with her. The beautiful Chanel suit she wore needed few accessories. A scarf or pin might enhance her ensemble. For the time being though, she would rest. It was still early. Dinner wouldn't be served for several hours. She would rest and think about the extraordinary past.

After Matilde had left her, Anna went to the room where she hid precious items belonging to her. It was a room of her own, a place of her own, like the one she'd created as a child so that she might hold on to past fantasies and remembrances. Anna unlocked a drawer and placed the gold watch that had belonged to her father in the drawer and locked it.

Anna knew she couldn't hide the watch forever. Eventually she would show it to her husband. Perhaps too she would someday show the watch to her sons.

Anna hesitated to leave the room where she'd hid so many precious things. There were photographs of her children everywhere even one of Micha. Anna wanted to stay in her special room. She opened a closet door. Inside the closet was the beaded ball gown that she'd worn the night her husband and Stalin had proposed to her. The ball gown still fit her but she'd never worn the dress again after she became engaged to the count.

That evening seemed so long ago. Koba now was ruler of Russia. Anna remembered the words she'd said in rebuff to his marriage proposal that night. "The prophetess, the old woman said my sisters and I would be wed to death." Koba had quickly left her side. Now he was back in her life.

It was almost time for dinner. Anna left the small room where she kept so many cherished memories and returned to her bedroom where she changed clothes. She chose the yellow dress worn with the emerald pin her husband had given her for her birthday. It was getting late. She knew they all were waiting for her. Matilde was busy talking with Stalin when Anna greeted them.

The count offered his wife her usual glass of chardonnay before she sat in a chair opposite the sofa where Matilde sat with Stalin.

Koba gazed at Anna. He couldn't help but notice how lovely she looked. She was no longer the frightened young girl of long ago. She wasn't the girl he had wanted to protect and rescue. She was no longer there. Anna had grown powerful. She was beautiful. He wanted her at his side. She belonged at his side. She belonged to the count.

Stalin placed his drink aside. He knew he had delayed his own departure back to Moscow partly because he'd wanted to be with Anna. He really hadn't wanted any increased security.

Anna smiled. There was tension in the room. She quickly glanced at Carl. He seemed to know what she was thinking. She was overtired. She was reeling from having to face the past. She was struggling with the thought that she owed her freedom and new found existence as much to Stalin as she did her husband. Anna set her wine glass aside as Carl rose from where he was sitting and suggested that it was time for dinner. He and Anna led the way into the dining room as Stalin and Matilde followed them.

It would be a leisurely dinner. The count politely proposed a toast to his guests as Anna, smiled across the table at them and listened attentively to Stalin whose quick wit, charming company and robust humor entertained them all. Anna and Carl smiled as Stalin proposed a toast to Matilde who laughed delightedly when she realized what the dictator had done.

Despite an outward festive mood, the warmth and gaiety they extended to their guests was at times a little strained. Anna and Carl seemed relieved when Stalin said he would be leaving early the following morning and needed a good night's rest.

It was early the following rainy morning when a car quickly pulled up in front of the count's home. Two bodyguards with umbrellas in hand started to escort the dictator to the car that would take him to the train depot. Stalin didn't mind a little rain. He started to wave both umbrellas away but instead took one of them from a bodyguard and held it for Matilde so she wouldn't get wet. He'd told her that she shouldn't be traveling by herself to Moscow and that he wanted to be sure that her journey there as well as her return to the South of France would be safe. Today Matilde had her own private compartment aboard the dictator's train. When Stalin wasn't being his usual workaholic self he would invite her to join him for lunch or dinner when they would laugh and reminisce about many things. Later when she returned home to her husband she would remark, "Regardless of how his critics scoff and the aristocracy balk, Stalin, for the time being seems to have saved Russia." Her husband wouldn't comment.

* * * *

Several days had passed. Although Carl and Anna were relieved that Stalin had left in such good spirits, the count hadn't belittled the need for increased security surrounding them. Stalin's visit had heightened outside curiosity and a need for increased protection to the highest level. He knew he and his family were being watched. He knew how vulnerable they were to danger, so one morning when Carl nervously looked around for Anna and didn't find her, he felt concerned. He thought she might have gone upstairs to her office or to their rooms. When he didn't find her there, he kept looking for her but not in the place he might have never thought to look for her.

For years Anna had walked past Dracula's apartments. She was still haunted by the shadowy figure she'd encountered when she'd exited Dracula's secret passageway after hiding important documents there. She wondered, if Dracula still wasn't one of the undead or had he really died decades ago when a stake was reputedly driven into his heart? Anna shivered contemplating the dread scenario. For decades no one had entered Dracula's rooms. The door to them was securely locked, and only her husband had a key he never used to open them. Today Anna's curiosity got the better of her. Instead of trying to peek through a crack in the door to see if she might discover any trace of him, Anna boldly turned the door handle on the heavy carved wooden door to Dracula's rooms. To her astonishment, the door opened. She cautiously stepped inside the semi darkened room and gazed at a well stocked bookcase near a desk and chair. Trembling with fear, and realizing she had entered a place no one, not even her husband dared enter, she turned to leave the apartments but not until she saw the same shadowy figure she'd seen only once before. For a moment she froze in fear. She thought she heard him say in an almost inaudible whisper. "Don't be afraid. The gate again will open for you." Anna gasped then quickly left the apartments as the door locked behind her and she quickly made her way upstairs to the schoolroom.

When the count opened the door to the classroom and found his wife talking with the governess, Anna turned to him saying, "Darling I believe the boys need to practice more self discipline. Carl Nicholas has been reading his Mickey Mouse comic books when he should have been doing his math lesson and Ivan hides his favorite dime novels inside his literature anthology book."

The governess politely interrupted Anna. "The boys need to adjust to a normal school room routine." The count listened to the discussion then turned to Anna and said, "The boys need to concentrate on their studies." Anna never disagreed with Carl's decisions in the way he raised their sons. After all, he was their father. If she thought he overindulged them she said nothing. If as in this instance, she thought Carl should take a sterner hand with the boys she didn't offer advice. She'd been through so much personal pain in life she only wanted her sons to enjoy their childhood free from fear and uncertainty. The count tried to be gentle with his children. When they deserved a reprimand, as they did now, he never raised his voice to them. In return for their father's fairness and kind understanding both his sons had grown very close to him. They were never afraid to confide in him even if they'd done something wrong. He was always there for them.

After the meeting with his wife and the children's governess, Carl left to go riding. If Anna thought her husband should have talked to his children first, she had to be satisfied when he told her he'd speak to them later. When she'd told him she wouldn't be accompanying him on his morning ride, he'd just assumed she knew he didn't want to get into further discussion regarding his children's lackadaisical school performance. Anna had another reasons for not accompanying him. She knew she had entered a forbidden place when she set foot in Dracula's apartments. She was feeling frightened and uneasy contemplating her morning encounter with the shadowy almost indiscernible figure she'd glimpsed. She wanted to tell Carl what she'd seen that morning. She wanted to tell him that she'd finally done the brave and daunting thing by entering Dracula's apartments but she couldn't do it. She was afraid that Carl might not understand or forgive her curiosity in entering the vampire's mysterious apartments. Anna realized Carl might suspect what she had done when she wasn't behaving like her usual self. Yet she had other reasons for not accompanying Carl on his morning ride.

In Marina's absence, Anna also planned the menus and supervised the servants in the care of their home all of which took time away from being with her family. Carl always missed Anna when she didn't accompany him on his morning ride. He wanted to keep her safe. He'd tried to tell himself that his concerns regarding her were unfounded. Anna had already proven to him and others that she knew how to take care of herself. Yet he knew there were those, who if given the opportunity, might do her harm. He wanted her by his side.

As Carl continued to ride alone around his estate, he remembered the time years earlier when he and Anna had been under surveillance. Lately he had sensed that he and his family again were being watched. Only this time the surveillance wasn't being done by the Bolsheviks or motivated by the struggle within the Communist regime. The count sensed a different sort of presence surrounding him and his family.

Stalin had told Carl that he wanted him to draw near to the Nazis. In doing so, he would also invite the observance of German agents. Carl wondered if he and his wife weren't already drawing their attention.

Several hours passed. It was beginning to get late and Anna was growing anxious about him. She nervously gazed through a window and was relieved when in the distance she could see Carl returning from his morning ride.

"Darling I was beginning to worry about you", she said, as she walked down castle steps and watched him dismount from his horse. A groom led the horse away as the couple walked through the castle's entranceway together. The count seemed a bit amused when after following his wife indoors he still saw a week's supply of menus waiting for her approval. He knew that if his mother still was living with them she'd already have approved and given the menus back to the chef with comments. He knew Anna was feeling insecure in taking over her mother-in-law's job. She knew the chef and other staff who worked for them might silently be comparing her inefficiency in menu planning to Marina's past proven efficiency regarding the undertaking. Anna knew she had to give approval to the chef as soon as possible. He had to order food for the household. Even though she knew her husband was comfortably well off Anna realized that Carl expected his wife to stay within a budget. Yet she wanted to make sure that he was as comfortable and satisfied with the way she ran his home as he had been when his mother was still living with them.

Carl had his preferences. "Did you enjoy the London Broil the other evening?" she asked him. Carl wasn't sure which dish Anna meant. If he didn't like the food served him, he'd always let his mother know about it so she could tell the chef. When the count simply agreed to her choices, Anna went boldly ahead and approved the menus. He wasn't thinking about food right now. He had other concerns.

"We're being watched" he said. "I noticed men moving about in the trees while I was riding. They're probably the same people who were watching Stalin before he left for the Kremlin."

"Since they no longer have Stalin to spy on they're probably out there hiding in the brush and hoping to discover something sinister about us" she laughed.

"I suppose you're right" he said feeling a little foolish for his concern and pretending to make light of the situation. "Now that they know we're friends with Stalin we're going to have to work even harder to bring the Nazis over to our side. We'll want to convince them that like Stalin we want to befriend them."

Carl knew how charming Anna could be. He'd always counted on her to get them through the awkward times. "You must do your best and try to make them feel at home" he said uneasily as Anna left his office and went to her own before returning with a pair of field glasses. Anna wasn't sure if turning on the charm with representatives of Germany's High Command would remove her family from unwanted scrutiny. If someone was spying on them then she was ready to reciprocate in kind.

"When I accompany the children on their daily walk today, instead of pointing out migrating birds from Arctic regions, I'll use the glasses to try and spot people lurking around the premises" she said gazing out an office window through the lens of the binoculars.

"Darling, I wish I hadn't mentioned anything to you about being watched. I don't want you to worry unnecessarily". Anna made no comment.

Instead, she put the field glasses aside, picked up the approved menus, and walked downstairs towards the kitchen so she could give them to the chef. On the way to the kitchen, a maid interrupted her and said, "Excuse me. There is a gentleman at the door who says he'd like a word with your husband."

Anna asked the maid if she had any idea who the man was.

"He has a German accent", she replied a little nervously.

Anna handed the pile of menus to the maid, and told her to take them to the kitchen and give them to the chef. She then quickly ran upstairs so she could tell her husband that there was a stranger at the door wanting to see him. Carl looked up from what he was doing as she peered around an opened door.

"Darling I believe the Nazi High Command's representative may be paying us a visit. He wants to speak with you" she said.

Carl left his office and walked downstairs toward the castle's entranceway where the man awaited him.

"Hello Boris", he said sounding relieved and extending a hand in welcome to the Soviet spy Stalin had sent to inform him that representatives from the German High Command had arrived.

Carl directed Boris to a corner hallway chair then sat opposite him and asked him if the rumor was true. "Has Hitler forced members of the Communist party out of the country?"

"Yes, I've recently returned from Berlin. There is a great deal of fear gripping members of Berlin's Communist party. Stalin's government has granted some of them asylum in Russia."

Knowing Stalin the way he did, the count knew that arrangement only could be temporary. He knew what Stalin had offered the refugees couldn't possibly be asylum. Eventually Hitler would want the political refugees back and Stalin would return them.

After his brief conversation with Boris, Carl showed him to the door and returned to his office where Anna waited for him. "I suppose it's never too soon to extend a welcome. One of Stalin's spies has reminded me that I need to make a social call," he said.

"You mean the Nazis are already here?" she gasped. Anna knew there would be no need for her to carry the field glasses with her when she took the children for a walk. The situation was out in the open.

"I'd like to accompany you when you pay them a visit", she said tidying up her husband's office space and putting aside the field binoculars.

"I think it's best if you remain here this morning. I'm not sure if my visit to the High Command will be welcome."

"Why shouldn't it be?" she asked. He didn't answer her. He was too busy watching her tidy up his cluttered office space to tell her why. He was sure Anna had done such a good job in tidying up his office that he'd never be able to find anything when he needed it.

Anna didn't try to change her husband's mind. She didn't stop tidying up his office either.

Carl realized his call on the Nazis had to appear to be casual. "I'll just engage them in some pleasant conversation. Then I'll invite them for dinner."

"Very well darling" said Anna locking one of her husband's desk drawers and placing the key in her pocket. "And speaking of dinner, I've already sent the menus to the kitchen but if you think there might be something special that our guests might enjoy, let me know."

The count smiled at his wife. "I think a steady reinforcement of vodka and champagne should be the order of the evening if we want to make our visitors feel at home."

"I suppose you're right. Sobriety shouldn't be the order of the evening if we really want to discover their secrets" she said laughingly as Carl asked her where she'd put his appointment book.

Anna smiled at Carl, unlocked the count's top desk drawer, and handed the appointment book to him. Carl returned her smile but seemed a little irritable. He understood what she was trying to do. He didn't say anything to her about nosing into his affairs. When he turned to leave the room, Anna called after him. "When will you be back?"

"I should be home in an hour or so."

Anna took a deep breath. She thought the Nazis might suspect that Carl was too eager to extend a dinner invitation to them. She knew Carl was impulsive. She would accompany him whether he liked it or not.

The count was already in his car and had started to pull the vehicle out of the driveway when Anna ran after him so he could stop the car, lean over and open the car door letting her inside. Carl then backed up the car and turned it around so he could drive down the castle's steep driveway and access the main road.

Anna gazed into the car's rearview mirror. "I hope I look alright. I didn't have time to prepare for any sort of meeting with anyone today." The sweater she wore over her wool skirt clung seductively to her. Carl rolled down the car window and Anna brushed the hair away from her face. He didn't answer her. He was too absorbed in what he would say to the commandant to concern himself with anything else.

They drove for several miles. Carl quickly put his foot to the brake pedal but narrowly missed a man escorting a small herd of sheep along a quiet village street. He then turned onto another road and sped several miles into the countryside. It was early fall. The day was pleasant. The morning air was filled with the scent of newly mown hay and wild flowers imbued the air with a false sense of peace and security. Anna kept brushing her windblown hair from her face. They passed a couple of small farms. Cows grazed lazily in an open pasture. The count pressed down the brake pedal again as the car rounded a sharp curve. He then slowed the car down and backed it up. He'd missed the turnoff. He turned the car around and sped back in the opposite direction until he came to the intersection before continuing down the right road. The car went over a bump. Anna told him to slow the car down. Carl irritably responded to his wife's insistence that he was driving too fast by suggesting that the next time she do the driving. Anna was silent. She knew he was nervous. Neither of them knew what sort of reception they'd receive from the Nazis. Then they spotted it. On the right side of the road was a rambling but comfortable looking farmhouse.

Guards surrounding the house stood behind a gate and fence and quietly observed the count as he slowed the car to a halt, rolled down the car window and a guard asked him what his business was. Carl presented the guard with some identification then introduced Anna before telling him that he'd like to speak to the commandant.

After looking over Carl's identification and realizing that he was a count and the woman with him was his wife, the guard allowed the couple to pass through the gate. Carl then brought the car to a halt and the couple emerged from the car and walked toward the farmhouse.

"We've come to see the commandant" said Carl stopping at a checkpoint entrance to the farmhouse. If the guard was suspicious of the count's reason for wanting to see the commandant he didn't reveal it. He directed Carl and his wife to a waiting room where they sat on a corner sofa directly beneath the portrait of the Fuehrer.

Anna shuddered. The shades in the room were closed, and an unfurled Nazi flag was placed in an opposite corner of the room. She was beginning to think that the impromptu visit had been a mistake. Silence engulfed them and she placed her hand in her husband's. Her heart pounded. She wanted to go home but she dared not tell Carl that they should leave. Instead she gazed around the semi-darkened room. An iron sculpture of an eagle was prominently displayed on a solid oak desk but the room was devoid of all décor other than the Nazi symbols scattered around the room.

Anna was about to whisper and tell Carl what she thought of the room's decor but hesitated. A door opened. Ribbentrop's representative appeared and extended a hand in greeting to them. The count rose and shook it but Anna remained seated as the man bent and kissed her hand. He couldn't help but notice how lovely and seductive she looked in her tight fitting sweater. It had been awhile since he or any of the men with him had been in the company of such a charming and engaging couple but the dinner invitation was accepted with an air of suspicion regarding the reason for it. The Nazis knew Stalin was the count's friend. Yet Stalin was for the time being, also Hitler's friend. Why shouldn't they enjoy the count's hospitality?

It was early in the day. Carl and Anna were offered a drink. Anna wanted to decline the drink but her husband nudged her. It would be rude not to accept the drink. She accepted the drink but unlike Carl she cautiously nursed it. The count was a man who could consume alcohol without it seeming to affect him. Yet he was cautious too. He knew he had to remain alert. He didn't want to engage in a drinking binge in which someone in the company, namely he, might be carried away to sober up.

The conversation was amiable yet guarded. Carl knew it would be stupid for him to ask ridiculous questions such as how long do you expect to remain here. He knew why the Nazis were making their presence known. He knew their reason for being in Romania was so they might establish a political presence and begin tapping the Romanian oil that flowed so abundantly.

He also knew there was little anyone could do to oppose their political expansion or to drive them away. The count slowly sipped his drink. Anna had put hers aside. When asked if he would like a refill, Carl politely declined.

Anna nervously twisted the single strand of pearls wound about her neck. It was getting late. She wanted to leave but said nothing. She waited for her husband to take the initiative. A time and convenient date for the dinner invitation was arranged. The commandant told them that they would be looking forward to seeing them for dinner. "If you get over our way before then do drop by and visit us" said Carl placing his unfinished drink aside.

He then shook hands with the commandant who escorted the couple outside and walked with them to their car. Carl was already sitting in the driver's seat when the commandant politely opened the car's passenger door so that Anna could get in beside her husband.

Then maneuvering the car around a bit Carl began backing out of the driveway. Anna rolled down the car's window and quietly watched as guards saluted the commandant. He smiled at her. She smiled back and nervously waved in return.

Anna was relieved. They were on their way home. She wondered if the commandant would pay them a visit before the dinner party. She wondered too if he knew who she really was. Perhaps it was something he'd said during her conversation with him. Perhaps it was something he'd said to her husband that convinced her that it would be futile for her to try to hide her real identity.

Now that Stalin had asked Carl to take an active role in spying for him, the count felt trapped. He'd made the overtures. He had opened the door to scrutiny not just for himself but for his family.

As they drove along the road together, Anna seemed strangely quiet. Carl thought she must be feeling frightened and alone. Anna didn't want to tell Carl that she didn't want to be scrutinized. They were living in extraordinary times. People like them couldn't live normal lives anymore. Anna wondered if it wasn't time for them to run--but where?

Anna pensively gazed out the car window. The count had slowed the car's speed to a leisurely pace. He knew she was feeling worried and wasn't in the best of spirits. Now that the visit with the Nazis was over, Carl wanted her to relax. He knew what she was thinking. He took her hand in his and told her to stop thinking of running.

It was a beautiful day so Carl suggested that they shouldn't go directly home. Instead they would enjoy having a little time alone together. For years, the couple hadn't ventured far from their castle retreat unless they knew that Stalin had provided them with bodyguards. Today Carl felt differently about the situation. Perhaps he and Anna could get lost if they just kept driving.

Where were Stalin's bodyguards? Where was the train that would take them to the Kremlin? Ever since she'd been a child, Anna had never gone to ordinary places such as restaurants and inns. She'd never ventured into the real world. When her family became imprisoned, she again was isolated. After she'd been rescued from prison Anna still had been in a sort of confinement. Her husband had tried to protect her by keeping her with him safely within his castle home. Even Countess Marina had had more freedom than Anna.

When they stopped for lunch, the couple enjoyed the quaint atmosphere of the quiet village inn where they enjoyed a simple lunch consisting of a bottle of wine and some fruit and cheese. Never before had Anna felt so free.

Never before had she felt so close to the real world. "I wish we could stay here forever", she'd said wistfully.

Carl was a realist. He knew they had to keep moving. He believed the only reason the Nazi officers accepted his dinner invitation was to see what they could find out from him about his friendship with Stalin.

Following their lunch, the couple slowly drove home along a winding country road. If they were being watched as the count thought they probably were, he was comfortable in the knowledge that for the time being, he and Anna had found respite from it.

After their return home, Anna opened the doors to the drawing room and sat down at the recently tuned beautiful grand piano placed there. She wanted to know if the Steinway was tuned well enough for a professional pianist to play upon. She'd decided that if she and her husband were going to entertain German High Command representatives that they must have some sort of diversion planned for the evening. Conversation might invite inquiry. The couple knew what questions they wanted to ask their guests. Once they got the answers to them they didn't want to be asked any questions in return. A musical evening might discourage unwanted meddling.

Anna had studied piano when she and her sisters were growing up together. Memories of the past flooded over her as she sat down at the piano and played familiar melodies by Brahms, Liszt and Beethoven. Tears came to her eyes. The music was harmonious, discordant, sad and unbearably beautiful, just like her life had been. When she played a piece her mother liked to play, Anna turned to find the count watching her. Keep playing he encouraged her. She knew she needed more practice. Carl sat down beside her on the piano bench and watched her long delicate fingers sweep across the keyboard. Anna had forgotten how much she used to like to play the piano. With her family now gone, it had seemed almost too difficult to play all the familiar pieces she'd learned to play as a child. Now she had a new family. Her children who knew their mother could play the piano but who'd rarely heard her do so, came and listened too. "Please Mommy continue to play," said Carl Nicholas standing behind his parents but Ivan saw tears in her eyes and refrained from asking his mother to continue playing.

"I need more practice. I make too many mistakes" she said getting up from the piano bench. She'd never told her children about her family's tragedy. They were too young to be burdened with it. Yet Ivan had seemed to understand without her telling him. He'd seen his parents alone together. He'd watched and listened when his father tried to comfort his mother when she cried for no apparent reason.

Anna suddenly turned to her children and said "Your father and I are going to entertain some visitors in a few weeks. We are going to make it a musical event and we want you to be present when we invite a professional pianist here to play for us."

The Russian composer, Rachmaninoff had written some brilliant works for the piano. On more than one occasion, Carl and Anna had heard him play his own music. Anna was determined that the planned evening's entertainment would focus on the music of Rachmaninoff. She had selected his music to be played because she knew he too had struggled with despair. Some of Rachmaninoff's most beautiful music had been composed when he'd overcome depression. Now that the piano was tuned she would find a pianist who could do justice to the composer's work.

Anna's tearful episode had passed. She regained her composure and again sat down at the keyboard. It was getting late in the afternoon. Her husband continued to listen to his wife play as the governess entered the room and led the children away for tea.

A week past; there was much to be done in preparation for the planned entertainment. Although he hadn't expected to be included, Anna had invited Stalin to the gathering. Hitler's own special envoy, Ribbentrop, had made it be known that he would attend Anna's entertainment. Regardless of whether or not Ribbentrop was present, Stalin knew he would outrank the other guests. Anna especially hoped that Stalin would be present for the occasion. She wanted to feel his support when she confronted Ribbentrop.

Anna knew how to throw a party. She'd done it many times before. Only this time her role would be more than that of hostess. She would be playing the role of an actress. What she was feeling in playing that role would be genuine. Anna knew what she'd say to Ribbentrop had to sound unrehearsed. What she would say must come from her heart. There would be flowers from the greenhouse to decorate interior rooms and several of the family's most prized paintings would be exhibited as well.

Carl watched his wife dust off one of the paintings they'd selected to be put on exhibit. She wanted to place the painting on the wall in just the right location so with heavy painting in hand she stepped onto the stepladder. "Here, darling" he said making Anna step down from the ladder. "Let me do that."

She watched Carl stand upon the lowest rung of the stepladder and reach upward as she handed him a small hammer and nails so he could hang the painting. She then gingerly lifted the painting up to give to him as he quickly took it from her grasp. Anna watched Carl place the painting in the desired place before stepping down from the ladder. Together they stood gazing at the magnificent Renaissance work from several different angles. They wondered if the location they'd chosen for the painting was the right one. After giving it careful consideration, they decided that it was. The room's artificial lighting brought out colors and background in the work they hadn't previously seen. "We'll hang the rest tomorrow", Carl said folding up the ladder.

The following morning, during their breakfast together, the couple decided that they needed to spend some time with their sons. It had been awhile since they'd had a family outing. Anna went to tell the governess that they were going to take the children riding with them and that they could resume their lessons later.

When Ivan heard the news their governess delivered to them, he closed his books and quickly put his pens aside. "I hope we're going on a picnic too", said Carl Nicholas stuffing his math book into a desk drawer and following his older brother from the classroom. The boys' governess was still in conversation with their mother but noticed their enthusiastic departure from the classroom and said confidingly, "They need some time away from school. They enjoyed the time you and your husband spent with them last evening." Anna smiled acknowledging her comment. The people who worked for her found Anna to be appreciative and understanding.

After the boys left their schoolroom, they quickly changed into their riding clothes and joined their parents waiting outside for them. The early fall morning enveloped everything in an atmosphere of expectation and promise. The aroma of late blooming garden flowers and forest greenery permeating the air mingled, as morning fog melted before the sun like magic. The family then mounted their horses and the boys rode just ahead of their parents before disappearing around a curve until Carl caught up with them. He told them to rein in their horses so he could have a word with them. Anna rode just behind her husband and listened as he said "a picnic lunch is waiting for us at the end of the trail overlooking the valley. Since your mother and I have something we want to discuss with you, we thought having a family picnic might be the best way to have the discussion." Anna wondered what sort of a discussion her husband had in mind but didn't ask as she and her family continued moving toward their destination.

The sun was high in the sky and the trail leading directly to the place where the mountainous hill overlooked the valley was steep. The day was getting warm and the horses no longer cantered along the trail but plodded up the incline where rest, water and food awaited them and a picnic table laden with food awaited the family.

The boys eagerly dismounted their horses and headed towards the picnic table where there were glasses and large pitchers of lemonade waiting for them. Anna dismounted her horse then waited for Carl. He was making sure that the horses were being watered and properly cared for too.

The picnic, prepared in the castle's kitchen and brought by jeep to the luscious green hillside was placed upon a rustic wooden picnic bench covered by a colorful checkered table cloth. Carl and Anna slowly approached their children before joining them then sitting at the picnic bench beneath the shade of a large overgrown forest pine. Fruit, sandwiches, cheese, nuts and pastries were passed around and glasses of lemonade refilled or poured from pitchers. The atmosphere surrounding them was relaxed and easy as the boys laughed and joked happily with their parents. Conversation was only interrupted when a pair of squirrels scavenging for food cautiously approached the picnic bench and waited at a safe but close enough distance for a handout. When the last squirrel had scampered off with what remained of lunch, and crumbs had been thrown to the birds, only the picnic bench with its tablecloth and pitchers of lemonade remained.

Carl watched his sons pour themselves another glass of lemonade before saying that he had something he wanted to tell them. He searched his wife's face before beginning the difficult conversation. He wanted her approval before he said anything. Anna gazed downward. She sensed what her husband was about to tell her sons but said nothing. He knew she hadn't given him permission to tell the boys what he felt they must know. He hesitated to say anything at all when he watched Anna slowly turn her head as if she wanted to avoid listening to what he was about to tell their children. The boys seemed bewildered by their parents' strange behavior. Carl Nicholas asked, "Is everything all right Mother?" Anna didn't answer him.

Instead, the count began the conversation by saying, "Like you, your mother and I were born to privileged families. We consider ourselves to be fortunate in that respect. Life's circumstances change though even for the most privileged among us. Perhaps you think it is strange that your mother has never introduced you to her parents, brother or sisters. I think it's time that you know the truth. You need to know who your mother really is. In your history classroom studies you may have heard that Russia's last Tsar was assassinated with his wife and children. What history doesn't reveal is that your mother didn't die with the rest of her family. She is Nicholas II's only surviving daughter. You are his grandsons."

The children were astonished. They didn't know what to say in response to what their father had told them. Anna almost cried. "You shouldn't be telling them this now. They're too young to understand. She tried getting up from the table and leaving but the count took her arm and made her sit down again. She knew Carl had to tell their sons her story.

Although they were young, the children understood their mother's emotion. They also respected their father for wanting them to know the truth about their mother's relatives. When all was said, Anna was grateful to Carl for what he'd done. She was sad yet proud that he'd done what she couldn't bring herself to do.

Ivan touched his father's arm. "Thanks for telling us about mother," he said. Carl Nicholas put his arms around his mother and hugged her. He knew his mother had wanted to hide her past from the world. He and his brother were her children though. Like Ivan, Carl Nicholas knew their father had done the right thing in telling them the truth about their mother's family.

The family's ride home was peaceful. Since the trail downward was steep, the count warned his sons to let the horses take their time in descending the hillside. When the terrain became more level, and it was easier to ride the horses, the children chose to remain close to their parents.

Since he'd been a small child, Ivan had sensed the strain sometimes between his parents. The whispers and quiet disagreements between them was something he'd grown used to. Since he loved both parents, he could never take sides. He'd sensed his father's past had been a difficult one. The legacy of Dracula still haunted the family and so did Carl's ties with revolutionists. Both parents had something to hide. Yet Ivan was convinced that the emotional strain he'd sensed between his parents had much to do too with his mother's tragic past. His father had tried so hard to cover it up. Ivan knew his father had been trying to protect his mother from the world's scrutiny. He hadn't known why until now.

Now that he and his brother had peaceably descended the hillside together, Ivan knew a burden had been lifted from their shoulders too. He and his brother wouldn't look for a cause anymore for their mother's crying jags or their father's impatience. They hoped all that was over. The boys, who sometimes bickered, much to their parents' dismay now were quietly engaged in friendly conversation with one another. There didn't seem to be any rivalry or competition for their parents' attention. The children felt at peace because their parents were at peace. Today the boys didn't try to outdistance their parents on the ride home. They were happy simply to be with them.

The count knew his sons were enjoying their time alone with them. The atmosphere was more relaxed than it ever had been. He and Anna quietly talked with their children and every now and then they would rein in their horses and Carl would point out familiar landmarks to his family. If they saw a wild animal from the forest dart out in front of them he'd tell them the name of the species. It was as if they were seeing the world around them clearly for the first time. Anna realized what a good father her husband was. His kindness and gentleness, the qualities that had drawn her to him, were being shown to his children.

After returning home, Carl let the boys help him hang the remaining paintings that he wanted to exhibit in the drawing room. Anna only intervened when there was a disagreement over where a particular painting should hang. If there was a dispute, she had the final word.

While the family was busy sorting through the paintings, Anna went and fetched tea for them. She knew her sons liked the thick icing on the warm buns that had been iced after being taken from the oven. She made sure there was an abundant supply of them on hand as they sat down for a tea break.

The children didn't ask their parents if they needed to return to school after tea. The count made it clear: They'd been given the day off. Today at least, he didn't want them to feel as if he and Anna were relegating them out to someone else's care. He wanted them to feel important and that they were a fixed part of his and Anna's lives.

Since it was getting late in the day and the room in which they now sat was becoming cool, the boys helped their father build a fire in the hearth as Anna sat across from all the activity and watched. She slowly sipped her tea as her husband heaped another log on the fire.

When it was time for the children to leave them, the governess came and fetched them. She knew there would be no schoolwork until tomorrow. Today had been busy enough. Both boys hugged their parents and thanked them for a wonderful day before telling them good night.

Anna at last was at ease with the knowledge that a matter she'd not wanted to discuss with her children had finally been addressed. When the boys had left them, she turned to Carl and said. "I'm glad you told them everything." Carl was relieved to hear Anna say that to him. He'd felt guilty for addressing the issue without first asking her permission though. It had been her life he'd been talking about not his own.

Carl then took Anna in his arms. For a long time he just held her. When he finally let her go, he walked into another room and fetched a bottle of champagne. While he was gone, she went and got the priceless Faberge egg that Stalin had given her. She would display the egg along with its portraits of her family in a glass case. Tears came to her eyes as she recalled seeing the exquisitely crafted egg sitting on her father's desk so many times before. Anna knew it was time to move on to other things. Yet the cherished memories, like the portraits of her family contained within the Faberge egg would remain a precious part of her life forever.

Carl returned with the bottle of champagne then poured her a glass of it before pouring himself one. He then picked up his champagne filled glass and proposed a toast to her. He knew she had brought him back from the brink of despair after his time in prison. In their love for one another each had given the other back a life. "This is to you, darling" he said clinking his glass against hers. Then placing his champagne glass aside, Carl again took Anna in his arms.

"I'm so grateful to you. Life would be almost intolerable for me if I didn't have you and the children" she said as he held her.

"We support each other. That's what makes us a family." Anna wearily rested against Carl's shoulder. She closed her eyes and thought about what he'd just said to her.

It was getting late in the evening. Both were tired but the tiredness each felt was partly relief. He took her by the arm and gently led her upstairs. "I love you", she whispered as they closed the chapter on another day and passed an important milestone in their marriage. "I've never felt so happy," she said to him before drifting off to sleep.

Chapter Thirteen

Stalin was sitting in his Kremlin office and preparing to leave for Berlin. Since he was sure his informal secret meeting with Hitler would be concluded by then, he had told his secretary to accept Anna's dinner invitation. His train could make the extra stop. Secretly he was always concerned about Anna's welfare. More importantly, Stalin wanted to be present when Anna confronted Ribbentrop. Stalin's insistence that Anna and her husband entertain representatives of the German High Command could only enhance the feeling of friendship Stalin wanted to convey to them. He wanted them to realize that his affection for Anna was genuine, and that he regarded her husband to be a loyal friend.

Stalin's greatest affection and loyalty was not to any individual though. His loyalty, first and foremost always would be to Russia. Anna must somehow convince Ribbentrop that events were moving too swiftly towards an aggressive turn in Europe. Stalin would hold back. He'd let Anna do the talking. He would remain on the diplomatic sidelines. He wouldn't even step in if her casual conversation with Ribbentrop appeared to be meeting an unsympathetic response.

Ribbentrop must be made aware of cold reality. Stalin was not yet ready to confront Hitler with the equation or proposition. It had to be presented at a lower level. Stalin didn't really want to form any sort of lasting alliance with Hitler. He was hoping that Anna, his beautiful participant in his power struggle with Hitler would stem the tide. He knew Hitler would never allow territorial lines to remain where they were in Europe. Yet Stalin was hoping that Anna's deliverance of her late father's peace message would stem aggression's tide.

Stalin stopped thinking about Anna's upcoming party. He removed the pipe from his pocket as the train carried him closer toward Berlin. He placed the stem of the unlit pipe in his mouth and gazed thoughtfully out a window before closing his eyes and listening to the train's even rhythmic movement. Stalin knew he must maintain a steady pace. He mustn't rush anything. His motives must be carefully thought through before he made his next move.

Stalin didn't want to ignite any feeling of hostility with Germany. He wanted to maintain an easy pattern of diplomacy with Hitler. Yet if there was to be a secret pact with Hitler, it would be understood: The Soviet Union must have the freedom to make territorial and political modifications too. Yet that train seemed to be moving too fast in an opposite direction. Stalin felt uneasy. He knew he couldn't fail in slowing that train down or better still, stopping it altogether.

The whistle sounded shrilly as Stalin's train, carrying him for his secret meeting with Hitler moved closer to its destination. Stalin had let Hitler know that he expected their meeting to be low profile and that Hitler should clarify his political position. Hitler must understand that he couldn't ignore the Soviet Union's political interests.

Upon arrival in Berlin, and surrounded by his own bodyguards, Stalin stepped from the train into an unmarked car for the meeting with Hitler at his Berlin headquarters.

Today's meeting was as shadowy as the room where the two leaders met. The shades were drawn and there was an unusual silence pervading the room's atmosphere. No one was around except the two leaders. Hitler's desk was bare. Not even a paperweight or anything giving the desk the appearance of frequent and normal use was visible. Only the Nazi flag with its ominous familiar symbol dominated the room. There were the usual polite exchanges between the two leaders including the handshakes. Stalin appeared to be in good humor but so did Hitler. Beneath the outwardly friendly manner and appearance though were two men raging over political issues that would end in war.

Hitler knew Stalin's visit to him wasn't a casual one. Stalin had every intention of making that apparent during their meeting. He wanted Hitler to know what he expected: Stalin wanted control of the whole of the Baltic States including Lithuania.

Hitler pretended to admire Stalin's forthright blunt behavior. Since Hitler was better prepared for war than Stalin, he thought the Soviet leader should be aware of what he wanted for the Third Reich too.

Secretly Hitler thought Stalin was being unrealistic when he mentioned that it was in the Soviet's best interests that they be given the Polish oil fields around Borislaw and Drogobycz. Didn't Stalin realize that the Third Reich was starved for oil?

Hitler smiled compliantly. Stalin was adamant and poker faced. He knew he was asking for something Hitler wasn't about to give him. Stalin was as generous in his maneuverings with Hitler as Hitler would be when he finally invaded Poland.

Before he left the meeting with Hitler, Stalin made it clear. Once he maintained control of the Polish oil fields, he would sell the Germans oil. Hitler smiled but remained unmoved by Stalin's overwhelming generosity. He shook the Soviet leader's hand and assured him that their meeting had been a productive one. Stalin smiled his usual tongue in cheek smile. He placed the stem of his pipe in his mouth, and left the dreary room.

Stalin seemed relaxed following his meeting with Hitler. When finally he stepped aboard the official train that was to return him to Moscow, he seemed even more relaxed. Hitler had pretended not to mind Stalin's bluntness. Stalin was no fool. He knew Hitler despised him for being so outspoken. Comrade Stalin nervously bit the stem of his pipe. The train rocked then jolted as it continued on the long journey back to Moscow. Stalin thought of the times he'd traveled to Berlin so he could visit Communist headquarters. That was a thing of the past now. There would be no revolution set in motion in Berlin of the mid late 1930's. Hitler's Nazi Germany was firmly in control. Any Communists not in hiding or in concentration camps already had fled the country. Stalin had pretended not to show any objection to Hitler's treatment of the German Communists. He'd never even raised the subject with him. He'd simply turned a deaf ear when he'd heard the Gestapo had picked most of them up. Stalin shuddered at the news though when his spies had informed him that Hitler was building up his armies. Stalin knew that eventually Hitler would pursue an aggressive policy with Russia. He had to play for time as best he could. He would continue to befriend Hitler. He would even ignore the threats if he suspected Hitler was going to attack Russia.

The train lurched forward again, and Stalin spilled the hot coffee from the cup he was holding in his hand. He placed the coffee cup aside and wiped his hand with a paper napkin. He then leaned back in his seat and closed his eyes. The journey to see Hitler had been a strain. He'd wanted to tell Hitler off. He knew he couldn't. Stalin hated playing the role of a subservient hypocrite. Yet that's what Stalin considered himself to be. If the Nazis invaded Poland and the English and French took arms against them in retaliation, Stalin would remain neutral. He knew how disastrous World War I had been for Russia once the Tsar's government had entered into it. He didn't want to repeat an historical blunder. He knew Hitler eventually would do something to provoke an attack. Stalin felt uneasy. He opened his eyes then closed them again. He would try to get a little rest so he could be his usual workaholic self once he got back to the Kremlin. As Stalin drifted off to sleep he thought of his little daughter. She always missed her Papa when he took long trips away from home. She wondered why he never took her with him. Stalin wanted his little girl to be safe. He didn't want her to miss any school. If Russia was ever attacked, he dreaded to think that his little girl or her younger brother would have to live through a Nazi German invasion of Russia. Stalin was close to his daughter. Her younger brother, like his half brother, the son from his first marriage weren't as close with their father. They were in awe of him and a little afraid of him as well. Stalin criticized his sons and daughter too if their performance in school or in life didn't measure up to his expectations.

The train continued on its path towards its destination and Stalin nodded off again. He had to get some rest so he could remain alert. There was work he'd brought with him: letters and documents that he needed to peruse. He was tired. He hadn't had much rest lately, and yet Stalin wasn't a man who required much rest. Perhaps the reason for that was because he'd spent most of his life running. As a young revolutionary, Stalin had spent his youth running from the authorities but the advent of middle age had caught up with him. Stalin knew it was time to stop running. He couldn't change the course of history. He wondered if he was trying too hard to stem the tide though.

Stalin gazed out the train's window. The train had gathered speed. The scenery outside the train window became a blur as the late afternoon sun nearly blinded him. Stalin pulled down the train's window shade then closed his eyes and nodded off for a few minutes.

Since he was looking forward to having a little time to relax, Stalin arrived a day early for Anna's party. Anna would see that he was accorded the necessary rest and hospitality that he sorely needed right now. She and the count graciously welcomed him to their home after Stalin's bodyguards preceded him. "Dear Koba" said Anna hugging the dictator as the count took his coat from him. "It is so good to see you again." Carl asked a servant to take Stalin's luggage upstairs to the room he usually occupied when visiting them.

Anna led the dictator to a comfortable room where he could enjoy a drink before lunch. It was a chilly fall day. Carl put an extra log on the fire in the fireplace before he sat next to his wife on the sofa. Stalin sat opposite the couple in an arm chair. Anna knew Stalin had just been to Berlin. It was rumored that he'd had a secret meeting with Hitler and she wanted to ask him about it but refrained from doing so. She would wait to see if Stalin invited her and her husband into that circle of secrecy.

When he didn't bring up the subject, Anna finally asked "How was your trip to Berlin?" Stalin sipped his drink and enjoyed the warmth of the fire in the hearth. He didn't answer her. Instead he tried to remain evasive. He acted as if he'd just returned from a holiday that he hadn't liked very much. "It was a waste of time", he said putting his glass of vodka aside. Anna dared not ask any more questions. She knew Stalin had seen Hitler. He'd never admit to the meeting or tell them that it had been a disaster. Anna sensed that the hope for a brighter future for Europe might rest on tomorrow evening's dinner party. The count wanted to replenish Stalin's empty vodka glass. The dictator politely shook his head when he tried to do so. Anna insisted that Stalin's visit to Berlin couldn't have been a waste of time. "Surely you accomplished more than you are giving yourself credit for doing".

Stalin still refused to reveal that he'd had a meeting with Hitler. It was up to his hosts to decide for themselves whether or not that meeting had taken place. Anna suggested that it was time for lunch. Stalin left his empty vodka glass behind and followed his hosts into the dining room. Anna knew Stalin wasn't in the best of spirits. She'd been expecting that he might be feeling overtired after his trip to Berlin.

"I've had the chef prepare one of your favorite dishes", she said as he sat down to lunch with them. The count took a quick sip of vodka from the glass he'd carried with him into the dining room. It never ceased to amaze him at how well his wife managed to buoy up the dictator's spirits even when he appeared tired or in a bad mood.

Anna placed the napkin in her lap then smiled across the table at Stalin and then at her husband. She acted as if nothing of any great consequence lay ahead for any of them. She carried on a conversation that would suggest that what she had planned for tomorrow evening's entertainment couldn't be anything other than a success. If Stalin's recent visit to Berlin had been something of a disappointment for him, tomorrow evening's meeting with Ribbentrop and the Nazi High Command representatives would make up for it.

Stalin relaxed in Anna's company. He knew he had to regain his confidence in being able to prevent the Soviet Union from entering into war with Hitler. After lunch he would take a quick nap. Later he'd join his hosts in their last minute plans for tomorrow evening's entertainment.

After lunch, Anna was sitting at the piano when Stalin joined her in the drawing room. The count was in another room. She looked up from playing the instrument when she saw Stalin standing next to her. "We've invited a pianist to play for us tomorrow following dinner. Perhaps you've heard of him. His name is Rachmaninoff. He's also a composer. Carl and I heard him play when he visited Switzerland. He spends all of his time now in the United States. We were so impressed with his performance I had to invite him to play."

Stalin was familiar with Rachmaninoff's music. He hadn't heard him play though. Like so many other artists, writers and poets Rachmaninoff had fled Russia. Yet Rachmaninoff would provide tomorrow evening's entertainment. Not all artists and writers found him to be intimidating. Stalin was pleased.

"I didn't tell Rachmaninoff you would be present at our gathering. Stalin winced at Anna's comment. "I didn't tell him that representatives of the Nazi regime would be present either. I've heard he has no sympathy for Nazism."

The count entered the room and heard his wife talking with Stalin. Anna glanced at her husband. She knew Stalin wanted to talk with him alone. Carl suggested that he and the dictator take a short walk. Stalin's bodyguards were guarding the premises. Whatever he and Stalin discussed would be private.

A servant brought them their coats and the men put them on. Stalin slowly buttoned a few buttons on his overcoat and casually accompanied his friend outside. The day was bright, sunny and windy. He began the conversation by saying. "Hitler has assured me. He wants peace. I suppose he may think I want peace at any price." Stalin's face appeared grave and pale as he contemplated the thought.

Carl wouldn't tell the dictator what he thought. Stalin might resent his friend's honesty. He would never trust him if he told him that war with Germany was inevitable. The count was a realist. Both men knew Hitler didn't want peace. Yet they must remain adamant in their denial. The worst scenario couldn't happen. It mustn't happen.

Stalin knew the count's German was excellent. Carl knew what Stalin wanted him to do before he asked. "They must come to trust you. Russia has to prepare for war".

Carl wasn't eager to take Stalin up on his suggestion that he draw close to men he knew would destroy him if they realized what his motives for doing so were. The count had his wife and children to think about. It was one thing to entertain representatives of the Nazi Regime. It was something else to actually become one of them.

"I will try to do what you ask me to do." he said when Stalin kept pressing him for assurances. "I think the Nazis are holding their cards too close. They have no war timetable for the Baltic States or anywhere for that matter, at least not one that's obvious."

Stalin didn't pursue the matter further. He knew the count was right. He knew the Soviet Union and the Baltic and Balkan States were always vulnerable. He reached for the pipe he carried in his pocket and placed it in his mouth. Stalin wouldn't admit it to his friend. He was scared. For the first time in his life he felt as if things were spiraling out of control.

Where were the alternatives to war? There really weren't any at least not in the game Stalin played with his opponent. Stalin knew he had to convince

Hitler that he was ready for war. He had to make Hitler believe that he was strong. He had to make Hitler feel as insecure in his position as dictator as he did. Stalin knew that wouldn't be easy. Hitler knew he was more powerful than Stalin. In Stalin's eyes that might be Hitler's major flaw.

Overconfidence in his evil regime's power would entice Hitler to become reckless. Stalin would underplay his hand in the bid for European power. He would hold back and make his adversary make the first aggressive moves. When Hitler suffered his first major defeat as that always happens with men who are overconfident, Stalin would have the opportunity to strike and eventually bring down his adversary. Yet he knew he was thinking ahead to situations that might never come to pass. He had to play the game that was in front of him for the time being.

Carl was feeling uneasy with the dictator. He wanted to go back inside the house where he might avoid further discussion with him. Stalin could sense Carl's uneasiness but ignored it.

For a few minutes each man seemed to move in his own world. Stalin placed his cold hands in his coat pockets. It was getting late in the day. He'd wanted to have a short visit with Anna before dinner.

When they returned from their walk, Carl was surprised. His mother and her new husband, Anton Beckov had dropped in on them unexpectedly. Anna was busy entertaining them in a sitting room when Carl and Stalin joined them. She seemed embarrassed. She'd neglected to invite them to tomorrow evening's dinner. She seemed a bit flustered as Stalin amiably greeted the count's mother and her new husband. He kissed Marina's hand then told Bockev that it was such an unexpected pleasure to see him again.

"We were just in the area, we thought we'd drop by for a visit" said Bockev as the count embraced his mother and offered them both something to drink.

After he'd handed his wife and mother a glass of wine, Carl poured glasses of vodka for Stalin, Bockev and himself. Anna suspected that Bockev had already heard about tomorrow evening's get together for the German High Command. She knew she'd made a social faux pas by not inviting Bockev and her mother-in-law to the party. She also realized that Stalin might want them there. Since Stalin was eager to prove to German High Command representatives that he was Hitler's ally, why shouldn't Bockev and Marina be at Anna's party? The Nazis knew that Bockev had been introduced to both Hitler and Stalin.

Anna gently touched her husband's arm as he turned then looked at her. She could see the look of embarrassment reflected on his face. She began the conversation by saying "We're having a little get-together tomorrow evening. We hadn't expected that it would be much, just a little entertainment for a few people in the German High Command. Stalin is adding the honor of his presence to the gathering too. The party has grown unexpectedly. Carl and I would be deeply disappointed if you didn't join us tomorrow evening."

Bockev was no fool. The fact that he and his wife hadn't been invited to Anna's party might appear to the Nazis as being not just a social blunder but a political one as well. Carl and Anna knew Bockev was a double agent so did Stalin and the Nazis. Bockev's absence from the party would reflect unfavorably upon the count and his wife.

Bockev realized the diplomatic necessity of accepting Anna's belated dinner invitation. He surmised that the real reason Stalin had arrived one day early to visit the count and his wife was so that he would be present when he and Marina dropped in on them for a visit. Stalin had told Bockev he wanted to be sure he would be present for Anna's party.

Bockev shifted a little uneasily in his chair before placing his drink aside and glancing at Marina sitting next to him.

Marina took the initiative in accepting Anna's dinner invitation. "Of course, dear, Anton and I would be delighted to stay over an extra day and help you entertain your guests."

Anna had always regarded Marina as a friend and not just a mother-in-law. "Your presence at social gatherings we've had in the past has always lent them an air of ease and grace. Carl and I are delighted you will be attending our party. Besides," she said turning to her father-in-law, "It will give us an opportunity to get to know you better."

Bockev smiled cautiously. He felt uneasy with his new stepson and daughter-in-law. The count had winced at his wife's remark when she suggested to Bockev that they would have a chance to get acquainted with him. There was probably very little Stalin didn't know about Bockev. Yet Anna sensed there was something about Bockev's behavior that would suggest he had his secrets. Not even Stalin could intrude upon them. He might be a double agent but like her husband Bockev had his hidden loyalties. This sudden realization made her feel less embarrassed. She made excuses for her social blunder by simply telling herself that she hadn't fully considered the political implications of not inviting Bockev and her mother-in-law to the party. She'd made an honest mistake. Bockev gazed at Anna as if he knew what she was thinking. He took a quick sip from the glass of vodka he held and smiled at her with a cautious yet fatherly look of the utmost understanding.

The count's mother had taken the situation in stride. She quickly changed the subject by asking Carl and Anna about their children. Anna made sure her mother-in-law knew how much her grandsons missed her. "You must have a visit with them today. They'll be thrilled to know you are staying with us tonight. They talk about you all the time and always ask us when you plan to visit us."

Marina was still feeling hurt that the son and daughter-in-law she loved had been keeping their distance from her and her new husband. “We have much to talk about. Anton has been looking forward to seeing you and your family. He wants to get to know you better. I realize that you think I’m always trying to spoil the children. We couldn’t resist bringing some presents for them. Perhaps they can open them after they’ve had their tea.”

Anna glanced at her husband. They smiled at one another. “You really shouldn’t have done that mother. Now they’ll expect you to bring them presents every time you visit us.”

Since Marina knew her visits to see her son and his wife had become so rare lately, she didn’t think there was anything wrong with showering the children with presents. “We just don’t want them to forget us”, she said putting aside her wine glass.

Stalin listened to the family discussion with a mild sense of amusement. He knew they were feeling uncomfortable in each other’s company. He took great pleasure in knowing the reason why.

Anna suggested that everyone might want to have a little rest before dinner. She then smiled and looked directly at the count before saying to Marina and Bockev,” You must stay with us tonight. Carl wouldn’t want you staying in an inn during your visit with us, would you darling?”

Carl quickly got up from where he was sitting and suggested that he show Marina and Bockev to their comfortable upstairs rooms.

Later when she had a chance to casually talk with Stalin, Anna asked him, “Why didn’t you suggest to us that we invite Bockev and Marina to the party?” Stalin’s face was grave before he said hesitantly, “I wasn’t sure that I wanted you to invite Bockev until I was certain that circumstances demanded he be present”, he lied.

Anna seemed puzzled with what Stalin had told her and wondered what Stalin knew about Beckov that he hadn’t told her. She started to ask the dictator that question but didn’t. She wasn’t sure if she wanted to know. She wasn’t sure if whatever Stalin told her about Bockev would be true. She knew she was playing a game of pretense with the dictator. Whatever pertinent information Stalin might say he had regarding Bockev might turn out to be of little consequence. Anna was relieved when Carl joined them and she knew she wouldn’t be tempted to ask Stalin any more questions. She was relieved too when Stalin decided he needed some time alone. The dictator had already talked with Hitler. He knew the political position Ribbentrop would have to take when Stalin met him the following evening. Stalin needed to think. He needed to consider how best he might face what lay ahead for him. He wasn’t just fatigued. He was feeling the weight of responsibility pressing upon him. Never before had Stalin felt so close to defeat. Even when he’d been sentenced to exile for his revolutionary activities, Stalin had remained positive in the face of adversity. The difficulties facing him now seemed so huge that they appeared to be outside the sphere of his or anyone else's control. He knew he couldn't confide in Anna or her husband. He had to keep the most important details regarding his meeting with Hitler a secret to them and the world. Stalin was alone with his burdens. Those burdens were exhausting him. He needed time to consider plans and options but time was moving too fast for him.

Stalin excused himself from Carl and Anna's company, and went upstairs where he entered his room lay down on the comfortable bed and fell asleep as a clock in the room's corner ticked away the dwindling hours.

After Stalin had left them, Carl suggested to Anna that they take a late afternoon walk together. They hadn't been able to be by themselves in awhile. They'd been too busy entertaining guests or seeing to the needs of their children to have any time left for each other.

Anna put on a coat and tied the scarf hanging loosely around her shoulders. A quick blast of early fall arctic air swept over them as the couple emerged from behind a heavily carved wooden door. Carl pulled Anna close to him. He wanted to protect her from the wind but more importantly he wanted to protect her from the harsh realities bearing down upon them. He was feeling uneasy about tomorrow evening's dinner party. He wanted to protect Anna from the dangers of becoming too involved in an increasingly dangerous political situation. He wasn't sure that he wanted his wife to confront Ribbentrop. "I think Stalin is just trying to use you", he said. "I don't know what he expects to gain from this deadly little game he's playing with the Nazis. Whatever you have to say to Ribbentrop though, I'm sure he won't seriously consider it. Hitler wants eventual war not peace. Your effort to present your late father's plea for peace isn't going to deter the Fuehrer from carrying out his plans for Europe."

Anna squeezed her husband's arm. She was shivering from the cold wind. "I have to try to do what I can" she said trembling.

He pulled her close to him again. He wanted to shield her from the bitter wind and from the unseen reality of that other wind that was beginning to sweep down upon them.

Anna was thinking about her late father when she said to her husband. "Even if I fail, I have to do what I know he would want me to do." The count started to say you can't be sure what you're father would want you to do under these circumstances. Instead he grimly gazed at the ground as they walked arm and arm together.

There was a silence between them. Finally Carl put aside any unsaid misgivings he had in Anna delivering her father's message. "If he were alive today, your father would be proud to know that you are carrying forth his message for a peaceful Europe." Anna was grateful that Carl understood. She leaned against him as if she were trying to draw strength from him. She closed her eyes as he held her before they looked up. The sun was beginning to set behind the mountains as arm in arm the couple continued strolling along a path that led back to the entrance to their home.

The sky's brilliant fiery color underscored the underlying passions surrounding a turbulent world as the couple watched the passionate silent red sun slowly descend behind a stark horizon. Anna shuddered. Brilliant crimson light slowly gave way to gray slate dusk. Somehow she wanted to prevent the sun from setting. She wanted to hold onto the bright light that awakened the world each day. She didn't want the world to fall into sleep and darkness. The sleep might become too deep. When the world finally awoke again, there might be nothing left but fiery passion in the wake of a brilliant fiery sun.

"We need to go inside" he insisted. "It's getting late."

Anna didn't answer Carl. She seemed too lost in thought to move. The cold stillness surrounding her reminded her of something else. She wanted to know warmth again. She wanted to be able to push aside the frozen cold reality that was about to enshroud the world in terror and tumult.

The count took her cold hand in his. He knew she was trembling "You're shivering" he said. "We need to go back inside he insisted". Anna shook her head.

"The cold reminds me of how vulnerable we are in the face of things we can't control." She knew she couldn't control the outdoor environment. She knew she couldn't control her destiny either. "The cold reminds me of how powerless we've become" she said turning away from him and gazing at the bleak horizon.

The count put his hand on Anna's shoulder and made her face him. "You're strong Anna. We're both strong." He placed his hand beneath her chin and kissed her. He wanted to keep her warm and safe.

He wanted to be alone with her before dinner. He wasn't sure how much more time together they really had. He knew the political climate was becoming such that European stability faltered from day to day. He knew he and Anna eventually would be caught up in the terrible maelstrom sweeping across Europe. He wanted to be with her even if it was just for a little while until something unforeseen and insidious separated them from each other.

Carl opened the door and they walked back inside the house, and handed their coats to a servant. For a long time he just held her. He wanted to tell her how much she meant to him. Yet words seemed inadequate to express the emotions he felt.

"I can't imagine being without you", she said as they held each other tightly. Anna knew her own life was inexorably linked to his. She knew that if anything ever happened to him she wouldn't want to go on without him. He knew that too.

"Promise me you won't take any risks. Promise me you'll always come back to me wherever you go" she said. He knew her couldn't give her that assurance. Carl knew their future together was uncertain, that war might separate them. He turned his back on her and slowly walked away from her.

Inherently Anna understood Carl's reason for leaving her. She stood alone at the foot of the stairs where he'd left her. She watched him disappear in shadow as he slowly climbed the stairs so he could go to his office. She didn't try to follow him. She knew there wasn't another woman. She had to learn to live without him. The uncertainty of what lay ahead for them, the fear of a terrible future looming ahead in their lives, was Carl's mistress.

After Carl had left her, Anna climbed the stairs leading to the room she'd first occupied after coming to live at the count's mysterious home. She didn't know why she'd been drawn to that room but memories of that time long ago flooded over as she fell across the bed and closed her eyes. The room was completely silent until half dreaming, she heard the same haunting train whistle she'd heard before when drifting off to sleep in the room. Where was the train taking her today? What did the future hold in store for her? The train whistle shrieked as the train with its mysterious vampire occupants aboard, lifted itself above the tracks, and continued to sweep her along in her dreams. Anna's life had been like a dream. The vivid image of that phantom train and its strange occupants continued to haunt her until she awoke suddenly to find her husband gazing down at her before bending over her and taking her in his arms. He didn't want to leave her alone in that room where she and now he seemed to find refuge. For awhile they just lay alone together shutting out the world and the future that for the time being couldn't enter their lives.

Chapter Fourteen

The couple took their time in preparing for dinner. Anna wanted to select the right dress for the evening. She wanted to wear something cheerful to dispel the gloom that earlier had accompanied their walk together. She chose a rose colored dress to match the ruby earrings he'd given her. Anna half turned then gazed at herself in a mirror before Carl took hold of her arm, and they slowly descended the stairs, entered a sitting room and greeted their guests who were already talking to one another. Anna amiably greeted her new father-in-law and Stalin. The count kissed his mother on the cheek. After a servant offered everyone something to drink, Carl suggested that his guests might want to follow him and bring their drinks into the dining room.

When everyone was seated at the table, the atmosphere seemed almost relaxed. If there had been previous strain with Carl's relatives the tension had eased a bit. Bockev sat directly across the table from his lovely hostess and tried to probe into Anna's complicated past of war and revolution. Stalin sat near her too and listened with quiet amusement as Anna quickly discouraged Bockev's probing by pretending not to hear what he'd asked her or by changing the subject. Marina had seemed almost embarrassed by her husband's rather nosy curiosity, also ignored Bockev's prying conversation concerning Anna's past. Instead she carried on a light but amiable conversation with Stalin. Later she would mention to her son that the dictator was not only astute. He had a phenomenal memory.

After dinner, Anna seemed relieved that her conversation with Bockev had ended and suggested to her guests that they might want to go to their rooms and prepare for the following day. Later that evening when she and Carl were alone, and they had a chance to visit with their sons, the boys seemed disappointed at not being able to have dinner with their grandparents and Stalin.

"You'll have a chance to visit with them tomorrow", said Anna quickly when she and Carl told them good night.

* * * *

The day of Anna's party was full of activity. She stood in the hallway and watched as servants carried huge vases of flowers and greenery from the greenhouse into the castle's rooms. Anna knew exactly where she wanted the flowers placed and how she wanted the rooms to look for the evening's dinner party. She quickly excused herself from all the busy activity though when she was interrupted by a familiar entourage.

The children and Oscar, the little terrier Carl had given Anna to replace Micha who'd recently succumbed to old age, suddenly burst into the room. Although she loved the new dog, Anna still missed Micha. She felt almost disloyal in welcoming the newcomer into her life. She knew she never could love another dog as much as the one that had followed her from imprisonment to freedom. Anna habitually laid a single garden rose on Micha's little grave near the sundial below the castle room she'd first occupied so many years earlier.

Anna seemed almost misty eyed when suddenly she said to her children, "Until Oscar is fully trained you must keep him with you outdoors, upstairs or in the school room with you". Then followed by her sons, seeming surprised by their mother's rather stern remark regarding Oscar's training, Anna donned a coat and carried the little dog outside with them.

They were busy playing with Oscar when the distinguished pianist she'd invited to perform for the evening's entertainment arrived. He walked over to her and graciously introduced himself as Anna turned from playing with the puppy and smiled.

"My husband and I have heard so much about you", she said handing the little dog to one of her sons, before introducing her children to the composer. "We are familiar with your wonderful compositions and are looking forward to hearing you play for us and our guests this evening."

Rachmaninoff smiled and nodded his head in response to her remark before saying, "I hope you don't mind my arriving a little early. I wanted to practice on your piano before I play for you and your guests tonight."

Anna smiled and said. "Not at all, I assure you the piano is yours to practice upon. We're so glad you've arrived early. You must have lunch as well as dinner with us tonight. My husband and I never thought that you would do us the great honor of playing your own compositions in person. I thought some other pianist surely would be substituted for you."

Rachmaninoff bowed slightly before saying, "Thank you for your kind words." Followed by her children and the little dog, Anna then led the famous composer, into their home so he could begin practicing the piano. When her husband saw his wife with Rachmaninoff he extended his hand in greeting to the composer.

"My wife and I are honored to have you in our home. We hope you plan on staying with us tonight."

"That's very thoughtful of you", said Rachmaninoff. "I'd be delighted to stay with you."

"It will be wonderful to hear you practicing", said Anna."

"Music brings such joy into our lives," said the count." My wife plays the piano too."

"There was a time when I felt unable to play. Just recently I started playing the piano again" she said as Carl placed his arm around her shoulder.

Rachmaninoff said nothing in response to Anna's comments. He seemed to understand without her telling him. He'd heard the rumor: Anna was Nicholas II's only surviving daughter.

"I'm sure circumstances have been trying for you", he said respectfully.

"My husband and I are looking forward to talking more with you later" said Anna changing the subject. "The piano is in the drawing room" she said leading Rachmaninoff there. "You can practice until it is time for lunch."

"That is a splendid suggestion", he said gazing at the beautiful Steinway before sitting on the bench in front of the keyboard and beginning to play.

"Please let us know if there is anything that you might need", she said leaving him alone to practice.

With the dog now in her arms, Anna accompanied the children upstairs to their schoolroom before leaving them and joining, her husband, Bockev and Stalin sitting in a downstairs room and talking. "You must meet Rachmaninoff. I think I'll invite him to join us," said Anna after carrying on a short conversation with them before leaving the room

Rachmaninoff looked up from playing the piano when Anna approached him and said, "My husband and I would like for you to meet our guests. They are waiting for us in the next room."

After following Anna into the adjacent room where he was warmly received and introduced to everyone, Rachmaninoff bowed respectfully to the dictator and told him what a great honor it was to meet him. Stalin smiled at the comment and responded to it by saying "I'm looking forward to hearing you play your work. I've heard only good reviews regarding your performances." Although Rachmaninoff felt a little uneasy with Stalin's praise: He knew the dictator was not an effusive man. He also knew Stalin could be a cruel and unforgiving tyrant if he didn't like a particular work of art. Rachmaninoff hoped that the compositions he'd chosen to play that evening would only please his listeners and in particular Stalin.

Since Carl realized too that Stalin sometimes could be unkind regarding the arts, he decided there should be no more unnecessary discussion surrounding music. It was time for lunch anyway so he quickly changed the subject by leading his guests into the dining room.

Although he seemed unmoved by Carl's quick maneuvers regarding lunch, Stalin took a quick gulp from the glass of vodka he'd been drinking and carried it with him into the dining room. He then set the drink aside. He wanted to remain alert and clear headed so he would be well prepared in answering any questions that might be directed to him during and after lunch.

Stalin stared down at his luncheon plate. He didn't feel especially hungry. He'd already had the informal meeting with Hitler. What possibly could be learned from tonight's visit with Ribbentrop that he didn't already know? Stalin had had the main course.

The count knew his guests didn't want to linger over lunch. Rachmaninoff wanted to continue practicing the evening's repertoire and Stalin wanted to take a nap. Anna was thankful to her mother-in-law for helping her with the last minute dinner plans and told her "I think the preparations for everything are complete."

Marina knew they weren't complete. She seemed a little disappointed that there wasn't anything more for her to do.

"Anna must want to take full charge of everything" she thought turning and starting to walk upstairs. Bockev followed his wife upstairs to their room. He could sense her disappointment at not being asked to do more to help. He reminded her that it was Anna's party. She ought to let her daughter-in-law take control of it.

"I just wanted to help her sort things out", she said feeling a little resentful that Anna was fast becoming as good a hostess as she'd ever been.

Bockev made his wife sit down in a chair next to him. "You forget that you and I are guests in your son's home now. Let Anna do her job as hostess. You do such a splendid job entertaining for me. You need to just relax and enjoy yourself."

Marina thanked her husband for reminding her that she was always the perfect hostess then commented "I think I might enjoy a warm bath and a nap" she said leaving him.

After his wife left him alone, Bockev sat in a chair, and thoughtfully gazed out a window. He considered the importance of this evening's meeting with the German High Command representatives. Although he wasn't a man to become deeply involved in politics, he'd seen the financial and political necessity of appearing to befriend the Nazis. Secretly he'd recoiled from many of the things they'd advocated. He'd been sickened by the way they treated the Jews. He was in no position to stop the persecution of them though. Like so many people who'd lived during his time in history, Bockev was silent as the terror and persecution continued to grow like some terrible plague throughout Europe.

Bockev reached into his vest pocket and removed his pocket watch. There was still plenty of time before dinner. He considered what he might say to Ribbentrop when he met him. Then he closed his eyes and started to doze off. He hadn't realized until now how tired he felt. He knew he had to remain alert. His thoughts kept shifting though. He thought about Marina's son and wondered where his true loyalties lay. He'd sensed the strain between Carl and Stalin. He'd learned through various intelligence networks how Lenin's regime had treated Carl, and that Stalin after succeeding Lenin in power, saved Carl's life but only after Anna intervened with him on her husband's behalf. Bockev admired his stepson for his courage in bearing up under a life threatening situation.

Anna was an enigma. He admired her courage in confronting Stalin and asking for Carl's life yet who was she? Had Stalin and the count rescued the real Anastasia or was the lovely fragile woman who thought of herself to be Nicholas II's daughter just an imposter? The count seemed to be in love with her. She'd obviously made him happy even if she'd come with what he'd heard to be a bit of emotional baggage.

Bockev reached into his pocket for one of the Turkish cigarettes he liked to smoke. He placed it in his mouth, lighted the cigarette then drew upon it one time before crushing the cigarette in an ashtray. He was unaware that Marina had just walked into the room as he watched cigarette smoke curl towards the ceiling. He then wearily closed his eyes and when he opened them he saw Marina standing in front of him wearing a red silk embroidered Chinese robe. The black brocade dinner suit she would wear for tonight's dinner party lay across the bed. He watched her pick it up before carefully smoothing the suit's creases and making sure there were no visible wrinkles there. She then looked up from what she was doing and suggested to her husband that he should begin preparing for tonight's dinner party.

Bockev gazed at Marina. Despite her years she was still beautiful and desirable. He wanted her to know that as she sat down on the edge of the bed they shared. For a short time they could enjoy a quiet interlude together. Then Bockev would close his eyes again as if he wanted to blot out the obvious. Tonight's dinner party was part of the polite prelude. Then there would be the beginning of something huge, criminal and terribly cruel. It would be only a matter of time before Hitler's military forces swept across Europe. People could only guess where his true loyalties lay. He would straddle a middle road. He'd pretend to be friends with both sides in an impending conflict. Yet deep down inside, Bockev knew he could never betray his wife's family. If the count's loyalty was with Stalin rather than with Hitler's regime, Bockev would do what he could to befriend his wife's only son.

Bockev rose from where he sat. He stood by a window and gazed outside. The sun was sinking fast on the horizon and the sky was almost dark. Only a golden outline of daylight remained. Beckov knew he had to change into dinner clothes. His stepson and his wife would expect them to join them and their other guests for cocktails before dinner. He knew Carl and Anna needed their emotional support if it was only to create a congenial social atmosphere. Vital information might be discovered amidst casual conversation.

* * * *

The count was putting on his dinner jacket matching his dark trousers when Anna turned and asked him how she looked. Although now 35 years old, Anna looked as lithe and slender as she had the day he had brought her home to later become his wife. Memories flooded over the couple as they gazed at one another. The count was still as handsome as he'd ever been when he'd rescued Anna and carried her away with him. The years had mellowed him though. He was gentler now than she'd ever known him to be. There was a trust between the couple that hadn't been there before. Their marriage had withstood the shocks that life had dealt it. They were strong in their relationship with one another.

"You look beautiful" he said as she turned then moved in a wave of white ruffles. As a child Anna remembered her mother dressing her and her sisters in white frilly dresses tied at the waist with colorful pastel sashes. It had been prior to World War I. Anna had been only fifteen the day she stood outside her father's office and overheard his conversation with the German High Command. The years had passed quickly. That young girl wasn't there anymore. In her place was someone else. So much had happened to make her grow and mature in her love and concern for others. Until recently Anna hadn't understood the importance of the conversation she'd overheard outside her father's office that day. Only the trials and the terrible trauma of the years that followed had made her realize how important that message had been.

The count helped button the back of his wife's dress as she turned and straightened the collar of his jacket. "I hope Ribbentrop will remember me?" she said going to her dressing table and gazing into a mirror before fastening the clasp of the pearl necklace she wore with the dress.

The dress bore a haunting similarity to the one the little girl had worn so many years earlier. Although long and not short it was a dress of impeccable design and beauty. Worn without a sash, the dress embodied a certain sophistication and innocence.

"You look beautiful" he told her. "How could anyone forget you?" She turned so he could take her arm in his and close the door behind them. He then led her down the hallway to the top of the stairway where they would ascend the stairs together. As they stood atop the stairs, Anna seemed lost in thought. It was if she'd stepped back in time. The whole haunting scene seemed to pass before her. She could hear two of her sisters laughing and talking as they hurried down the corridor. It was time for their school lessons. "Hush you mustn't disturb your father", the tutor had said to them as they obediently returned to their schoolroom upstairs. Only she remained behind, standing in shadow, listening to the conversation in her father's office. Nobody seemed to miss her absence from the schoolroom. It was just like the day in Perm when she'd passed through the gate unnoticed. Nobody had missed her that day either.

When the men began leaving his office, the Tsar saw his daughter standing alone outside it. He wondered why she wasn't in the schoolroom. He didn't say anything to her then about her truancy. Instead, he introduced his youngest daughter to the men of Germany's High Command. Anna hadn't forgotten that moment or that day so long ago.

When they reached the foot of the stairs, Anna could see that the drawing room door had been left open. Marina and Bockev were listening to Rachmaninoff play one of his lighter compositions. It was still early. The couple's guests hadn't yet arrived.

Carl and Anna approached Rachmaninoff. "We've been enjoying your playing so much today", she said accepting a glass of wine from a tray being passed around, as the composer looked up from the piano and the count enjoyed a glass of vodka.

Rachmaninoff put aside the glass of vodka he'd been offered. He started to play the piano again but hesitated when he glanced up and saw that Stalin had just walked into the room.

"Please don't stop on my account" said the dictator. "We all enjoy your playing" he said walking towards the composer as Rachmaninoff stood up and extended his hand in greeting to Stalin.

A maid entered the room. The representatives from the German High Command were beginning to arrive. The count left his wife's side so he could greet his other guests at the main entrance.

Handsome in the dark suit he wore, Carl strangely resembled the striking image of Dracula whose portrait was displayed prominently in his home. He held his head high as he moved towards his arriving guests. He was about thirty feet from his guests yet despite the dimness of the room's light he saw their faces clearly. The finely woven oriental carpet beneath his feet cushioned the sound of his footsteps as he quietly approached men he considered to be his foes. There were six representatives of Hitler's High Command including Ribbentrop whose uniform and demeanor indicated that he was the one clearly in charge.

The dim light shining through the room's dark stained glass windows created almost a foreboding atmosphere as the count moved within the near darkness and watched his guests enter his home. He knew the men were doing more than entering his home. They were entering his life and the lives of his wife and children as turbulent events within Europe would unfold in the years to come.

The count's face and form now seemed partially hidden by an unseen shroud as he drew closer to his guests watching his approach from a distance. It took less than a minute for Carl to greet his guests but it seemed much longer to him as he approached the representatives of Hitler's Third Reich.

"Welcome to my home" he said smiling at Ribbentrop and extending a hand in greeting to him. Although the welcome and warmth seemed a little forced Carl tried to hide his sense of discomfort in the presence of representatives of a regime he knew he couldn't embrace. "My wife and our guests are awaiting your arrival in the drawing room", he said leading them forward.

There was plenty of light surrounding Carl and his guests but the corridor leading to the interior of the count's home seemed dark and unwelcoming. Carl glanced at the ceiling as he led his guests beneath a glistening 18th century chandelier. Shafts of light emitted from the chandelier created myriad hues of purple, violet and blood red as Carl's guests stood beneath the portrait of Dracula. They seemed both intrigued and intimidated when he described the artist's characterization of his famous ancestor before saying, "I'm told that Dracula met just once with the artist before the painting was commissioned. He made only quick sketches of him. Dracula never actually stood for the portrait."

The count's guests studied the Dracula portrait with unfeigned nervous interest and contemplated a being they knew not only personified evil but had become a popular symbol of it in diabolical circles. Carl laughed with inner satisfaction and realized he'd actually instilled some fear within the representatives of Hitler's evil regime. "I assure you Dracula no longer wanders castle corridors. He rests eternally now, perhaps even in peace." As he spoke, a flash of lightning followed by a tremendous clap of thunder was heard, and outside the castle confines rain came down in torrents.

A servant opened the door to the drawing room. Rachmaninoff had been playing a composition but rose from the piano bench and directed his attention to Ribbentrop who extended a hand in greeting to him before saying "you play beautifully". Rachmaninoff smiled acknowledging the compliment but Ribbentrop's attention quickly shifted. His gaze turned to Stalin who was standing beside Bockev and Marina. Anna was now standing alongside her husband.

Ribbentrop made his way towards the dictator. Through a high level source he'd heard that Stalin and Hitler had recently met. He knew the details of the meeting. He knew exactly what Hitler had said to him during the course of it.

"The Fuehrer sends his regards", said Ribbentrop shaking Stalin's hand. The dictator smiled but the smile quickly faded. He'd sensed Ribbentrop was on the defensive. Ribbentrop knew Stalin would dig for information that he would not or could not give him regarding Nazi Germany's future yet inevitable wartime schedule. A servant carrying a tray filled with glasses of champagne offered Ribbentrop one. The count had been watching Stalin and Ribbentrop interact with one another. He stepped forward and left Anna's side. He was eager to hear more of the conversation. He knew Stalin preferred vodka over champagne. He knew that Ribbentrop would join the dictator in a glass of vodka. He would pretend to embrace the same tastes and ideals of a secret opponent. The count motioned for the servant to offer Stalin and Ribbentrop vodka as he joined them in a toast and the three men clinked glasses. From outward appearances the world and the powers that be in it were enjoying a sustained and amiable truce. The peaceful interlude conveyed on a very personal level though soon would disintegrate. The count knew Stalin wasn't to talk alone with Ribbentrop. He also knew that Stalin wanted Anna to be introduced to him alone.

As Bockev and Marina interacted with the representatives from the German High Command, the count quickly turned and walked over to his wife who was busy talking with the wives of the officers present. She had already accepted their invitations for tea but she politely excused herself from their company as her husband took her by the arm so he could introduce her to Ribbentrop.

Anna smiled graciously as Ribbentrop bowed slightly and kissed her hand. "Your Imperial Highness" he said, "It is such a great pleasure to see you again." For a moment, Anna forgot that tonight's dinner party was secretly about politics. Almost no one ever referred to her in that manner anymore. Tears welled up in her eyes. He'd remembered the secret meeting he'd had with her father prior to World War I.

"Yes", she managed to stammer "My father introduced me to you the day you had the meeting with him". Anna fought back the tears. "Thank God he remembered me" she thought. Her true identity had been acknowledged.

"My father was so pleased to have me meet you. I was proud as well. I'm afraid I was quite truant though. Later my parents admonished me for not being in the schoolroom with Maria, Tatiana and my brother Alexei. We were supposed to be studying for final exams that day. I thought what was taking place in father's office was far more interesting than what was going on in my schoolroom. I think I learned something about world affairs that day."

"It has been too long", said Ribbentrop. "I should have liked to have seen you long before today. That charming little girl of years past is gone. In her place is a lovely young woman."

Anna beamed in response to the compliment. "After my father was forced to abdicate, life became very difficult for us." Ribbentrop bowed his head in remembrance of the tragedy.

From a distance, the count watched quietly as Anna interacted with Ribbentrop. He didn't try to join the conversation. He knew it was important that she alone should have his attention. Anna never glanced in her husband's direction. Ever since the tragic loss of her entire family, she had found it difficult to engage others in conversation unless her husband was there too. The fear of being alone, of being without family and friends temporarily had left her. Anna felt whole and complete. Ribbentrop continued to talk with her and quietly listened sympathetically when she said: "Father was a good man. He only wanted peace not just for himself but for others as well. When he met with Bloch he convinced my father that war in Europe would have wide reaching effects on Russia as well as other European nations. Father understood Bloch's insight into what eventually would happen in Europe perhaps better than most people. He knew that Europe would undergo great social upheaval and chaotic turmoil following a World War. I remember during World War I my father meeting secretly with an official of the German government. They were trying to help establish a secret peace between Russia and Germany. Even in war my father wanted peace. Without refuge from war our family and country was doomed to revolution. The civil war and hatred magnified by a war continued to drag Russia downward. Unfortunately the meeting came to nothing."

Ribbentrop didn't try to stop Anna from talking. He politely listened even though he knew his thoughts and loyalties must lie elsewhere.

"I was still quite young when my mother, sisters and I visited and comforted our country's war wounded. We saw firsthand the terrible toll war took upon our country's brave men who fought in Russia's defense. You know what a toll the war took upon Germany's fighting men too during the last war" she said, "The repercussions of World War I were severe not just in Russia where we had revolution and civil war but throughout Europe and the United States.

"I miss my father. Revolution aggravated by war deprived me of his love and compassion. It deprived me of my entire family. I have only the memory of their dear faces. I weep to think I will never see any of them again."

Ribbentrop appeared moved to think that Anna had spoken to him with such heartfelt honesty. He also was concerned. He'd realized the last war had shattered Europe. It had shattered lives and had taken away loved ones from families who grieved for them.

"Please tell me another war won't happen" she said gazing directly into his eyes. Ribbentrop felt uncomfortable talking with Anna. He knew what she'd asked of him was impossible. She knew as well. He couldn't tell Anna that war in Europe wouldn't happen. He was part of Germany's High Command. How dare she ask for any such assurance from him? Was she being realistic by even asking him such a preposterous question? From a distance the count slowly sipped his glass of vodka and watched his wife interact with Ribbentrop. From another corner of the room Stalin pretended to be listening to what a German officer was telling him but his gaze was on Anna still talking with Ribbentrop. He was being polite with her but from the expression on his face Stalin knew Ribbentrop wanted to escape Anna's company.

Ribbentrop's eyes searched the room uncomfortably as if he were trying to focus on something other than the conversation he was having with his hostess. Hitler was firmly in power. Didn't she realize that he wasn't free to disclose his true feelings regarding a war that might not happen? Ribbentrop was fooling himself. He knew war would take place. For Ribbentrop to disclose information regarding Hitler's plans and leadership would be suicidal not just for him but for anyone who did so. Ribbentrop took a quick sip from the vodka glass he held in hand. Like a garden that one found to be too sweet and intoxicating, he wanted to excuse himself from the lovely woman who held him trapped by her overwhelming charm. He wanted to back away from having to answer questions that were not just frank but embarrassing as well. His face was grave as he considered the message the lovely woman had given him. He knew she was a wife and the mother of two young sons. He knew that whatever the cost she wanted to protect them. What could he say to this young woman who'd lost her parents, brother and sisters and so much in life?

As if she could understand his thoughts Anna said: "Surely you have loved ones. You have children and grandchildren. Only a peaceful Europe can insure their welfare and the safety of us all."

Ribbentrop's face was distraught. Anna had spoken to him perhaps a little too frankly. "The Fuehrer wants only a peaceful Europe" he said wanting to end their discussion.

"I realize that", she said." Please give the Fuehrer my message. Since he has no children, please remind him that other people do. Remind him that as

Fuehrer he must see all the people in his country as his children. They must be cared for and protected".

Ribbentrop thought of Hitler's persecution of the Jews and so many other innocent people. He knew Hitler's priority wasn't the preservation of human life. He knew Hitler and the Nazi regime would trample anyone and anything if they saw fit to do so. He knew he could never deliver Anna's message to the Fuehrer. Was she being a fool or was he for allowing Anna to rattle on about such an unacceptable thing to say to Hitler?

Ribbentrop nearly spilled the glass of vodka in his hand as he backed away from Anna. She didn't try to follow him. Instead, she saw her husband smile knowingly at her. The count knew his wife could be tough. She was a survivor. She'd seen and lived through the worst. They both had. The hard times had bound them together. The hard times would hold them together. Their inner strength would carry them through the most turbulent times yet to come.

Anna discreetly returned her husband's gaze. She then walked across the room towards the piano where Rachmaninoff, much to the enjoyment of her other guests was playing.

The count came and stood beside his wife as she listened to the composer play a selection from his second piano concerto. When Rachmaninoff had finished playing it, the count suggested to his guests that they follow him into the dining room where dinner was waiting to be served. Carl took his wife's arm in his and led the way to the dining room followed by Stalin who was busy talking with Marina and her husband.

Anna sat beside her husband who sat at the head of the table. The count would refrain from interjecting any comments regarding the necessity of maintaining a peaceful strife free Europe. Inwardly Carl doubted if anyone would pursue the subject. Although he hadn't overheard their conversation, from the look on Ribbentrop's face, Carl was convinced that Hitler's Reich minister had heard and said enough on the subject. Ribbentrop turned to Rachmaninoff, who was sitting opposite him and asked him about his life in the United States. Stalin who also was seated across from Rachmaninoff eavesdropped on their discussion. Stalin knew Rachmaninoff and his family had fled Russia in 1917.

"It was a difficult decision for us to have to make. We have always loved our homeland" he told Ribbentrop.

Stalin knew Rachmaninoff's family was of the Russian nobility. The dictator's face clouded at the remark. Like Ribbentrop, he was feeling uncomfortable listening to or discussing matters that might reflect in a negative way on current events or past history. He seemed almost conciliatory when he said, "A talented man like you is always welcome in the Soviet Union."

Rachmaninoff had known the Russian composers of his day: Tchaikovsky, Scriabin and others. He admired their work and often played their compositions along with his own. He also knew the other composers, who like himself had fled Russia. Like many of the talented people he'd known, he and his family feared persecution if they remained in Russian. "We crossed to Helsinki in winter in an open sleigh," he said." We left behind much that was dear to us but we never looked back."

Following dinner, the count's guests again listened to Rachmaninoff play more of his music. Although he appeared outwardly polite and relaxed, Ribbentrop was relieved. Music was drowning out after dinner conversation.

Chapter Fifteen

The following morning after Stalin had boarded the train returning him to Moscow, and their other guests including Bockev and Marina had left them, Anna felt isolated. "You should have intervened" she said to Carl when they had a chance to discuss what had transpired the night before. Had she really done the right thing in confronting Ribbentrop? "I only did what you and Stalin wanted me to do," she said trying to defend her actions. Her husband seemed a little distant. Anna had looked beautiful but she had done little to make Ribbentrop feel comfortable. "Perhaps I should have been more subtle" she said. "Perhaps I shouldn't have seemed so eager for his attention. I don't think he liked any of the things I said to him."

"I don't think we need to leave for England just yet" he said with a bit of a smirk on his face. Anna playfully kicked her husband gently from underneath the table as he enjoyed a mid morning cup of coffee. She knew he wasn't taking her seriously. Perhaps Ribbentrop hadn't taken any of the things she'd said to him seriously either. She still felt remorse. Her late father's peace message had been ignored.

"I sensed a distinct froideur in the room after you confronted Ribbentrop and told him all the things you say you said to him. He was pale as a ghost."

"Surely nobody overheard our conversation", she said. "All of that lovely piano accompaniment must have drowned out everything."

"Never mind darling" he said getting up from the table, "You'll have a chance to make amends for all the things you said to him last night when you start attending those teas you've been invited to by the wives of the Nazi High Command."

Anna wasn't amused. She was upset that Stalin and Carl had put her up to confronting Ribbentrop. "I promise darling that I won't say another word to anyone about the dangers of someone going and starting another World War. I'll let you do it instead."

The count smiled at Anna's chiding remark. He knew only a beautiful woman like his wife could have gotten away with saying the things she'd said to Ribbentrop. Anna wasn't so sure.

She feared Ribbentrop might never forget what she'd said to him last night. She knew how ruthless and cruel the Nazis could be.

"Look darling" he said, "You gave Ribbentrop and that regime he works for legitimate reasons for not going and starting another world war. Let's just hope he listens to your advice and takes your message back to his boss."

Anna sighed with relief. "I still love you" he said bending over and kissing her on the lips. "It took courage to do what you did last night" he said leaving the room. At last her husband was giving her credit for her words and actions. Anna smiled a look of the utmost satisfaction.

She idly picked up her cup, slowly sipped her coffee, and thought about what a stunning evening last night had been. Rachmaninoff's musical performance had been wonderful but it hadn't outshone the one she'd put on during her conversation with Ribbentrop.

Anna opened the daily newspaper the maid had brought to her. She was busy reading the front page when the governess interrupted her and said that while walking the dog, she and the children were approached by a man who said he knew her husband, and that he needed to talk with him.

"Where is he, and what did he say his name was?" asked Anna putting the newspaper aside as the boys curiously looked on. "Please take the puppy upstairs to the school room" she said to the children. "We'll have a visit later."

After the children had left them to go upstairs, the governess told Anna that she'd asked the man to wait outside the front door where she assumed he still was. "The gentleman said his name was Boris and that the count would want to know he had come to see him."

Anna immediately asked a maid to invite the man inside. "Offer him some coffee. Tell him to wait outside the dining room. I'll go and tell my husband that he has a visitor."

Anna quickly left the governess and went upstairs. The office door was slightly ajar when she peered from behind the opposite side of it and saw Carl sitting at his desk. He looked up from what he'd been doing when he heard his wife's familiar voice. "Boris is downstairs waiting outside the dining room. He says he needs to talk with you, that it's important."

Carl left his office but Anna didn't try to pursue him. When he met Boris, the count could see that he looked disheveled and he didn't appear to be especially buoyed up in spirits. "I've been traveling non-stop ever since I left Berlin. I knew I had to find someone who might be able to help me. That phony id you obtained for me enabled me to get here."

The count invited Boris to take a seat at the dining room table. The servants had left them alone and no one could hear their conversation. "You look as though you could use something to eat" he said walking towards the kitchen then asking a servant to bring Boris some breakfast and them both some coffee.

When Carl returned, Boris gratefully thanked the count for his hospitality. "I'm afraid I can't return to Germany. My association with the German Communist party has made it impossible for me to remain in Berlin. I'll be sent to a concentration camp if I return to Germany. I have no money. I only managed to scrape enough cash together to get this far."

Carl hesitated before responding to what Boris told him. He didn't want to offer Boris permanent asylum within his home. For the time being, at least until he could figure out a way to help him move on he could remain within its confines.

"I'm going to have to give you a job to do while you're here. I know that by profession you're a surveyor. There is some new fencing that needs to go around the estate grounds but the land should be resurveyed in certain areas. I can put you to work in that way. You can sleep downstairs in a small room we have. Keep to yourself. Don't talk to the servants. Tell them as little as possible about yourself. I'm not so sure Stalin will welcome you back to Moscow now that you've fled Berlin. Some of the other Communists who thought they'd found safe haven in Russia have been sent back to Germany."

Boris looked pale. "Do you really need to tell Stalin that I'm here?"

"I'm sure eventually Stalin will find out that you're with us. I'll do what I can to help you evade deportation back to Nazi Germany."

"Could you possibly help me find safe haven in England?" he asked nervously twisting the corner of a napkin he held in hand.

Not wishing to pursue the subject and getting up from the table, Carl said "perhaps something can be worked out to get you there."

By employing Boris as a surveyor Carl decided he could accompany him around the estate and disguise the real purpose for hiring him. While Boris scoped out the land, the count would disarm any listening devises found on the property that the Nazis might have planted around the estate.

Several weeks passed. Carl didn't trust Boris, and felt uncomfortable with him. He wasn't sure if Boris was being honest in telling him that he had no money. If by working for him, Boris earned the cash to travel to England, Carl would do what he could to help him move on. He was determined he would never help Boris obtain another phony id but since Stalin knew too of Boris' travel plans, Carl didn't need to be concerned. The dictator was determined to prevent Boris from traveling to England. The Nazis soon learned that Boris had contacted Carl and that he'd found temporary refuge in Carl's home but they were being smug about it. They knew Boris was a spy. They also knew that like Bockev his loyalties might be questionable. They might be able to use him to their advantage.

* * * *

Stalin rose from where he sat at his desk in his Kremlin Office. The sunlight was almost blinding Stalin felt vulnerable and uncomfortable sitting under the sun's terrible late afternoon glare. Could no one have secrets anymore? It was impossible to keep anything from the enemy. Stalin got up from his chair, crossed the room, adjusted the window shades to block the sun's glare then returned to his desk. He was exhausted from all the thinking and planning. He sat down, closed his eyes and fell asleep. After he'd taken a short vacation from the burdens he carried, he would devise a plan to insure that Boris wouldn't make it to England. He also would devise a plan to make sure that the count and his family would find safe haven in the Kremlin away from their new Nazi neighbors.

Boris' new identification and documents arrived sooner than usual. So did those of the count and his family. After he opened the heavily sealed envelope that a government courier had delivered to him, Carl read Stalin's short note and examined the documents accompanying it. "I want you and Boris along with Anna and the children to travel aboard a train that I'm sending to transport you to Moscow." The count's heart pounded. "What could Stalin's reason be for calling him back to the Kremlin? Hadn't it been agreed upon that he and Anna would remain in Romania with their family so they could spy upon the Nazi High Command?"

Unbeknown to Carl and Anna, the evening of dinner and music meant to entertain their Nazi neighbors hadn't been well received by them. Stalin had learned that Ribbentrop was miffed and thought that Anna had used the occasion to confront him with a matter that should not have been discussed at a dinner party. The count's hands shook when he handed Stalin's letter and the documents to his wife.

Anna lowered herself into a chair. She took a huge breath when she saw what Stalin had sent them. She stared at the words, "You must return at once." Her face blanched pale as she studied the handwriting. There could be no mistake, the familiar signature was his.

"We must do what Stalin asks for us to do" she said looking up from the letter. "Our lives and those of our children may depend upon it" she said sadly handing the letter back to her husband.

"What about Boris is he to trust Stalin too?" asked Carl

"Of course" replied Anna. "Boris wouldn't have made it this far in his journey if Stalin hadn't wanted him saved too."

"You can't be sure of that" replied Carl. The unexpressed feeling of tension between them was apparent. The count didn't want to compete for his wife's affection. He detested the dictator. Anna could sense her husband's emotion when searching his face she said.

"I could never love him if that's what you're thinking" said Anna trying to dispel Carl's suspicions regarding her past relationship with Stalin. "I could never forgive him for the pain and emotional upheaval he's brought into our lives. These are difficult times. We have to fight for our survival. If this is the only way we can survive right now then we need to do what Stalin wants for us to do."

The count turned his back on his wife. The strain in their marriage was apparent. "You're naïve Anna" he said walking towards a window and gazing outside as the rain fell in torrents from the sky." You don't understand Stalin the way I do", he said turning and facing her. "He has no regard for human life and suffering. He will trample anyone who stands in his path. He will annihilate, conquer and kill until he achieves his totalitarian goal."

Anna began to weep. "Please don't say that now." She knew her father had lost Russia because he'd failed to keep it under his control. Anna knew Stalin had an iron fist. He'd never would lose control of his rule. "We have to trust Stalin. We have to remain loyal to him".

Carl felt grim. He didn't bother to reply to Anna's remark. Nothing needed to be explained. Both knew how dismal their options were. Carl wouldn't tell Anna that he thought Stalin's reason for having them spy upon the Nazis had been the dictator's way of creating a situation that eventually might force them to leave Romania and flee to Russia. If that had been the case, and Anna could never believe that it was, then Stalin's plan had worked. The count gazed into his wife's eyes and saw the pain reflected in them. They knew the choices offered them weren't what they wanted in life. They had to survive as best they could.

"We'll go" he said like a defeated man and with a distinct sound of misgiving in his voice. "We have no other choice."

"Thank you," she whispered as she embraced him.

Carl picked up the envelope containing Stalin's letter and the documents and started to leave the room.

"Are you going to hide the documents in the usual place?" she asked.

"Of course, why not?" he replied turning and facing her.

Anna remembered the time, years earlier when after hiding documents in the secret passageway she later discovered them in her desk's drawer. Do you think hiding the documents is even necessary?" she asked as if she were waiting for him to reveal a secret to her.

The count didn't comment. He turned his back on Anna and left her gazing after him as he closed the door behind him.

It was mid afternoon. The servants were taking a tea break, the children were in the schoolroom, and Boris was outside surveying property surrounding the count's estate. The count hadn't realized that Anna had followed him when he quickly made his way downstairs. She watched from behind a corner in the hallway as he pushed open the drawing room's huge mahogany door before quickly stepping inside the room. Anna then watched unseen as her husband slipped behind the tapestry and opened the door leading to Dracula's secret passageway. As Carl entered it, leaving the door slightly ajar, Anna could see the dim light from the lantern her husband held in hand shine from beneath the passageway's door. As she waited for him to return she seemed almost breathless with anticipation. She half expected to see Carl and Dracula come face to face. Instead she saw something else. On the floor was an envelope addressed to her. Anna picked it up and read the cryptic unsigned message contained within the envelope. "The light of day surrounds us but night's darkness alone will prevent us from becoming light's slaves." Anna's heart pounded as she wondered who had placed the envelope on the floor for her to find.

After the count had hidden the documents in the passageway, she heard him close the passageway's door and watched him slip from behind the tapestry. It was late in the day. The shades in the drawing room had been drawn so the room was dark. Strange shadows jumped at them as Anna made her presence known to Carl. He started to say something to her but hesitated as they listened intently to unfamiliar noises. The muffled sounds Anna thought were voices were merely the wind's howling around the castle's heavy exterior walls. Anna reached out to Carl who quickly took her arm in his before saying to her, "Darling you seem so suspicious lately. You don't need to snoop around the premises and follow me everywhere. I don't follow you around so why should you follow me?"

Anna knew she'd been spying on Carl. She tried to make light of his accusation and cover up what she'd been doing by saying, "Just because we happen to bump into each other you don't need to think that I'm following you around. Actually I was looking for something I'd lost. I thought I might have dropped it on the drawing room floor", she lied. Anna was of course referring to the note she'd discovered there.

Once they were standing together outside the drawing room, Anna breathed a sigh of relief. She was sure no one had seen them enter or exit the room. They quickly went upstairs to the count's office where they remained until a servant knocked on the door and asked them if they'd like some tea. Anna knew her husband would rather have vodka but he accepted the tea.

When they were by themselves again, Anna leaned towards Carl and said as if she were confiding in him "I think that passageway is one of the most fascinating and forbidding places I've ever been inside. But whatever hidden mysteries lie within passageway walls might be no more mysterious than the missing note I found while searching the drawing room floor."

Anna poured her husband a cup of warm tea then handed the note to him and said "The messages Dracula managed to scrawl upon the rough stone wall within his hiding place deserve closer examination." After he'd read the note Anna had shown him, she asked, "Does this note's message and handwriting match the handwriting and graffiti on the passageway's wall?"

"The light of day surrounds us but night's darkness alone will prevent us from becoming light's slave." Carl's demeanor was calm. He wasn't about to suggest that there possibly could be any connection with the note and what was scrawled upon a passageway wall. He evaded answering her question by getting up from where he sat and leaving her alone to sip her tea. "I'm afraid I don't have the answer to your question" he'd said closing the door to the room behind him.

Chapter Sixteen

"The servants mustn't know that we are going to Moscow" Carl said when later he and Anna discussed the plan for leaving." We'll simply leave a note for them to find informing them that we've gone on a short holiday and that we plan to return in a couple of days. When they realize we aren't returning, a courier will inform them that we will be gone for an undetermined length of time but that they will be paid and should remain in our employment."

"Perhaps our visit to the Kremlin may turn out to be an impermanent stay" Anna hopefully suggested yet at the same time feigned to be naive."Eventually we might be able to return to Romania."

"To whom would we run to then?" he asked sarcastically, sounding exasperated and answering his own question-- "The Nazis?" The count didn't mention what the worst scenario might be. He didn't want to burden his wife with that possibility.

Anna knew what her husband was thinking. Carl knew neither of them was being completely straightforward in the conversation they were having. Anna had known Stalin long enough to realize that he trusted no one---not even the people he loved. Yet she felt guilty for even entertaining the idea that Stalin might betray them.

Over a week had passed. No one had learned of the family's plan to flee aboard the Soviet train that would return them to the Kremlin. Anna and Carl lingered alone together in his office following breakfast the day before they were to leave. The children hadn't started the school day yet. Carl glanced at his watch. It was time for them to leave his office so they could have their usual visit with their sons. When they entered the room where they waited for them Anna began the conversation by saying, "Tonight before you go to bed you must be prepared to leave with us. Place warm clothes-- jackets, gloves and boots next to your bed. Your father is taking us on a secret adventure that nobody is to know about. Do you understand?" The boys seemed puzzled by the request but they were excited about the prospect of going on a family adventure.

"May we take Oscar with us?" asked Carl Nicholas. Anna glanced at her husband who nodded his head in assurance that it was all right for him to come with them.

"When it's time for us to leave, Oscar will go with us with a leash attached to his collar" said Anna quietly. "I'm used to traveling with small dogs so I know he needs one on the journey ahead for us." The boys sensed that the adventure they were about to embark upon wouldn't be an ordinary family outing.

"Will we be gone long?" asked Ivan turning to his father. The count was evasive. He didn't want to alarm his children.

"We'll be gone for just a little while?" he replied gently.

After they'd left their children and were standing alone together in the count's office, Anna asked. "Shouldn't we give Boris warning that he is to leave with us tonight?"

"No" he replied. "Tell him nothing. Don't even tell him where we're going. When we are aboard the train we'll just hand him his identification papers."

"What if Boris demands that we let him off the train?" asked Anna nervously. "He wants safe passage to England."

"We'll simply tell him he has no choice but to stay aboard the train and accompany us."

"If you say that to Boris he'll know that he's on his way to Russia."

Carl seemed a little impatient with the conversation he was having with Anna. "I don't think either of us should concern ourselves with what Boris wants or will be thinking in regard to the journey. He's coming with us whether he likes it or not" he said leaving the room.

It was nearly 1:00 A.M. the following morning when Carl and Anna prepared for the journey. "Meet me in my office along with the children in twenty minutes" he said placing a gun inside a holster he'd strapped beneath his jacket. "If I'm not back by then don't go looking for me."

"Let me go with you" replied Anna. "We'll fetch the children together."

"No" he said emphatically. "You and the children must remain behind in my office until I return. I'll go to Boris and tell him he is to come with us tonight."

Anna shuddered. She didn't trust Boris. She didn't want him accompanying them on their secret journey. She was afraid that Boris might say or do something that might jeopardize their safety. "Perhaps Boris is a double agent. What if he manages to contact the Nazis somehow?" she asked.

"He won't contact them. That's why we're taking him with us." Carl thought it was strange that Boris had so easily discovered so many wires and listening devices set up around the castle estate. He wondered if he'd helped plant them there. "We have to do what Stalin wants for us to do" he said realizing that further discussion regarding the conversation they were having was going nowhere.

Anna refrained from making any more comments. She gazed at the gun in the holster visible beneath Carl's jacket. She knew the count was prepared for the worst. "Please hide the gun from the children. They'll be alarmed if they see you carrying one. They'll wonder what's wrong. We'll wait for you in your office," she said.

The boys were already dressed and ready to go when their mother knocked upon their door. "Neither of us could sleep" said Carl Nicholas who along with his brother greeted Anna in Ivan's room when she came looking for them. The boys wore the warm clothes and boots their parents had instructed them to wear and each wore a jacket with gloves stashed inside the pockets.

The family's beloved pet Oscar had spent the night with them. His leash was already attached to his collar when Anna told her sons to follow her quietly to their father's office where they would wait for him to meet them.

After the count had left his wife and was on his way to fetch the documents, he was unaware that Boris secretly had been observing him from behind a corridor pillar. Boris hadn't tried to follow the count after he'd entered the drawing room. He'd realized that Carl had locked the drawing room's door preventing anyone from doing so. Instead Boris waited and watched as Carl left the drawing room so he could follow him but he seemed frightened and confused when he saw the count knock upon his room's door. Boris knew the count would know he'd been snooping around the premises when he didn't find him in his room. He also realized it was time to make his presence known to him.

"I'm afraid I couldn't sleep" he said as Carl heard his voice, turned around then faced him.

Carl didn't reach for the gun still in its holster strapped inside his jacket. Instead he casually invited Boris upstairs to his office where he knew his family waited for them. Anna suspected nothing when she saw Boris standing alongside Carl. The count handed the envelope containing the documents to Anna and told her to keep them with her. "It's time for us all to leave" he said turning to her and the children. "Boris is coming with us. I believe there is a car outside waiting for us now."

Boris's hands trembled. He had no gun. He'd forgotten to bring one with him. Boris cautiously watched as Carl casually removed the gun from his holster, and told Anna to lead the children downstairs where the black sedan waited for them. With gun pointed directly at Boris's back, the count followed his family downstairs and outside towards the castle driveway where the sedan was parked. Anna, the children and puppy were already in the sedan's backseat when Carl instructed the sedan's driver, to place handcuffs on Boris. If Ilyich seemed shocked by Carl's request he said nothing. He knew the count must have good reason for pointing a gun at Boris. He also knew Carl was Comrade Stalin's friend. Illyich never would dare question Carl's actions in regard to Boris.

No one spoke. Anna and the children seemed very subdued. The driver got back into the car, turned it around and hastily began driving it down the steep castle driveway and onto the main road. Within a half hour the sedan met the train and only Illyich lingered behind those who quickly boarded it. He hastily hid the sedan in bushes alongside the road then ran and boarded the one car train that already had started moving.

Anna knew the Nazis might dare to stop and search the train before the border crossing. She clutched the all important envelope containing their documents and gazed across the aisle where her husband sat a few rows up from where she and their sons were sitting. Even though Boris was handcuffed, the count watched him closely. Without turning around in his seat, Carl told Anna to please give Boris his documents. As Boris leaned forward and with his manacled hands, took the documents from her, Carl removed a small knife from Boris's vest pocket and handed it to Anna. He then sat down in a seat directly in back of him so he could easily point a gun at Boris' head if need be.

Boris hung his head in despair. He knew he was on his way to Russia. He knew that what awaited him there might be something he dared not contemplate.

The train continued on its journey. There would be no unnecessary stops and there were no other passengers aboard the train. Stalin had wanted the count and his family to be sheltered from the curiosity of others and by the darkness of night. With just its one car to pull, the train continued to gather speed and momentum as it easily moved towards its destination. Anna and her family must be protected at all costs.

Several hours had passed. It already was dawn and Anna lifted a window shade revealing a foggy bleak early morning. The exhausted children sitting on either side of their mother had fallen asleep beside her. The sleeping puppy was curled up in her arms.

The early morning fog surrounding the train on its journey gradually dissipated in mid morning sunlight, and Anna nervously glanced through the train window as if anticipating the worst. She only hoped the note she'd left for the governess would deter any curiosity regarding her family's absence: "We'll be gone for just a few days", the note had said. "Boris is assisting my husband with some work. We've decided to make it an out of town holiday for the children too." Anna only hoped no one would discover the abandoned black sedan hidden in the bushes on the dirt country road near the railroad tracks.

Carl was exhausted. He had to rest. Boris was handcuffed to the seat where he sat so the count told Iylich to keep an eye on him while he took a break. It was 7:00 am.

Trays with warm tea and food were passed around and Carl finally had a chance to join his family for breakfast before having to return to his seat so Ilyich could have his breakfast too. Boris' manacles were removed only long enough for him to eat. As soon as he'd finished his meal he again was handcuffed to the seat.

Another day passed. The boys seemed restless, and Anna continued nervously gazing out a train window. The scenery had become a blur as the train sped onward trying to outrun the unknown and ominous. Soon they would be coming to the Russian/Ukrainian border. Anna only hoped the Nazis dared not board the train before it reached Russian territory.

Her greatest fears were realized. The train was only twenty miles from the Russian/Ukrainian Border when a Nazi blockade brought it to a halt. The count quickly removed Boris' handcuffs when he realized they were going to be searched but he kept a gun pointed at Boris but concealed beneath a jacket as a Nazi guard checked everyone's identification papers.

Anna's heart pounded furiously. She was almost in tears. She knew she must make every effort to conceal her emotions. She smiled at the guard as he checked her family's identification papers. When she was asked the nature of their visit to Moscow she simply said it was a family holiday. She and her husband had been invited to Russia for a visit. The Nazi guard asked no further questions. He knew from looking at the all important seal on the documents that only a high Soviet official could have issued such an invitation. Finally the guard finished checking papers and left the train. Anna breathed a sigh of relief but she still was in near tears.

The train moved hastily towards the border. Twenty miles seemed so far away. Twenty miles seemed like an eternity. Anna's hands were still trembling. She knew her husband had held a concealed gun pointed directly at Boris during the Nazi guard's search. She wondered if the guard hadn't seen the suspicious awkward lump hidden beneath her husband's jacket.

Anna solemnly gazed out the window at heavy snow was starting to fall. The boys were very subdued. The count again had manacled Boris. The snow outside the window now was almost blinding. The train had slowed down but it still made steady progress towards the border.

If the Nazi guard had seemed convinced that there was nothing out of the ordinary regarding the family's journey from Romania to the Soviet Union his commandant thought there was. He'd just learned that the black sedan that had transported the count and his family to the train's stop had been found abandoned in bushes not far from railroad tracks. He was furious with the guard for not detaining the train, and ordered a small swift train vehicle immediately be dispatched in pursuit of the Soviet train that now was within less than ten miles from the border. As if sensing something was wrong Ilyich left his seat opposite the count. He moved to the back of the train and stood on the open rear iron platform. A shot was fired and Ilyich nearly lost his footing but managed to regain it. A railed vehicle was so close to them that Ilyich was sure it would overtake them and the train be boarded. The train's engines were working furiously. The engineer was afraid to increase speed. The intensity of the storm was such that the train easily might derail. Then the unexpected happened. The small light vehicle along with its hostile occupants went flying off the tracks. The storm and icy conditions had derailed it.

The train now was less than four miles from the border but in the perilous blizzard conditions it might as well have been 40. The Nazis had set up a small barricade in an effort to derail the train but miraculously it kept moving forward after blindly crashing through it. The engineer had assured Carl that the border crossing had to be less than a mile away. For a few minutes it stopped snowing. The border crossing now was in clear view but hostile shots were being fired at the train's occupants lying on the floor as the train plowed through snow drifts. Suddenly the train stopped moving and there was an eerie silence. For a moment no one dared even breathe. The sound of hostile gunfire had subsided. The border had been crossed and Soviet guards quickly boarded the train to check passengers' documents. The guard's leader had been told by his superiors that the people aboard the train were Stalin's friends and shouldn't be delayed. He hadn't needed to be told. He'd recognized Stalin's seal upon the documents. He dared not ask the count any questions regarding the near disastrous encounter with the Nazis. Russian guards waved the train forward and it continued on its journey.

Carl removed the handcuffs from Boris' hands then said, "Nobody aboard the train wanted to manacle you. We knew you were afraid. We couldn't be sure that you'd voluntarily come with us. I had to make sure you would.

"I tried to get you papers so you could get to England" he lied. "Even if I'd been able to obtain the papers for you to travel on, you might not have made it there".

Boris was full of fear and rage. He hated the count for what he'd done to him.

"Were you ready to kill me if the Nazi guard saw the gun you had pointed at me when we were stopped?" he asked.

"The gun was pointed at the guard not you", said Carl unconvincingly.

Boris hung his head in despair. Desperate to get off the train, he got up from where he sat and ran towards the metal enclosure serving as the car's entrance and exit. Carl knew he had to stop Boris from jumping from the train. He grabbed hold of his arm and pushed him against the metal enclosure. Ilyich and the count then led Boris back to his seat.

"Get a hold of yourself" said Carl. "You wouldn't have made it this far if Stalin hadn't wanted to keep you alive."

Boris said nothing in reply to the remark. He silently wept as Carl again manacled him to the seat.

Anna brought Boris something to eat. "Everything will be all right" she said feeling a little guilty and handing the cup of tea to him with some bread and cheese "None of us needs to be afraid," she said as he took the food offered him before staring at the floor.

When Anna returned to her seat, she took the puppy from Carl Nicholas and sat down beside her youngest son. "Mommy why did we ever leave home", he wept. Both he and Ivan were sure that it was now impossible for them to return there. The terror they'd gone through while crossing the border was something they'd never forget.

"We can't go home not for a long time. Stalin has invited us to come and live near him in Moscow. We'll be safer there than at home right now. Someday when you're older and the world is a more peaceful place we'll return home" she replied.

* * * *

The servants in the count's employment soon learned that the family wouldn't be returning home. After they'd crossed the Soviet border, a courier was sent to inform them that the count was living abroad but they should maintain his home and estate and remain in his employment.

When the Servants learned that the count's absence from home would be an extended one they were both puzzled and concerned. The wolves surrounding his estate didn't need to be told though. They'd sensed he was gone and that he wasn't coming back. Their howls had been heard for miles as in vain they tried to call back the one man who loved and protected them. As the wolves howled amidst the snowy landscape they were unaware of how far nature's storm extended.

The heavy snow covering the world for miles had halted humanity's busy activity and forced the world to surrender to it. If the world was trapped by hills and valleys of frozen crystals then men with their struggles, and contentious behavior temporarily were buried by something greater than themselves. A natural disaster had saved the count and his family as they'd fled across the border. A natural disaster now prevented men from succumbing to their own evil. The purity of deep valleys of ice and snow had cleansed the world, and a raging blizzard had offered escape to those who found refuge in it.

The storm's icy fingers had encompassed the train and imbedded it in deep mountains of snow. Exhausted passengers, grateful for what little warmth the train's heaters provided them with had found rest beneath comforting silence. The boys, bundled up in the warm clothes they wore, removed their mittens so they could play a card game before falling asleep with their heads against one another. The puppy chewed happily on an old leather shoe he'd found beneath a carriage seat, and Boris, was resigned to making the best of his situation. Several hours passed. Carl glanced out a window before nudging Anna who'd been sleeping. He wanted her to know that the storm had ceased and the train was underway again. The wind miraculously had blown away the powdered drifts covering tracks. Anna groggily mumbled something in reply to him before drifting off to sleep again. Finally Carl closed his eyes and rested too in the comforting knowledge that he and his family had outrun their pursuers.

For the time being Carl was too tired to think about new concerns regarding what the future might hold in store for him and his family. Instead he rested in the passenger seat beside Anna and dreamed of the familiar sights and sounds he'd left behind. He almost could hear the wind in the trees and the distant lament of wolves calling him home. Someday he and his family would find their pathway homeward so they could connect with the natural world they were leaving behind.

The train suddenly jolted forward and Carl awoke. He gazed down at the floor half expecting to find some omen of good there, only to discover shattered glass and fragmented pieces of the train's interior.

Despite the bullet ridden train compartment and shattered glass, Carl was certain that the violence he'd just witnessed and the violence that might yet come wouldn't deter him and his family from finding good and peace in life. The things he'd taught his children to know and love would be preserved.

Later when it was again daylight Carl and Illyich occupied their time in trying to make the train more habitable. They tore old pieces of cardboard from boxes found in a corner and used them to patch up broken windows or to cover bullet holes in the carriage's interior. Carl then sat down again next to Anna before reaching upward and adjusting a shade so that he could see the morning sunlight streaming through an unbroken window. As the sun enveloped him, his hopes and dreams for a better future remained unbroken too.

Suddenly the sun's brilliance was obscured by clouds. Darkness encompassed them again and Carl closed his eyes. He knew darkness could only be temporary. Despite the despair he felt, he was determined that someday he would return to the beautiful forest landscape and the natural things that had become so important to him in life. He would fight for them because they were symbols of his and others' freedom.

When the sun was high in the sky again and its splendor once more apparent, Carl Nicholas pressed his nose against the window and stared. Commune farms covered in snow extended for miles. "Are we going to live on a farm?" he asked. "Are we going to stop running so we can live here?" he asked his voice tremulous. He'd been terrified by the bullets and the shattered glass. He wasn't sure if it was safe to continue their journey.

"No. we're not going to live on a farm here" replied his father who'd remembered hearing of the tragic famine of the early 1930's when so many died of starvation. "We have our own farm at home. We'll return there someday after we've lived in Moscow." Ivan put his arm around his younger brother. He thought he was still too young to understand the dangers of returning to Romania. Carl Nicholas was growing up. The bullets that had shattered train windows hadn't been fired at them in play as Anna had told them. He knew his mother had pretended that the violence they'd experienced had been just a game. Ivan would never tell his younger brother how dangerous the situation they'd been through had been. Carl Nicholas had held the small dog in his arms close throughout the entire ordeal. He understood the terror and danger of what they'd been through. He'd never forget it.

"We'll be arriving in Moscow tomorrow" said Carl turning to his sons.

"Will we like Moscow?" asked Carl Nicholas who with questioning eyes gazed at his father. Carl looked at his youngest son and said. "We must get used to living in new places. You'll find Moscow to be very different from our home in Romania. You'll meet new people, see new sights and take full advantage of all the experiences living in a different place offers one." Carl Nicholas wasn't sure if he understood what his father had told him. He'd loved their home in Romania. He'd loved the horses his father owned and the wildlife that they saw when they went riding together. He'd liked to look out his window and gaze at the distant mountains when he got up early in the morning. "Will there be any mountains in Moscow? Will we be able to go riding there?"

"Don't ask your father so many questions" said Anna listening to the conversation. She didn't want her sons to see the tears in her eyes. She wasn't looking forward to returning to Moscow. Anna's ties to Russia, her memories of living there during childhood and more recently ran deep. She belonged there. She only hoped the place didn't break her heart.

"When your mother was little she used to live in the Kremlin" said the count when Carl Nicholas kept asking him questions about it. She can tell you what it was like growing up there. Anna didn't want to relive the past. She didn't want to tell her children what her childhood was like. She wanted that chapter of her life to remain closed and an enigma to them all. Sometimes the children wondered if their mother had had any childhood at all.

"Mother, why don't you tell us about your brother and sisters?" asked Carl Nicholas. "Why don't you tell us about all the things you used to do when you lived in the Kremlin?" Anna quickly glanced at her husband. She didn't want to talk about her family. Past memories concerning them were too painful for her to bear right now.

"Darling, tell them about the happy times" he whispered. "They don't need to know about anything else."

Anna hesitated. She knew Carl was right. She knew she had to come to grips with the past. She had to blot out the sadness. "We used to play hide and seek" she said. "There were so many wonderful places we found to hide in at the Kremlin. If it was a rainy day and we couldn't go out of doors and play we would pretend that we could step into another world by hiding from everyone. Sometimes it was so hard to find one another that we had to give up and stop playing hide and seek."

Anna broke off in mid-sentence trying to tell her sons what it was like to play hide and seek. She knew she'd never stopped playing it. In her heart she was always hoping that somehow she would be able to find the missing members of her family. "Perhaps they're just hiding" she thought grimly.

There were tears in Anna's eyes. "Will you play hide and seek with us?" asked Carl Nicholas, seeing her tears and gazing at his mother. Anna didn't answer him. Instead she said, "When we get settled in our Kremlin apartment, perhaps I'll be able to show you some of the places where I used to play. I'll show you the room where I had school and I'll show you all the things I once did. Perhaps everything is still there just waiting to be found" she said before thoughtfully saying, "My sisters, brother and I kept a secret journal together that we hid behind a small corner bookcase in our schoolroom. I've never tried to retrieve the journal even when your father and I were living in the Kremlin I left it where it was. With your help I might be able to retrace steps of long ago and find it."

"That sounds like an adventure" said Carl Nicholas."

"If we discover the old journal hidden so many years ago, you and Ivan must write another one to take its place" she said.

"What sort of information did your journal contain?" asked Ivan who'd been listening to the conversation his mother and brother were having with one another.

"We made up games and stories to tell one another or we drew pictures of the things we saw. I liked to draw when I was little. Some of my sketches along with those of my sisters and brother depict our daily lives and family experiences."

"Do you suppose someone has already found your journal?" asked Ivan a little hesitantly.

Anna was thoughtful but her face was sad. She'd never told her sons that before they had been imprisoned, she and her sisters had burned their diaries. Perhaps their journal had been confiscated by the authorities. Had Ivan guessed the truth regarding something she didn't want him to know?

"You'll both get used to living in Moscow" she said quickly changing the subject without answering him.

The train continued on its slow journey to Moscow. "Thank God we're almost there" said the count gazing out the window. "This trip was far worse than anything I could have imagined." Anna grimaced at her husband's remark. She couldn't imagine any journey more terrifying than the one she'd taken after her escape from the Perm house. Did Stalin know the final truth? Would he ever tell her if he knew? Darkness surrounding her family and what might have happened to them after she left the Perm house made everything easier to bear.

Anna gazed down at the heavy wool coat she wore. Inside the coat's lining she had sewn her marriage certificate, her children's birth certificates and her own as well as her husband's true identification papers. Someday when it was safe for her and her family to leave Russia they would use those documents to cross the border and return home to Romania.

It was late in the afternoon. Anna pulled down the train's window shade to block out the sunlight. She'd seen enough of the new Russia. She hated what the Communists had done to beautiful old homes where the privileged nobility once had lived. The homes looked ill kept. Was Stalin alone responsible for Russia's new downward trend? He couldn't be. Anna knew Stalin too well. He had an appreciation for the finer things in life. He'd never known them fully until he was dictator but he'd learned fast. Stalin remembered what the grand Russian homes prior to the revolution looked like. They resembled her husband's castle estate in Romania.

Chapter Seventeen

Stalin sat alone in his Kremlin office. He knew Anna and her family had escaped Nazi pursuers. He smiled to himself. He regarded the family's safe arrival in Moscow not just a victory for them but one for him too. In Carl's absence, Stalin's spies would make certain that the Count's Romanian estate would remain secure. The Nazis were fooling themselves if they thought the count and Anna had been the only spies there ready to inform him of the Nazis' activities.

The Nazis had reason to respect Stalin. He knew how to protect his own interests and those of his friends. Yet Stalin regarded few people as friends. He trusted Anna and Carl as much as he was capable of trusting anyone---which wasn't much. "Anna's home must remain unmarred by unwanted intruders," he thought taking his pipe from his pocket. He then drew upon it one time before emptying the pipe's tobacco into a waste can then restlessly getting up from where he was sitting. "This entire day has been a waste of time," he said grumbling to himself then leaving the room.

It was getting late in the day. Stalin wanted to make sure Anna was escorted safely to the Kremlin. He'd been informed of her family's progress throughout their harrowing journey to Russia. He knew their arrival in Moscow was less than an hour away. He'd made sure that an official car was standing by to deliver them to the Kremlin. He wouldn't be there to meet them of course. He wanted them to think he had more important things to do, and he did.

It was late afternoon when the passengers prepared to leave the train. Their arrival in Moscow couldn't have come soon enough. "If I had to spend another day aboard that train I think I'd have gone mad" said Anna glancing at shattered glass and bullet ridden coach seats. "Sorry darling, it was the best

I could do to get us here. I believe we arrived a little ahead of schedule", said Carl chidingly as he helped her from the train. Ivan handed his mother the puppy before he and his younger brother quickly jumped from the train as Illyich and Boris followed them.

The driver of the car who was to deliver them to the Kremlin met them at the station and led them to the car. Anna knew Boris and Illyich lived in Moscow too. She nudged Carl who asked the driver if he could deliver them to their homes as well. "Of course", replied the driver as the car sped away from the train depot.

The Moscow city sky was dull and gray. Industrial smoke mixed with fog permeated the atmosphere and the frosty late afternoon air seemed to penetrate any warm escape from the cold. Pedestrians bundled in heavy coats and wearing fur hats appeared tired and weary as they quickly walked homeward or toward a warmer destination along city streets.

When the car transporting the family approached the Kremlin, Anna was quick to point out familiar landmarks such as Red Square, Basil Cathedral, and Lenin's tomb lying at the foot of the Kremlin. "There is much to see in Moscow" she said turning to Ivan and Carl Nicholas. In fact, there is so much to see that one can live for years here and not take it all in" she said stepping from the car into the cold late afternoon air.

"Look" said Anna taking hold of Carl's arm and noticing the baskets of food and delicacies greeting them. "Someone has been generous". She then glanced at Carl, who nodded his head as she said, "Please take one." Ilyich and Boris thanked the couple for their kindness and realized that the trying ordeal they'd been through together hopefully had ended.

After the car taking the men to their homes drove away, and the family was alone, Anna didn't speculate on who'd sent the baskets. She was rather certain that she knew who he was though. She then turned to her children and asked them to carry the remaining two baskets into the Kremlin with them. Stalin hadn't been there to greet them but he'd watched their arrival from an office window as the family walked towards their luxurious apartments within Kremlin walls.

When Carl was handed the key to unlock the door to their new home Anna was delighted with their accommodations. Their apartment faced the gardens and was larger than the one the couple previously had shared while living in the Kremlin.

The couple watched as their sons quickly found their rooms and Carl Nicholas bounced upon his bed as the puppy made up for lost exercise."I believe your new school room is just a little distance down the hall", said Anna interrupting the joyful reprieve. "We'll have to find a new tutor for you tomorrow so you can begin your lessons" remarked Carl. The boys grimaced at their father's remark about having to start school so soon after their arrival and quickly made the puppy stop tugging on the drapes.

"I think Oscar needs a quick run in the gardens" said Ivan turning to his father for his approval. "Can Oscar stay in our rooms with us?" asked Carl Nicholas. "Of course," replied Carl glancing at his wife who nodded her head in agreement.

Anna then opened closet doors in the boys' rooms. The clothes she'd ordered had arrived and were ready for them to wear. "You need to take showers before you change into new clothes and join your mother and me for dinner," said Carl as Ivan quickly answering for Carl Nicholas but at the same time departing with Oscar in tow said "I'll make sure we do".

Anna laughed to herself as she noticed the boys' quick departure. "I think I'll take a bath before dinner too", she said excusing herself so she could luxuriate in a tub of clean warm soapy water.

Later Anna examined the new clothes she'd ordered hanging in closets alongside ones she and her husband had left behind months earlier in their haste to return to Romania. She then carefully hung up the coat with the precious documents sewn into the lining alongside the other coats and items in the closet.

"I wonder when Stalin will invite us to visit him?" asked Carl, busy dressing for dinner when Anna walked into the room and began brushing her newly shampooed hair.

"I'm sure he'll meet with us soon. I doubt if there is anything about our difficult journey that he doesn't already know though, she said gazing at herself in a mirror. We probably won't have much to tell him about it."

Carl shuddered to think that Stalin probably had already heard how they'd evaded Nazi checkpoints and had to handcuff Boris and force him aboard the train to get him to Moscow. "It's too bad we couldn't have left him behind. Taking Boris with us turned out to be a huge liability" he said. Then turning from the room so he could make sure their sons were getting ready for dinner Carl left Anna and walked down the corridor towards their rooms.

When the family was gathered together at the table, Anna was relieved that they finally were sitting down to the first warm meal they'd had in days. Bread, cheese and tea had been the main staple aboard the one car train bound for Moscow. Tonight they gratefully dined on roast chicken and vegetables. Tonight Anna didn't need to tell her sons to eat their greens and carrots. They relished them.

It wasn't until after dinner that an envoy delivered a message to their apartment's door and Carl realized that the note might require an immediate answer. After reading Stalin's short note welcoming them to Moscow, Carl handed it to Anna.

"We must thank him for the baskets of food he sent us, as well as our delicious meal tonight" said Anna opening a desk drawer and quickly finding some stationery and a pen before writing a note thanking Stalin for his hospitality. She then handed the note to Carl so he might sign his name and give the note to the envoy.

It was getting late in the day. After giving their dog a bath in a wooden washtub they'd found in the corridor, the children dried Oscar off then led the little dog to the kitchen where he received some delicious leftovers, a bountiful reward for his love and patience.

When Anna saw that her sons had taken care of Oscar's needs too, she commended them for their thoughtfulness. "Now that he is clean and well fed he may spend the night in your rooms with you. Your father and I will check on you both later so don't stay up all night talking to each other either. Get some rest" she said watching her children with Oscar at their heels disappear into their rooms.

It wasn't yet dark outside. The family's arrival in Moscow had evaded a storm now encasing the world in ice. The grayness of a wintry evening drew the boys to a bedroom window. Basil Cathedral, with its onion shaped domes covered in icy crystals loomed ahead in wintry splendor. Ivan held Oscar in his arms as he and his brother gazed at the wintry scene below. They watched with fascination as the gray outline of trees beneath their windows became so heavy laden with icicles that small branches broke and fell to the ground. They were still too young to realize that another storm far more devastating soon would freeze, burden and paralyze a world not in ice but in fear.

The count knocked on his eldest son's door before opening it as Anna slipped into the room alongside him. "You must prepare yourself for tomorrow's busy schedule" said Carl watching Carl Nicholas, with Oscar in his arms climb into bed in a room adjoining Ivan's. "Good night" they said as their sons reached out and embraced each parent.

Chapter Eighteen

Commandant Urhart smiled as he sat at his desk and leaned back in a comfortable office chair. Urhart had admired the count's home when he'd visited it. He also knew it now was impossible for Zurofsky to return to that home. The count's family had evaded Nazi guards stationed at check points during their recent flight to Russia. Returning to Romania was no longer an option for them. If they dared return there they would be dealt with severely. It would be only a short time before the Nazis occupied the count's stunning home. It would be only a matter of time before the count's home was stripped of its art treasures and other valuables.

Commandant Urhart knew that Dracula's curse, like a dark forbidding cloud hung over the count's ancient castle estate. Yet he wasn't a superstitious man. He didn't take the rumor seriously. He yawned then rose from his desk and put on his coat. It was late afternoon when he left his office and walked outside towards his car. He wanted to have a closer look at the count's estate alone.

The sky was cloudy and almost dark. Evening like some foreboding omen was setting in early. Urhart got into the car and turned the key on the ignition before starting the car's engine and driving along the winding country road leading to the count's estate. He was only several miles from his destination when a blown tire forced the car off the road, over an incline and into a ditch. He tried to free himself from the wrecked car but he was pinned behind the steering wheel and couldn't move. He reached for the car's emergency radio but found it had been damaged in the accident and didn't work. He then shouted for help but he was in an isolated area. There was nobody around to hear his cry and bushes surrounding him made it impossible for the wrecked car to be seen from the road. An hour passed. It was completely dark outside now. Urhart shivered with fear and cold. He kept trying without success to free himself from the wrecked car.

His hands were so cold that they hurt. Then the unforeseen happened. A tall thin man with face hidden behind a scarf slowly made his way through the brush and stood before the wrecked car. Then with superhuman strength he managed to tear the wrecked car door off its hinges. Urhard was so astounded at what he was seeing he couldn't even let out a stifled cry of terror. He mercifully fainted as the stranger slowly leaned towards him, grasped him by the throat and fangs penetrated Urhart's flesh before drawing the living blood from his body.

When Urhart's wrecked car was discovered several days later with him inside it, everyone assumed he'd died from wounds incurred during the horrific accident. The fang marks around his throat were almost invisible. Since the body had decomposed immediately and the stench from it was overwhelming, Urhart was cremated and his ashes placed in an urn to be sent home to his family. No one dared suggest that Dracula's curse had anything to do with Urhart's death. Nobody, not even the Nazis wanted to speculate on that terrifying possibility. Yet the rumors quietly persisted.

In the count's absence, no one else wanted to approach the estate. Only the few servants, the courier or those with business related to managing the estate's upkeep dared venture on the premises.

* * * *

"I do hope everything is running smoothly at home" said Anna looking over her husband's shoulder as he wrote a note enclosed with the servants pay stipends to be delivered by courier to them. The count didn't answer her. Instead he looked up from what he was doing and gazed into her eyes as if they both knew what the other was thinking but dared not mention it. They'd heard the news regarding Urhard's bizarre and untimely death.

"I have to meet with Stalin today" said Carl slipping his pen into his shirt pocket and placing the note in an envelope so he could give it to the waiting courier. "I probably won't be here for lunch," he said getting up and putting on the jacket he'd placed on the back of the chair where he'd been sitting. He then gave Anna a quick kiss, walked towards the door, handed the courier the envelope and left the apartment.

Anna was uneasy regarding Carl's meeting with the dictator. She knew Stalin must know how tough their journey had been. There was little about their lives that escaped his attention. She also felt defensive. If only Stalin had been able to see the train's bullet ridden interior and its fragmented glass everywhere, she nervously thought. She was relieved that Carl hadn't had to kill the Nazi guard who'd boarded the train. Surely Stalin would realize how difficult their ordeal had been. She walked across the room and stood at a window so she could watch Carl step into a car for the short ride delivering him to Stalin's office. Instead of taking the elevator, Carl quickly took the stairs leading to the dictator's office. A guard stood outside Stalin's opened office door. He watched Carl enter the room as the dictator extended a hand in greeting to Carl before closing the door behind them.

Stalin directed his friend to a chair before saying, "Your safe arrival here has caused a bit of a stir. German diplomatic sources have informed me that you would have been arrested if you hadn't crossed the border before they caught up with you."

Carl appeared somewhat pale before replying, "We were fired upon. I didn't dare return their fire. I was sure that if we were stopped again at another unscheduled checkpoint my family's journey to Moscow might have ended abruptly."

Stalin drew upon the pipe he had in his mouth. He then sat down in a chair opposite the one where Carl sat. "I know you did what was necessary to insure your family's safe arrival. No one should be criticized for trying to avoid danger. I've received a full report regarding your harrowing journey. In response to Nazi allegations that you were trying to evade checkpoints, I've told them that the whole matter appears to be blown out of proportion and that you, your wife and children were mistakenly fired upon by Nazi guards, who had they known who was aboard the train, would have held their fire. I'm not asking that the Nazis apologize" said Stalin a bit smugly. "I don't think I'd try to return to Romania any time soon. As you know, you and your family have been granted permanent asylum here. Since I've been so generous in extending such a welcome, I expect your loyalty in return. I also expect you to earn your keep by working for me. I commend you on returning Boris to Russia. I have no definitely plans regarding him right now. I'm not patient when it comes to dealing with men who are so cowardly that they can't trust their friends. I know Boris tried to run. I know he didn't want to return to Russia" said Stalin looking directly at the count. "If he hadn't returned to Russia, however unwillingly, I would have been forced to take extraordinary measures regarding him and those with whom he is closest: I should have him shot and his family exiled to Siberia. For the time being, I'll be lenient with him."

"Loyalty isn't bought", said Carl. "You must know that I could never work for the Nazis. My political leanings make it impossible for me to do so. I know I have no future in Romania so long as the Nazis are in control."

Stalin's face was grave. He watched sunlight stream in through a window before he got up from his chair and adjusted the shade. He felt uncomfortable with so much sunlight surrounding him. He wanted his life and future plans to remain in darkness. He also wanted to assure his friend that his loyalties could never be with Nazi Germany either. Since he knew he couldn't give the count that assurance, Stalin said nothing. Instead he changed the subject, "I want you and Anna to join me tonight for dinner."

"Anna has been looking forward to seeing you again. We'd be delighted to join you" he said relieved that their meeting had ended. Carl started to get up to leave but hesitated. He was searching for a sense of mutual loyalty. Was Stalin really his friend or was he just using him as he had so many people he'd had shot or sent to the camps? There was an uncomfortable silence between the men until Stalin opened a desk drawer and reached for a sealed envelope. He drew upon his pipe as he handed the envelope to the count. The envelope, addressed to Count Carl Zurofsky had been sent to the British Consulate who'd forwarded it to the dictator.

Stalin watched his friend open the sealed envelope. Enclosed was a letter and check from his stepfather Anton Bockev. Stalin placed his pipe in an ashtray and said. "After your gracious dinner party for the Nazi High Command representatives last month, Bockev and your mother immediately left for England. They were living in an apartment there when they realized that the Oxfordshire home you'd bought for your family was for sale. Bockev's purchase of it coincided with your family's flight to Russia. Since he didn't want to draw attention to your flight, Bockev didn't mail the letter until after he'd heard from inside sources that you'd safely arrived here in Moscow. "You can securely deposit the money from the sale of the house in any Moscow Bank" said Stalin as he observed Carl's reaction to the letter's news. Carl appeared to be pleased. Then smiling and leading the count forward he opened the office door for him, and said, "I'll have a car pick you and Anna up for dinner at 7 pm".

When Carl told Anna the news she was overjoyed. "Thank God they made it safely to England" she said sitting down and reading the letter Carl had handed to her. "We miss you and the children but we are relieved to learn that you have found safety and asylum in Russia. We pray that our family someday soon will be reunited. Until then we are caring for the house that was meant to be yours." Love Mother.

Anna placed the letter aside and said "The children will be so glad to know that we've heard from them. I'll show it to them after they've had their lessons. I think it's wonderful that Anton and your mother are living in the house that you bought for us."

"Bockev is just keeping it in the family" said the count a little sarcastically. Anna ignored Carl's remark by changing the subject and asking him how his meeting with Stalin went.

"It went as well as might be expected. He seemed to know the details involving our difficult flight to Moscow. I'm not sure if he approves of the way we managed to evade the Nazis."

"What did Stalin expect us to do? Get off the train so the Nazis could arrest us?"

The count smirked before saying to his wife, "Don't be so hard on Stalin I'm sure he understands what we were up against during our harrowing ordeal." Anna didn't comment.

"He asked after you and sends his regards. He wants us to join him for dinner tonight."

"It's about time he decided to meet with us" she said sounding relieved. "I wonder if a dinner invitation is for recognition of our loyalty."

The count's facial expression was uneasy. "I don't think Stalin ever finishes testing a person's loyalty to him."

It was about quarter to seven when Anna and Carl stepped into the car that chauffeured them to Stalin's apartments in a building opposite the one where they were staying. The early evening air was crisp and cold. Anna felt snug and comfortable in the heavy fur coat she wore. She ran her hands over the smooth fur and suddenly thought of all the wonderful beautiful wild things she and her family had left behind in their flight to Moscow. Anna felt guilty for leaving them behind. She felt even guiltier for wearing a coat made from one.

"If only we could step back in time" she thought wondering if she and her family ever again would hear the primeval howls of wolves at night or glimpse the beauty and mystery of creatures that lived on the fringes of the civilized world.

She seemed lost in thought when Carl asked her if she and the children had found the journal that her brother and sisters had hidden near their apartments so many years earlier. "We haven't had a chance to look for it yet. The boys have been busy getting involved in their studies and I've been encouraging them to do so too."

"You should realize how interested the boys would be if you could show them the journal. A family connection might be established" he said as the car stopped in front of Stalin's residence. "The children know almost nothing about your family. The journal would give them a glimpse into your childhood as well as that of your brother and sisters."

"Of course you're right" she said stepping from the car. "We'll look for the journal some stormy afternoon when the weather invites us to remain indoors."

As the couple walked towards Stalin's official residence, Anna carried in her hand a carefully wrapped package. She recalled that Stalin was a man who preferred informality. He also appreciated thoughtfulness. She was always the perfect guest as well as hostess. She hadn't forgotten to bring a gift along with her that evening. "Tell him it is from us both" she said handing the rare biography of Ivan the Terrible to Carl so he could give it to Stalin. Anna knew Stalin liked to receive interesting gifts and that he had read almost everything he could find on the life of the notorious Tsar.

The couple was surprised when Stalin opened the door for them. "Dear Koba" said Anna giving the dictator a hug as a guard stood behind him so Stalin could welcome his dinner guests.

"It is so good to see you again" he said. "I'm afraid I know all about your perilous journey. I'm so glad you and your family arrived here safely" he said as a guard took their coats from them and Stalin led the couple into the sitting room. He then opened a cabinet, and reached for a couple of glasses before pouring himself and the count a glass of vodka and handing Anna her usual glass of wine.

"I want your children to meet my daughter and youngest son sometime" he said turning to the couple. "At present they are at school near my country home. Some evening when they are here you must bring your children to dinner so they may meet them."

"I'm sure our sons would enjoy meeting your children" said the count handing Stalin the present they'd brought with them.

"Hmm-- The biography of Ivan the Terrible, a favorite Tsar of mine. Thank you," he said.

Following dinner, the evening spent with the dictator proved to be cordial but host and guests were guarded in their conversation with one another. Although nothing sinister had been proven regarding Urhart's death, Stalin had heard about it and knew it had created a bit of a stir. He nervously drew upon his pipe as he and his guests discussed trivial matters that might be left unsaid. Anna shifted uneasily in her chair. Before the evening ended, she wanted to ask Stalin a question of personal relevance and importance. "We hid it behind a bookcase in our old schoolroom", she said telling Stalin about the childhood journal. "Do you know if it was confiscated along with my family's other papers?" she asked. Stalin hesitated before getting up from his chair then saying, "I believe you may find your journal in a Kremlin archive. If you'll check with our archivist I'm sure he'll be able to show it to you. In fact, I'll personally request that the archivist contact you so that you and your family may see the journal." Carl and Anna thanked Stalin for dinner as he led them to the door, bid them good night, and a guard handed the couple their coats.

It was only after they were in their own apartments that Anna alluded to the journal by saying, "I'm glad I took the initiative to ask Stalin about it.

I dared not ask him for the return of it. I know the journal might be looked upon now as property belonging to the state but I thought Stalin's generosity might override the issue".

"You mustn't grumble" said Carl. "You have other family souvenirs. Be grateful for them." Anna sighed as Carl changed the subject, and said to her that at times during the evening he found Stalin to be subdued.

"If he seemed a little distant tonight, I think it's because the matter regarding Urhart's death has become an embarrassment for him. Stalin wants to know the truth." she replied.

"What do you mean?"

"Is he really dead?" she asked pouring him a hot cup of tea he hadn't asked for. "I'm not going to rest easy tonight until you give me a straightforward answer."

"Who are you talking about?" he asked, throwing an extra log on the hearth fire in their sitting room.

The expression on Anna's face was insistent. "Dracula who else" she said placing her warm cup of tea and saucer down and setting them on the table in front of her.

Carl didn't want to confide in anyone regarding what he knew about Dracula. He didn't think it safe to divulge a family secret to anyone not even to his wife. She was only a relative by marriage and not one by blood.

"He's still alive isn't he?"

"Don't be absurd. Dracula is dead. Vampires don't survive after a stake is driven into their hearts."

Carl didn't want to tell Anna what he'd learned. He didn't want her to know that he knew Dracula had taken the form of a wolf the night the stake had been driven into a vampire's heart but not Dracula's heart.

"Dracula is alive" she said gazing into Carl's eyes for the answer to her question yet sounding breathless and insistent. "He has to be alive."

"Yes" said her husband finally. "Dracula isn't the diabolical being fiction has made him out to be. An escape from annihilation has made Dracula into a better being. Dracula is committed to saving the things in life he feels are most worthwhile saving." Carl knew what Dracula's priorities were. The world or more importantly the natural world had to be saved. There would be wars in the 20th C. and beyond. Preservation of the natural world was the one means by which all life including human life in this physical world might be saved. "If there is another war men will either have to fight or die. No one will be able to escape into nature's protective wilderness. No one will be out of the path of devastation if war wreaks havoc on everything."

"Do you suppose Dracula killed Urhart because he wanted to frighten the Nazis enough so that they might flee back to Germany, and leave the pristine wilderness surrounding our home?" She asked.

"Dracula is our friend. He obviously is guarding turf that he believes to be ours and his. I doubt if anyone not even Dracula would be able to scare the Nazis from our home and country though. Their presence appears to be a fixed one".

"Dracula is a fixed presence too" she said. "He is a protector and a friend of the forest. He is not an evil being if he voluntarily has taken on the image of other life forms possibly in an effort to convince others that we all are connected to the natural world and its inhabitants, and we must stop civilization from destroying man's natural heritage."

Carl considered what his wife had said to him. "Since Dracula is a solitary being, and since he can't move freely within the human realm, he would have had to have drawn close to nature. The natural world is the only society in which Dracula freely can move. Carl seemed earnest as he searched for the right words." Perhaps the natural world is the only society in which any of us can freely move. That's why we all must strive to protect it."

"What if Dracula fails? What will become of the life we've come to know together? Worse still what will happen to people everywhere?"

Carl was thoughtful before he answered his wife. "People will become victims of power struggles and territorial disputes continuing without end until men realize there can be no peace in dominating the will of others? Such dominance only ends in pitiful struggles for human rights that become obscured as the natural world and personal privacy disappear and the power struggle among nations wreaks havoc on nature and the individual. Our children will have no place to flee to in such a world".

Anna rested her weary head against Carl's shoulder. They both knew the world around them was growing too fast, and that vast tracts of land that once had been wilderness were disappearing at an alarming rate. "When human expansion continues to grow without check or balance there only can be more violence as men fight for territorial rights" said Carl. Anna knew neither of them wanted to live in such a world. It was certainly not the world they wanted their children to inherit. They dared say no more to each other. They knew they couldn't stop the inevitable any more than they could stop a war. For a few minutes they silently sat on the sofa in front of the hearth.

Carl hesitated to throw another log on the fire. Instead he wanted to watch comforting embers die in the wake of cold impending reality. When he finally got up so he could stir the fire's dying embers, he gazed down at Anna. She had fallen asleep in front of the dwindling fire's warmth. The room and environment around them eventually would grow cold. He didn't want to disturb her. He didn't want her to face the cold reality slowly encompassing them. He finally threw another log on the fire then lay down beside her and covered her with his body as she slept unaware of his protective presence.

Chapter Nineteen

While they slept, Dracula wandered the halls of a Romanian mansion recently abandoned by owners who feared the Nazi presence. The vampire relished the darkness to accomplish what he knew was impossible for him to do in daylight. He knew he had to behave with utmost caution. Since the world no longer believed in him he wanted people to continue to think that he was mere myth or legend. The aura of disbelief surrounding him enabled him to do almost anything possible for a vampire.

For the time being, Dracula realized he had to distance himself from the count's estate. Urhart's death had raised suspicions and some wondered if he had caused it? He vowed that he wouldn't set foot on his family's estate unless an emergency called for him to do so. He was determined that in the count's absence no one would suspect that he was guarding Carl's home. Yet if another Nazi official dared to take up residence in the count's home during Carl's absence, Dracula would intervene. Such a residency only could be temporary.

Dracula stepped from the mansion's cold dungeon and relished the cold night air. Tonight he decided he wouldn't take the form of anything other than himself. He didn't need to do so. There was no moon. He felt secure within the blanket of darkness surrounding him. He knew he'd been cruel during his life as a vampire. Tonight Dracula felt guilty for taking the form of any animal. Dracula loved animals especially wolves. He understood the count's affection for them. They lived close to the earth. Yet men were afraid of them. Perhaps it was because the men who hunted wolves resented their freedom, and dignity. Wolves distanced themselves from men. Yet they were loyal to any human who showed them kindness. Tonight Dracula wouldn't even want to take the form of a bat, poor creatures---so reviled by some men for no reason at all. He wouldn't want to bring more condemnation to any species that was already persecuted. Even snakes had his sympathy. There weren't too many snakes in Romania's rather cold climate. But often men would conjure up some reason for blaming an animal for any unexplained misfortune.

The night air was cold but tonight Dracula felt strangely warm in the knowledge that the evil he'd embodied slowly was slipping away from him. He was becoming something he hadn't been for awhile. For the first time in many centuries, he was aware of what it was like to be benign. He had no thirst for blood tonight. He wanted merely to breathe and feel the cool night air embrace him like a comforting shroud. The cold was his warmth and the night sounds his music and song. The distant hooting of an owl and the calls of wolves told him he was home. He was among the things he'd always loved and wanted to protect but couldn't. Perhaps he'd kept himself alive these hundreds of years because he had a mission to accomplish.

Dracula wanted somehow to change the world by making it a better place. He would do so by opposing the enemy in such a manner that those who would want to fight him would discover they couldn't.

Dracula spread his wide black cape around himself as falling snow fell around the cape's folds. He smiled with inner satisfaction. The look of cruelty that always had been in that smile had disappeared. He knew Carl and Anna had found only temporary refuge from danger. He knew war eventually would break out in Russia. Dracula was determined that he would help save and protect Carl and his family for like him they appreciated the wondrous beauty of nature.

Dracula continued to walk along and listen to the snow crunch beneath his boots. He contemplated all the things he wanted to accomplish. He vowed he would taste no blood from anyone until he'd helped make the world a better place. His sheer desire to live long enough to instigate the changes he wanted to make in his environment kept him strong in body and soul.

Ah yes his soul, what had happened to his soul? Dracula dared not contemplate the possibility that perhaps his soul already was damned to eternity. He would change that. The omnipotent power from above would see how he'd made amends and would recognize what an instrument of good Dracula had become and forgive him for his sins. Someday Dracula would be known only for his goodness in saving the lives of others.

Somehow Dracula had to meet Carl. He had to assure him that he was his protector, and that no harm would come to him or his family. Dracula smiled the smile of inner satisfaction. He didn't want to live forever. He'd done too much in one interminably long lifetime and he was tired. He had just enough superhuman strength and courage in his supernatural body to live long enough to help keep civilization from crumbling. He would show Carl how to achieve the same things he'd been able to do in life. Yet he would tell him that it wasn't necessary for him to become a vampire to do them.

It would be daylight in several hours. Dracula was tired. He had to rest. Instead of blood he would drink milk but he still needed darkness to accomplish the things he wanted to do in the days and weeks ahead. It was beginning to snow again. Was he becoming something akin to a mere mortal? He felt almost weak. He could feel the biting cold penetrate his thin body like a sword piercing armor. Tonight he again would return to the mansion outside the village and seek comfort near the furnace he'd stocked with coal. His heart was no longer cold. It was warm and Dracula was only going to drink the sweet warm milk of kindness that he now searched for almost on a daily basis.

When he made his way back to the mansion and found the hidden entrance he used to enter and leave the building, he stopped to gaze at himself in a mirror. His appearance had changed. His eyes were no longer full of hatred. His entire appearance had taken on a gentler demeanor. He hardly recognized himself. Yet he knew he must rest.

In the evening when he awoke from his slumber he would write the count a letter. He would tell him how important it was for them to meet. Carl would understand the urgency of the request. Dracula found the coffin where he habitually rested and wrapped the blanket around his tired thin body before listening to the rooster crow. How he longed to be part of the world of sunlight. For so long that world had been denied him. Before he died he wanted to enter that world again. He wanted to be part of it so he could watch the sun's brilliance glance off newly fallen snow. He wanted to watch the snow slowly dissolve in the penetrating sun's rays foreshadowing spring's brilliant foliage. He wanted to walk through the forest with all its majestic daylight wonder and understand the reason for his very being. He and all men were created only to appreciate the natural wonders of the Creator's hand.

Dracula felt humble. He didn't want to be an instrument of evil anymore. Yet he'd used violence for so long to get his way that he hardly understood any other means of dealing with the world. Dracula had chosen the living death within the coffin and cheated life. He didn't want to go on half living as he now was doing. He wanted to escape instead into the world he'd once known as a boy centuries ago. As he slept within his coffin he remembered what it was like to be young and he remembered all the wonderful things about living. The comfort of friends and a daily routine full of the insignificant yet fascinating minutiae that made everyday life so worthwhile were Dracula's dream fantasies.

Dracula's slumber was disturbed only by the noises he heard outside the mansion's thick dungeon walls. He could hear people laughing, talking and arguing but those noises were muffled by something else. In the distance he heard the whistle of a train that carried one towards the pain and reality of living as a mortal. Dracula ignored that train whistle. He preferred to travel aboard a vampire train where he could escape from the real world and find the timeless mystery of night hanging upon the dark fringes of eternity. That train took him to far off unreachable regions. That train offered him a choice to accomplish something truly heinous or something of unimaginable and incomparable goodness and beauty. Tonight Dracula traveled aboard the vampire train drawing him upward where stars fell around him in all their splendor and galactic mystery. Tonight Dracula rode the vampire train across the heavens and drank in the moon's dim glow that like dewdrops fell upon him until he awoke from that mystery and majesty and almost touched the forbidden garment of light's early morning daylight. Dracula preferred that spectacular and majestic vampire train above all others. Yet all too often Dracula had traveled aboard a vampire train that had taken him to strange out of the way places where out of a sense of duty, and the need to accomplish some heinous deed Dracula had ridden. Today Dracula was feeling guilty for ever riding such a train. He was feeling guilty for all the negative energy he'd wasted in the years when he could have done something really good with his life. He knew he had to reverse the direction of the vampire train that he rode. He knew he had to stay aboard the train that drew him towards the incomparable beauty and perfection of the nighttime's heaven.

He wanted to love others even though in the past others had been cruel to him. He wanted to use his newly found positive energy before his gaunt haggard from simply disintegrated into dust. Dracula was going to wipe the slate clean. He was going to forget the past. The one way he could start life anew, the one way he could make amends for all his past mistakes was to seek out and befriend the family descended from him. Dracula knew how trying Count Zurofsky's life had been. He knew too well how the count and his wife had had to curry favor with Stalin's regime if only to survive and insure that their two sons were protected. Dracula was sympathetic with their plight. He knew how evil the world could be. He understood evil in others and this understanding grew out of his own terrible familiarity with evil yet powerful men. When he'd been a young man, Dracula had known power. He'd felt the only way to remain in control, to remain in power was to utilize evil. He understood men like Stalin. He wanted even more to understand a man like Carl. Dracula was proud that this descendant of his had shown such courage in the face of injustice. He slowly drifted off to sleep trying to devise a way he could have a face to face meeting with the Count. As he slept, Dracula began to dream. It was a pleasant dream. A dream of a new life: a life he had been denied because of evil. Dracula's sleep was deep. It was a struggle for him to awake. He had to keep going. Like a butterfly emerging from a cocoon, Dracula wanted to spread wide his black cape and embrace a world he'd forgotten. He wanted to become mortal or at least live like one.

Chapter Twenty

Several weeks passed. Anna and her husband were enjoying their morning coffee together when an attendant said there was a messenger at the door with a letter for the count. Carl rose from the breakfast table and retrieved the letter from the messenger. He then returned to the table and opened the letter before slowly reading it. The person who had sent the letter hadn't signed his name as Dracula. Despite the notorious vampire's effort to hide his identity his descendant knew it was he. Only Dracula could have had the intelligence and cunning to do what the count soon would learn his ancestor was planning to do.

Anna placed her coffee cup in its saucer and gazed across the table at Carl. "What's wrong?" she asked. "You look like you've just seen a ghost" she said glancing down at the letter her husband was holding in his hand."

"I haven't seen a ghost. I've heard from someone who might be even more startling than a ghost" he said crumpling up the letter in his hand. Anna got up from where she was sitting. She walked towards a window and pulled the drapes apart allowing morning daylight to stream in upon them. Then turning to her husband she said quietly, "Let me see the letter." Carl didn't want Anna to see the letter. He didn't want her to become party to something from which he wanted her to remain distanced.

"He knows where we are and he wants you to contact him, doesn't he?" she said.

"Yes" he replied quietly.

"You must contact him. You must finally meet him if only to satisfy a curiosity that is gnawing at your soul and his."

Carl didn't want to admit to Anna that he wanted to meet with a being the world still reviled. "Dracula doesn't have a soul" he replied sounding insincere. "If he does have one it's so dark that it's not worth saving."

"You mustn't say that" she said walking over to Carl and facing him. "You know you don't really feel that way or else you and your ancestors wouldn't have helped to hide and shelter Dracula all these years."

Carl knew his wife was right. Something inside him told him that it would be alright to face Dracula, that something positive might emerge from the meeting.

Carl thought of the many times he'd had to face down evil. He thought of how often he'd lived with terror almost on a daily basis. Now he would face down fear once more. He had to trust him. He had to believe that Dracula was going to help him and his family through the terrible ordeal that awaited them.

"When and where will you meet him?" asked Anna, her voice a mere whisper.

"He's already here in Moscow. I'll have to go alone" he said quietly. "He's told me where we should meet."

Anna said nothing in reply to her husband's remark. She knew Carl would never tell her where he and Dracula would have their meeting. Instead, she gazed at the crumpled letter in his hand and asked, "Did you always believe he was alive?"

"I've always presumed so. My father always told me Dracula still lived as one of the undead. I wasn't sure until now."

Anna wasn't sure if a meeting with Dracula would solve their family's current problems. Yet she wanted her husband to meet with him because she sympathized with him. Like Dracula, Anna and her family understood what it was like to hide or to be on the run. She wanted to believe that Dracula, this supernatural being she thought she understood, could somehow help them stop running.

"I always fear for the children" she said softly. "There is no safe place for us to run to anywhere anymore."

"Don't say that", said Carl thoughtfully. "We are safe because we have each other. Dracula is my ancestor. We are blessed because I believe that Dracula will lend us his support."

Anna was pleased. Her husband was seeing things her way in regard to Dracula "Perhaps you are right" she said smiling a secretive smile.

"Perhaps there is now someone other than our friend Stalin who will be able to lead us out of harm's way", said Carl feeling almost elated by the realization. "The hour is fast approaching when the world that seems so out of joint may be torn to pieces as powerful ruthless men strive for dominance in it. Our association with a notorious vampire may be our only means to escape domination and slavery".

"Please don't say that" she said. Anna knew Stalin had betrayed and destroyed anyone he believed was in the least way disloyal to him. Anna knew that she and her husband only had been loyal to Stalin. She wanted to believe that Stalin could never turn on them, that he always would protect them, and if need be help them escape danger.

Carl could see how pale Anna appeared when he took her by the shoulders and made her face him. "Stalin has always been in love with you. Don't think I don't realize that he still wants you. You must never let him know that you no longer love him."

Anna wouldn't tell her husband that she still loved Stalin. He wouldn't understand. She knew she owed what little freedom she had gotten in life partly to Stalin.

"Please don't say any more" said Anna breaking away from Carl and tearfully leaving the room. Carl didn't follow her.

* * * *

It was a dark rainy evening when Carl took a lonely walk by himself to a familiar park not far from the Kremlin. The wind blew the cold rain sideways as the leaves that stuck to the pavement crushed beneath his feet. There were no street lights surrounding them when Dracula and Carl met behind the statue of a rider and horse. Rain dripped from the bronze statue and fell to the ground in neat little puddles covering up any footprints or evidence that a meeting was taking place.

"I want to help you and your family" said the tall gaunt man wrapped in a black cloak with hood hiding both face and features. "This man Stalin who you and your wife look to as some sort of a savior is a cruel man. Yet he has shown you, along with the pain, much kindness and goodness. You must perceive him as a friend and not as an enemy.

"You have no choice but to partake of his hospitality for the time being. When the opportunity arises, and one soon will arise, you may leave the confines of your comfortable Kremlin refuge and escape."

"No one can escape Stalin's treachery" said Carl sounding tired and hoarse. He trembled inside the rain drenched trench coat he wore over the thick sweater and trousers with cuffs already encrusted in mud.

"You are moving in your own circle of evil and not Stalin's if you believe you can't escape the treachery. Trust me. I know well the road from the past. I've seen the future. It will be only a matter of time before Russia is at war with Germany. Russia and the allied forces will win the war, but the struggle will be great. Stalin will emerge as a victor but he will forever be remembered as a cruel and ruthless tyrant who mercilessly drove his people to gain the victory they so needed. There will be few opportunities during the war for you and your family to escape from him. You mustn't try to do so. Stalin has always befriended you. You must return his friendship by remaining loyal to him. Yet your safety and future is uncertain if you remain in Russia. These are evil times. The conflict between men and nations is cruel but not Stalin's cruelty. Like you, he too is caught up in evil's maelstrom. Like you, Stalin is vulnerable to evil. Evil will attempt to destroy him. Evil will attempt to destroy us all. You and your family must find a pathway to freedom away from the evil that surrounds you. I have come to show you the way. Until then, you won't always see me but you will be aware of my constant presence. I will not leave you alone to face the world's treachery."

"How can I be sure that we can trust you?" asked Carl following after Dracula who had abruptly turned from him indicating that their short meeting had concluded.

"You have no other choice" he said calling from behind as rain pelted down over the hood the vampire wore covering his face. In the darkness Carl wanted to confront him again. He wanted to believe Dracula was real and not some spy sent by Stalin to test his loyalty. It was too dark. He couldn't see the vampire's image. Instead, Dracula hesitated, turned around and walked back towards the count. He reached deep into a pocket and pulled out a jewel encrusted ruby ring. The ring had been in the count's family for centuries but had been lost nearly 100 years earlier. "Surely you will recognize this ring. I wore it in the portrait you have of me that hangs beside the staircase."

Carl took the ring Dracula offered him as the vampire melting into night's mist and darkness said, "I will contact you again soon". Carl had many questions of his ancestor. He was dissatisfied that they remained unanswered. He started to pursue Dracula but was deterred by his warning.

"Don't try to follow me" he said, his voice muffled by a darkness so deep that it hardly seemed as if he and the count could have found their way through the shadows. Only the priceless ring that now was in his possession was proof that Carl had at last met his famous ancestor.

"Will he help us?" Anna breathlessly asked him when Carl showed his wife the vampire's ring. She starred at the ring before examining it and returning it to Carl. She was sure the ring must be some sort of symbolic gesture of good will as well as a gift. Carl appeared emotionless and almost indecisive and unwilling to tell his wife that Dracula was ready to help evacuate them.

Since he was not a man to enlist help offered from others in situations that required careful consideration, Carl remained strangely unresponsive to Anna's question. "We need not run at least not yet" he said quietly as if something inside him was telling him that Stalin had the capability to become the victor and not the vanquished.

Anna sensed the reason for her husband's hesitancy in responding to her question. They both knew Stalin well enough to realize that he would lead Russia forward in a valiant campaign against the Nazi aggressors if he had the support of his party.

"If Dracula has a plan to help us escape from Russia we might discover ourselves prisoners of the Nazis in transit to one of the camps. Our only hope is to remain here," she said quietly and thoughtfully.

"Dracula is no fool. Your fears in that regard won't be realized. Dracula will know when the time is ripe for our departure from Russia. We will wait for circumstances to come about that will thrust us forward" he replied.

Chapter Twenty-one

In the several years that they had been living at the Kremlin, the children had grown up. Ivan and Carl Nicholas now were students at Moscow University yet they remained close to their parents and lived at the Kremlin where the advent of war slowly continued to close in on them. Anna and her family rarely saw Stalin anymore. He spent most of the time at his country home away from Moscow and tried to ignore the German troops concentrating on the Russian border. Stalin had firmly maintained that Hitler wasn't going to attack Russia in 1941 but he had been wrong. The Soviet-German Non Aggression Pact was about to become a worthless agreement.

"The night envelops us. There is no daylight now" said Anna turning to her husband. "The darkness of night complements war's bloody vocation".

"Stalin is moving in darkness if that's what you mean", said Carl. "He ignores the continuous German reconnaissance flights over Soviet territory. He thinks that perhaps the flights are mere threats being used to extract concessions from him. General Zhukov has asked Stalin for orders to fight the Nazis, but Stalin still hopes that the war might be settled in peaceful terms".

"I won't agree with Stalin's critics who say Stalin might be drawn to the twisted Nazi regime. We know him too well for that", said Anna. Carl had to agree with her. They knew the dictator too well to believe that Stalin could ever become a Nazi ally. Yet Carl questioned Stalin's actions. With the collapse of the Polish state Stalin's loyalty had wavered. When Ribbentrop had visited Moscow, it was agreed that Germany should get all ethnic Poland but at Stalin's insistence, Lithuania would go to Russia. "Stalin is trying to convince himself that the pact with Nazi Germany is not just a non aggression pact but one of friendship" said Carl bitterly. "He has sacrificed men who have told him the truth about Hitler's warlike intention towards Russia by having them shot or sent to the camps,"

"He has to be buying for time with the Nazis" whispered Anna as they softly talked together and strolled alone amidst Kremlin Gardens.

"Is Stalin really buying time for Russia or is he sacrificing Russia and her people?"

Anna gazed at Carl disapprovingly before she said, "You know Stalin better than that."

Carl hung his head in silence. He knew Stalin would eventually push the Russian people towards victory over the Nazi invaders. There had to be another reason for Stalin's reluctance to enter into war. The great sieges of Stalingrad and Leningrad had not yet taken place yet they would become desperate battles that only revealed Stalin's and the Russian people's determination to be the victor against an unforgiving adversary.

Through secret channels of information to which Carl had access, he knew as did Stalin which German personages were opposed to Ribbentrop's pact policies of collaboration. "Stalin believes that only factions within the German military and not Hitler himself are advocating war with Russia" said Carl.

"Stalin continues to play a game of deception." answered Anna.

A few days later following the couple's quiet discussion, the deception game soon was to end. Carl learned that Stalin finally had taken a bold course of action when the Nazis tried to direct Soviet support in a war against Britain. The final break had come when hoping to draw military expansion away from Britain and towards the Persian Gulf Stalin joined the Tripartite Pact with Italy and Japan. Hitler never formally signed the agreement that had other conditions attached to it. But Stalin who'd approved the pact had shown his hand. Operation Barbarossa, Hitler's invasion of the Soviet Union had begun. During those critical hours Stalin turned a cold shoulder towards Carl and his family. He refused to meet with the count. Stalin was too preoccupied with his own political impending downfall to give anything else a thought. He knew he needed the support of his party before he could declare war with Nazi Germany. He didn't have it. He knew as did they that Russia might be entering a war they couldn't win. Stalin remained in seclusion at his country home where he sat in a room's dark corner waiting and half expecting his comrades to come and arrest him. When they finally came to Comrade Stalin he seemed distant and downcast. "Why have you come?" he asked, with head bowed and eyes gazing downward.

"We have come, Comrade Stalin to ask that you form a Supreme Defense Council so Russia may declare war against Nazi Germany", said a party spokesman.

"Alright" agreed Stalin slowly getting up from where he sat yet seeming shaken by the visit. He reached for the pipe he always carried in his pocket and began filling it with tobacco. "I will immediately form one."

The new political turn of events had been too slow in coming for the count and his family. Ivan and Carl Nicholas had already withdrawn from classes at Moscow University. Their parents were afraid that anything might happen now that the clouds of war and uncertainly encompassed them. "We must prepare to leave at any time" said their father. His sons wondered what sort of an evacuation plan their father had in mind but refrained from asking. They knew their father was feeling desperate and that he had no such plan. The family lived from day to day hoping to work something out. Then just when they were about to give up hope, a plan came about in an unexpected way.

It was nearly dusk one day when Carl and Anna were strolling along a Kremlin walk and Anna noticed a wall nearly obscured by foliage. The thick wall attached to the Kremlin looked very ancient and apparently had been there for centuries. "I don't know why Stalin doesn't have the wall torn down" Anna remarked. "It serves no purpose at all" and then she remembered a rumor she'd heard prior to the revolution. "During the 15th century a wall was supposed to have been built hiding a secret entrance leading to an underground passageway so that political prisoners, sometimes within the Tsar's own family might escape the Kremlin. In more recent times the passageway's location had been forgotten but I believe we may be looking at the ancient wall that hides it", she said pointing.

Carl was astounded at what she'd told him. "So that's how Dracula came into our midst. There must be a passageway behind the stones" he said.

"He had to have traveled that way. For him to have taken any other route would have been too dangerous even for a vampire", she replied.

No sooner had Anna finished speaking when she was startled to see the vampire standing in front of them. "Now that you know how I enter your world I've come to lead you from your present circumstances. Even though you have Stalin's protection it is unsafe for you to remain here."

"I shall lead you and your family on your long journey to safety this evening. Meet me here at 12:00 midnight. I will take you into my world. I assure you no one will follow us."

"We will meet you. I promise." said the count, his voice trembling and sounding hesitant.

* * * *

"I wish we didn't have to run" said Ivan, who like Carl Nicholas was saddened at having to leave friends and girlfriends behind. "When do we ever stop running?" he asked his younger brother who placed a sympathetic hand on Ivan's shoulder. Both sons knew their parents were distraught over having to look for an uncertain haven. If they were dubious regarding Dracula's reason for helping them, desperation was thrusting the family forward and like their parents, Ivan and Carl Nicholas stood ready to leave their present surroundings.

All wore heavy hooded cloaks and boots as they awaited Dracula's arrival. Like the vampire, they appeared to be hiding not just their identity but their very existence behind night's comforting shroud. When Dracula finally appeared almost out of nowhere, he stood behind them and spoke in an even soft voice as Anna who had sensed his presence turned and recognized him. Even though his face was heavily hooded to conceal his identity, Dracula didn't have to reveal it. The family knew who he was and they weren't afraid of him. Dracula made a courtly bow in Anna's direction as the little dog in her arms trembled but didn't bark.

When Dracula finally dropped his hood revealing his identity, the count cautiously gazed into his ancestor's dark eyes and felt as if he were being drawn into a tunnel from which there could be no escape. Dracula could sense but ignored the count's uneasiness with what might lie ahead in the journey. Instead he used his superhuman strength to remove a heavy stone blocking the wall opening so the count and his family could follow him through it. Then after they were standing on stairs leading from the opening in the wall, Dracula sealed up the wall opening behind them and they descended stairs that twisted then turned and finally led to a passageway taking them from the Kremlin and beyond.

The lanterns and torches the family carried with them flickered in the darkness as Dracula carefully stayed ahead of everyone before saying, "There is plenty of food and water placed for you to eat and drink along the corridor. Hopefully the sealed food containers found along the way will discourage rats from invading them before we do."

Anna grimaced as she thought of the possibility of rats invading the food supply. She also realized that she was too nervous to consider whether she or her family would be able to eat or drink anything during their perilous journey.

Her agitation was further exacerbated by gruesome encounters with the unexpected. In terror, Anna clutched Carl's arm when they encountered a grisly sight. Lying on the passageway's floor was the ancient skeleton of one whose skull had been crushed by pursuers leaving behind the weapon used to decapitate their victim.

The damp passageway was forbidding in other ways too. Dripping water seeping through the ceiling had cause fungi and foul smelling mold to grow upon walls, and the acrid air the family breathed seemed unhealthy.

All sense of time seemed to be suspended in this strange cavernous underworld where bats slept in corner crevices or an occasional underground animal that had dug into the earth snarled then quickly disappeared from view. Night was day and day was night. It really didn't matter. There was no reason to check a calendar to record earth's daily movement. None of that seemed relevant in this environment where reality seemed to merge with illusion and the unreal took on the aura of reality.

When a small hole in the passageway's ceiling created a healthy oasis away from the stagnating claustrophobic misery of their environment, Ivan pointed to the beauty of moss, ferns and strange flowers never before seen growing beneath light streaming from above. Huge mushrooms grew in profusion away from direct light and evidence of life seemed everywhere in this corner chamber of near darkness.

Dracula stepped back from the light streaming from the passageway's ceiling as if he were backing away from a lightning strike. He seemed more afraid of the ceiling light than he was by the explosions and noise above them.

"Hurry" said Carl as earth around them trembled and the sound of explosions in the war zone above prodded them forward. Carl wasn't sure if his family was safe in the strange passageway environment. Dracula assured him that they were safe even behind enemy lines as small rocks continued to fall around them. Carl didn't want to hang around to find out. Even though they were exhausted, he knew he and his family needed to get away from the mayhem above them.

Within days of continuous walking and listening to the noise of explosives from above, the manmade passageway had ended and in its place the natural beauty of a wonderland unfolded. Ivan and Carl Nicholas raised their lanterns and directed their light on myriad hues of lavender, exotic pink and white crystals growing like some petrified garden surrounding them. In this strange otherworldly environment the chaos of war and turmoil had simply melted. In its place was a subterranean cavity and cathedral of unmatched beauty.

"Why we've stepped from an underground passageway into a miraculous cave" said Carl who marveled at the cave's natural splendor.

"But where does the cave lead to?" asked Anna seeming frightened and uncertain.

Dracula didn't answer her question. Instead he signaled for them to follow him.

Like a mirage that had slowly dissolved, the marvelous cave behind them had melted. Before them in the dim lantern light were stone stairs winding upward and etched into the side of the passageway.

The family stared at the wall in amazement before Dracula finally said rather cryptically "All good things must come to a close". Then reaching for one of the bottles he'd reserved along the way he poured wine from it into glasses.

Anna sipped with gratitude the well aged burgundy but she was hesitant to eat the cheese and bread that had been preserved in tins. She wanted to ask Dracula how long the tins had been there waiting to be opened but she was feeling so faint and exhausted she decided to eat whatever food was available to her.

Dracula knew Anna was tired from their harrowing journey. It wasn't just the food she found almost unable to eat. The pathway she and her family traversed seemed to be going nowhere. As if reading her thoughts, he finally said to her, "It won't be much longer. You will see daylight soon and you will find yourselves rejuvenated and ready to embark on another venture.

"Now that you have climbed these stone steps you will board a train that will breach the distance between time and place." Dracula had hardly finished speaking when the family saw before them an underground tunnel and a mysterious looking train waiting to transport them beneath land and mountain range.

"The train will protect you from the terror of light's forbidding glare" he said to Carl as he and his family boarded the steel futuristic streamlined vehicle appearing to be a replica of another time and place. The family uncertainly took their seats aboard the amazing train and gazed around them. The train's occupants, some appearing old and others young, looked like ordinary passengers aboard any train yet they seemed oblivious to the family's presence as if there was some sort of unknown barrier preventing them from communicating with them. Anna wondered if what she and her family were experiencing aboard the train wasn't illusion similar to the hypnotic dreams she'd had during other encounters with Dracula. "Don't try to speak with them" warned the vampire before taking a seat directly in front of Carl and Anna. If they were moving in a hypnotic dream, the strange train, even though seeming to be illusion, delivered the count's family to a destination they might otherwise have found impossible to reach.

When they stepped from it, they realized the train miraculously had transported them to familiar looking territory. Anna didn't need to say anything to Carl regarding the validity of their strange journey. He didn't need to be told but he was rather sure that the amazing journey beneath land had to have been some mesmeric illusion devised by Dracula to get them safely through the most harrowing and frightening leg of their journey. "I won't ask how we got here" he said turning to Dracula who told him that they had crossed the Russian border, and the castle home the family had left with such misgiving now was only meters away from where they stood.

She placed her arm in Carl's and asked in astonishment, "How did we get here so quickly?"

"The earth has strange secrets. It offers detours to those who wander its hidden passages. It twists and turns but if you have faith it finally takes you alive and safe to where you want to be," answered the vampire.

"For a few days you and your family may rest within the confines of your home without disturbance from those who would rob you of your peace and security."

"Surely our home is being occupied by the Nazis" said Anna contradicting the vampire.

"No, everyone has fled from your castle. They are afraid of becoming one of the undead if they remain in it too long."

Carl listened to what Dracula had to say then asked, in a tremulous voice, "Will we become like the undead too?"

"Please, you must trust me" replied Dracula assuring the count that the family's castle sojourn was only a temporary haven on the way toward a new land.

"You are my descendant. Your family's name and good reputation must go before you. It is your duty to undo the evil that for centuries has been associated with me."

The count bowed to Dracula's gracious words and reminded him that whatever evil he had done was nothing in comparison to the evil now sweeping over Europe and the world."Before we entered your dark corridor we were vulnerable to evil beyond measure. For days we have safely walked a corridor that has led us to the threshold of the beloved home we had to abandon" he said.

"Your home is yours to keep. You may visit it only temporarily now. Someday you will return to it permanently. First you must re-enter a world of turmoil but I assure you that you will find haven there and wherever else your treacherous journey takes you" he replied.

The shadowy outline of the castle's turrets was visibly etched against the sky as a half moon cast a pale ghostly light along a narrow stone pathway leading towards the family's magnificent ancestral home.

As Carl and his family approached the castle entranceway, Dracula warned everyone that it was necessary to take precaution and to use the hidden underground entrance that he habitually used. "We mustn't take the chance of being seen" he warned, removing a huge stone slab from the ground that revealed the hidden stairway he used to enter and exit the castle's passageway.

Once they had emerged from the passageway and were standing within the castle confines, Anna asked Dracula if there was any food left in the pantry fit for human consumption." There are canned goods, tea, flour, powdered milk and eggs, sugar, shortening and enough food to sustain you until you and your family begin another leg of a journey ultimately leading you to your final destination ", he replied.

Anna was adamant when Dracula mentioned future travel plans."I don't think my family wants to go anywhere until we've had a little water and luxury lather. We haven't been able to bathe lately, and we need to change into fresh clothes."

"There is still running water and you should be able to find soap that I've saved and hidden for your use. You mustn't invite curiosity by turning on any lights" he warned. "Candlelight will have to suffice. The old wood stove can be used for heat or to warm food."

When Anna walked up the stairs and entered rooms she was relieved to find clothes still hanging in closets even if they were a bit out of date. As for her sons, she knew they had outgrown the clothes in their closets. The count would have to share his leftover wardrobe with them.

The family was so grateful to find such basic necessities surrounding them that they forgot to look around for the unseen and unusual. The following morning when Anna pulled aside a curtain in a downstairs room near a door, she was surprised to discover an envelope lying on the floor and just inside the door. After tearing the sealed letter open, she was astounded to realize that it was from Stalin. He knew about the Kremlin's hidden passageway and their miraculous escape from Moscow. His spies who'd infiltrated Romanian Nazi occupied territory near their castle estate (if needed) would assist them in their planned escape to England.

Anna gasped. "Boris will be accompanying you. I've given him the opportunity to help you and your family in your perilous journey."

When she showed Carl Stalin's letter Anna was furious with Stalin for wanting to make them take Boris with them. "How can Boris possibly be of assistance to us?" she asked.

"I don't think Stalin believes that Boris will be able to help us at all. I think he is testing our loyalty," he replied.

Anna was thoughtful for a moment before quietly saying, "Perhaps Stalin doesn't expect Boris to accept the invitation to journey with us."

"I don't think we're going to want to take Boris on another train ride if that's the only way we're going to get to Tirana" he replied slowly and rather cryptically.

Anna took the letter from Carl's hand before saying to him "Darling you haven't finished reading Stalin's letter. He says something about us boarding a captured Nazi U boat near coastal Tirana then making our way across the Adriatic Sea to the Mediterranean Sea through the Straits of Gibraltar then to England."

"We'll have to get to Tirana first. Has anyone considered how we are to travel by train over enemy territory to reach that impossible destination?" he asked sounding exasperated.

Anna didn't answer him.

They were unmindful that Dracula, accustomed to adopting other forms, had been listening to their conversation. "Like a fly on the wall I'm afraid I've overheard every word you've said" he cryptically remarked, seeming to appear out of nowhere. Boris may not make it to England or even as far as Tirana. I am here to insure that at least you and your Family do."

The couple readily accepted Dracula's offer for help, but were curious as to what method of travel he had in mind.

"A safe pathway to Tirana will be yours once you board a freight train manned by vampires" he assured her.

Anna gazed at Dracula questioningly. "Who has their loyalty the Fascist or Communist regime?"

Dracula smiled a cruel yet understanding smile. "Neither, their loyalty is to me. Since the vampires serve me it won't be necessary for me to accompany you on your journey. In my absence my army will protect you" he said disappearing into shadow.

Anna wondered when and how Boris would contact them. "He must have placed Stalin's letter near the entranceway for us to find," she said. "Her husband wasn't so sure."

"Surely one of Stalin's other agents placed the letter near the entranceway for us to discover" he said.

Later when Boris finally contacted the count, both seemed insincere and evasive in discussion of any plans regarding the forthcoming journey. They were unaware too that Dracula had stood in shadow listening to what each had said to the other during that meeting.

Later after Boris had left him, Carl turned and saw Dracula standing before him. "Don't worry. I'll make sure that nobody discovers Boris after you are safely aboard the train." If Carl thought Dracula's remark strange, he said nothing, and Dracula didn't bother to explain his rather bizarre comment. He had something more important to tell him. Carl listened with interest as Dracula explained to him why for centuries he'd lived the way he had.

"Now that you and your family are leaving, there is much you should know regarding me. I've been caught up in evil's maelstrom. I've been living in a nihilistic world devoid of values and morality. Unfortunately I am still an evil man but I look to a brighter future when I may regain what I've lost and become whole again. I've seen the goodness you and your family exemplify. I want to be like you again. Until then, I live as a vampire until I can earn release from the vampire's curse."

Carl contradicted Dracula by telling him that he had already won release from evil by helping him and his family escape war torn Russia. "You tell me that the vampires aboard the train my family and I will be boarding serve you. They serve you rather than political systems that are both amoral as well as immoral."

Dracula's smiled in response to the count's remark was almost benign as he listened in appreciation to the praise his descendant had bestowed upon him. "I'm glad you understand. We live in such decadent times. Even I cannot comprehend all the evil things that are now taking place in the world."

Chapter Twenty-two

It was a moonless night when Dracula led his family through the forest where the distant wolves howled beneath a spectacular array of starlight. The freight train had stopped less than a mile from the castle's confines and the family had to make their journey through the forest. "The wolves will miss you", said Dracula stopping to listen to their howls. They are bidding you farewell. I will miss you as well." If only Carl and his family knew how lonely I am, thought Dracula.

As if sensing Dracula's sadness, Anna said. "We shall meet again. We must someday somehow return the enormous kindness you have shown us." Dracula made a courtly bow to Anna but he didn't try to kiss her hand in farewell. Instead he stepped into shadow.

Unbeknown to Carl and Anna, Boris had been watching the family prepare to board the supply train. He knew the Nazis would want to know the identity of the strange tall man who'd accompanied the family through the forest. Boris also knew he had no intention of accompanying the family on their journey. The Nazis were winning the war and Boris wanted to stay in Romania and ally himself with the winning side. Yet he would pretend that he was going to accompany the count and his family to Tirana. As if sensing that someone was following him, Carl turned and saw Boris step out of shadow before approaching him. "Sorry to be turning up a little late" he said greeting Carl. "I hope you weren't holding the train for me" he said with a sinister smile.

Carl watched uneasily as Boris lagged behind him and his family preparing to board the train. He suspected that Boris might have come to kill him and that in doing so Boris hoped to ingratiate himself with a Nazi regime that considered the count to be a fugitive from justice. Carl had seen the gun Boris had placed inside his belt. He wasn't about to be the one to die. He didn't hesitate to do what he felt under the circumstances was necessary for him to do. Carl reached for his revolver and shot Boris dead.

Anna stared in shock at Boris' outstretched body before quickly going to her husband's side and embracing him. Carl held the revolver limply in hand and stared at Boris' lifeless body as Anna continued to embrace him. No one spoke until Carl placed the revolver back in its holster and said, "I guess Boris didn't want to accompany us."

"You only killed him before he had a chance to kill you" said Carl Nicholas.

Ivan agreed saying, "You had to do it Dad."

Dracula had been watching transpiring events from shadow but finally intervened. He picked Boris up in his arms then turned to the count and said, "Don't worry. I'll dispose of the body." No one made further comment. The vampires aboard the waiting supply train who'd also witnessed the evening's brief and shocking interlude behaved as if what they'd just seen was merely something encountered in a normal night's work. They calmly watched as Dracula slowly carried Boris away.

Once aboard the supply train, Carl, Anna and their sons tried to remain inconspicuous. They knew their presence aboard the train was dangerous and might expose Dracula's army to more than the usual risks encountered when delivering food and medical supplies to those needing them. The journey was no ordinary mission. Yet the vampires seemed genuinely interested in the count's family. One of them drew Carl into conversation and said, "We must travel only at night. We don't want to arouse suspicion. The stolen food and supplies we deliver are for the oppressed people of Tirana. We only pretend to be serving the Italian army."

The remark proved to be true when the train was forced to pick up a suspicious Italian officer insisting on accompanying the train and its cargo to Tirana. Within less than a few hours into his journey aboard the train, the officer's bloody unidentifiable body lay at the side of the tracks. No one dared accuse the vampire army of killing him so the train continued undeterred towards its destination.

"Our schedule seems to blend well with yours" said one of the vampires. We are pleased that you and your family are beginning fully to appreciate night's shroud for we find night to be flawless in that it offers perfect camouflage and protective coverage", he said in his perfect Italian that was understood by the count easily conversing with him.

"Few people understand the utter beauty and mystery of night that is enhanced by the majesty of a clear and brilliant starlit sky. There is nothing in daytime to compare with night," he said. "Any nocturnal creature whether it be owl, bat, wolf or cat understands the advantages of living by night rather than by day. Night creatures revere darkness as much as do those who praise daylight. Yet we miss the sun's light each morning when it touches night's shroud and allows night to disappear and sleep" said the vampire. Carl watched the vampire leader partially open the train's sliding car door step, forward and stand at the car's edge so he could gaze at the night sky.

As the train traveled forward, Carl and his family became fascinated by the the nocturnal creatures aboard the train. The night's cosmic rhythm swept the train and its occupants forward and the train seemed to float effortlessly above the tracks as in deep darkness it moved closer towards its destination. During that journey the count's family drew to understand Dracula's vampire army. They knew that army was extending services to those during wartime who otherwise might be denied them.

When they finally arrived in Tirana and were met by a Communist leader of the Albanian Resistance movement Carl's family saw firsthand that Tirana was a desolate place under the loathsome yoke of Italian Fascism. The late afternoon sky was overcast and the poverty of war was reflected in the sad faces of people who had lost everything but their individual dignity. That dignity was reflected in the tired lined face of the man who drove the car that transferred the family to a rocky coast where a fishing boat waited and was ready to take the count and his family into the deep waters of the Adriatic Sea for a planned rendezvous with a u boat. The day was cloudy and the sea surrounding the rocky coastline appeared gray and forbidding but the rain had held off as the family climbed aboard the fishing boat that took them nearly ten miles off shore.

As the fishing boat moved across the waters of the Adriatic, the sea seemed relatively calm but the fishing boat bobbed up and down as tidal currents created small waves upon the sea's surface. The sky was almost enveloped in near darkness when a u boat suddenly surfaced alongside the waiting boat. For a few moments, there was confusion. The count couldn't be sure if he and his family were boarding the Russian captured Nazi u boat or another one. In dusk's dim light Carl could see that the boat he and his family were to board bore the dreaded swastika symbol. It was only after a man dressed as a Russian officer lifted the u boat hatch and beckoned for the count and his family to come aboard that the transfer from fishing boat to u boat was made. The hatch then was closed and tightened after one at a time the members of Carl's family came aboard the submarine and it submerged beneath the sea's dark surface. "We were startled by the swastika symbol" said Carl shaking hands with the captain, a thin middle aged man dressed entirely in black before introducing Anna and their sons to him.

"You must bear in mind that these waters are infested by Nazi ships and submarines. We don't want to erase the u boat's swastika symbol and draw attention to ourselves." Carl seemed satisfied by the captain's explanation and gave him an understanding nod as he, Anna and their sons were shown to their quarters.

For a family that was used to the outdoors and open spaces, life aboard the small cramped u boat seemed like a challenge. Anna grimaced holding her small dog in her arms but said nothing about how much she loathed being introduced to such an incredibly cramped place. She quickly realized that while she and her sons were aboard the u boat they wouldn't see much of Carl either.

After becoming settled in his family's quarters, the captain took the count aside and told him that the rescue of him and his family had been only the first step in a mission that Stalin wanted fulfilled. He knew Carl was an explosives expert and that during the Russian Revolution he had helped the revolutionists. Now his services again would be required.

"In a few days we'll be passing through the Mediterranean, and approaching the Straits of Gibraltar. There is a Nazi ship anchored in the channel blocking access to Allied movement and shipping. We need to destroy it. Our mission must remain secretive though. Your wife and sons must know nothing about this."

The count nodded his head agreeing to the secrecy as he was led to the small room where the explosives for the mission were being worked upon and assembled. The two men introduced to him, said little to each other as the count joined them and quickly became involved in the task at hand. For the next few days, Carl saw little of his family. It was only late one night when Carl took Anna aside and told her what he must do. She didn't want for him to see her cry. She didn't want their sons to be alarmed either. She and Carl wouldn't tell them about the dangerous mission their father was about to undertake. In her heart she knew they must have known when they watched them hold each other tightly before their father left her side and prepared to embark on a mission that for days had been planned in advance.

* * * *

The u boat approached the Nazi ship at anchor in the channel when it would be most vulnerable to sabotage. The sea was calm and the sky completely dark as the submerged u boat partially emerged less than 100 feet from the Nazi ship. The boat's hatch then opened as the count clothed in black, slipped into the darkness. Night's shroud that for centuries had protected his ancestor, hovered over him as Carl left his companion-in-sabotage behind and made his way alone towards the ship. The count had told the man assisting him not to follow him in the dangerous mission unless it became apparent that Carl needed rescue. The count quickly paddled the rubber craft carrying the deadly explosive filled barrels across water. As he approached the ship floating like some monstrous black duck atop an inky glasslike surface, Carl nervously wondered if the Nazis hadn't had a plan in place for detecting potential saboteurs. He hastily searched for any sort of counter device hidden upon the watery surface that might set off an explosion tearing him and his craft apart. Seeing none, Carl drew closer to the dark ship silhouetted against an even darker sky where there seemed to be no separation between sky and sea. Carl felt as if the darkness surrounding him had swallowed him but he detected no danger as he magnetically attached the deadly barrels against the ship's hull. As he prepared to disengage himself from his dangerous encounter with the ship, Carl also wondered if there wasn't anyone on land or sea who'd seen what he'd done. Even though it was a moonless night there was still just enough light shining from offshore that made total emersion in darkness nearly impossible. Carl's hands trembled as for the last time he adjusted and retested the explosives' timing devices that were timed to go off after the u boat had passed through the Straits and was safely at sea. He then paddled his craft away from the deadly barrels and made his way back towards the u boat. To any possible nearby observer, the deadly barrels took on a benign character and appeared like flotsam and jetsam bobbing harmlessly upon the water's surface. Carl didn't look back to observe his handiwork though. He quickly boarded the u boat that looked like some partially submerged black whale swimming through the dangerous Straits and into the Atlantic Ocean. Less than an hour later and still enshrouded by deep darkness, the u boat emerged from the sea. An explosion was heard and an enormous red fire ball seen for miles around leaped into the sky. Carl hastily scrambled to open the u boat's hatch so he could have a look. "Mission accomplished" he said before quickly ducking down beneath the hatch and tightening it behind him.

The Captain shook Carl's hand and commended him and the man with him on a job well done. If he'd been fearful that Carl might have failed in his mission, the captain never let the count know how terrifying his ordeal had been for them but Anna quickly went to her husband who held her tightly in his arms. The count's sons patted their father on the back and commended him on his success too as the captain said, "We'll have to refuel at some point so our next destination will be a small out of the way island in the Azores."

* * * *

It was dark and late one evening when the u boat pulled alongside a hidden station in the Azores where the job of checking the vessel's seaworthiness took place. The count, his two sons and the other men all with rifles in hand stepped off the u boat so they could guard the vessel as it underwent refueling. Although Carl had wanted Anna to stay aboard the boat while it was refueled, she insisted on accompanying her husband and sons as they briefly stepped ashore. Carl handed Anna a revolver as she waited for the men to complete the task of carrying extra boxes of food and drinking water aboard. As the men worked, Anna had observed. She had shivered in darkness when she saw lights of a distant ship drawing closer to them with each passing moment. Then after the u boat was again boarded and had slipped into open water the ominous shadow of the distant ship with its twinkling lights came into clear view. The captain who'd wanted at all costs to conserve the u boat's batteries during the last leg of the voyage said that they might have to dive.

"We won't have to do that", said Carl knowing that the u boat was capable of evading an approaching vessel by using night's shroud as protective armor against attack. "We won't have to outrun the ship we will simply slip away from it unnoticed." The captain pulled his black turtleneck up so it was almost around his ears and said, rather mockingly "do you mean we hide like this?"

"I'll show you how it's done" said Carl now wearing the protective black cape similar to the one he'd worn the day he'd saved Anna. He pushed open the submarine's hatch, and stood atop the vessel. The moonless night and calm sea surrounding him enveloped him and the vessel in a canopy of solid darkness as Carl became at one with his environment. He then cautiously watched the ship slowly move away from the u boat as if it were a mere phantom before quickly stepping down into the u boat and closing the hatch behind him.

Several days passed. The u boat's swastika symbol that had been camouflage in enemy waters now was becoming a matter of concern to the u boat's crew. They were drawing closer to the English coastline. Hopefully the allies would realize what the dangerous mission had entailed, and had been briefed about the necessity of retaining the swastika symbol prominently displayed upon the captured u boat's bow. Carl cautiously pushed the hatch open and looked up at a partially gray and cloudy sky. Thankfully a few allied planes had acknowledged their dangerous mission now completed. They flew overhead guarding the final portion of a perilous journey as dawn began to envelope the sky in its stark gray shroud.

Carl then stepped down from the hatch so Anna could have a look too. She gazed at a foggy distant landscape and sighed with relief when she realized that she and her family had made their impossible journey a reality. Gradually the foggy blur came into focus and the sun made its way above the horizon as land sharply came into view. Later a nearby craft transported the family safely ashore. Once there a fellow agent met Carl and Anna and told them that their sons would be shown to temporary quarters. "You may accompany them there and rest first but later, a car will pick you and your wife up and deliver you to Stalin's secret compound. He is concluding meetings with British commanders today and he'd like to see you this afternoon."

Carl's dangerous mission had not escaped Stalin's attention. Although he was exhausted with the burdens he carried in regard to directing war efforts at the Russian front, Stalin realized that Carl had scored a stunning Russian victory at sea. He carefully perused the intelligence report providing him with details of the mission and only looked up from it when a guard led the count into his presence.

The dictator reached out and shook Carl's hand before inviting his friend to be seated in a chair opposite his. Then drawing upon his pipe before placing it aside he said in his usual gruff voice, "If you hadn't shot Boris before you boarded the train for the Albanian coast I would have had you both shot upon arrival there. Fortunately you chose the proper course of action for self-preservation. You shot Boris before he killed you."

Carl appeared rather uncomfortable with Stalin's remarks regarding that fateful night. "He was lagging behind the rest of us. He was armed and wearing a Nazi uniform when I shot him. He's a traitor!" Stalin again picked up the pipe he'd been smoking and carefully considered what Carl had just told him. He then slowly got up from where he'd been sitting, walked towards a window and gazed outside at the peaceful English countryside. He then turned and walked back towards his desk before sitting down again. Comrade Stalin hesitated before he told Carl what he knew he wanted to hear.

"I commend you for destroying the Nazi ship anchored in the channel blocking access to the Gibraltar Straits. In fact, had you not done so, I might have looked upon your actions as disloyal." The count who appeared rather pale still said nothing. Then getting up from where he sat Stalin slowly paced up and down the room before turning and facing Carl. When he did so, he spoke slowly and deliberately. "Your service to me and to Russia is not just recognized and appreciated. Your contribution to Russia's cause will be needed again in the difficult times ahead."Carl smiled and thanked Stalin for the acknowledgement yet he knew whatever service he extended to Russia would have to take in the broader Allied cause. He knew he had passed through freedom's gate and must continue moving forward. He then warmly shook hands with Stalin who led him to the door.

After Carl left his office, one of Stalin's aides handed him a letter. Carl took the letter from his hands then sat down beside Anna. Since Bockev's letter was to them both, Carl gave the letter to Anna which she quickly opened and began reading aloud.

"He wants us to live in the house that he bought from you. He and your mother are living in the specious guesthouse behind it. The house is ours. How kind!" she said.

Since finding proper housing was a problem during wartime, Carl was grateful to Bockev for his generosity.

Anna had missed her mother-in-law and Bockev. "The boys will be delighted. There are horses and a stable" she said handing the letter back to Carl. As she did she glanced at his face. He seemed sad and uneasy. He knew Stalin wanted to see her too. Sensing her husband's mood, she said softly. "Remember that day following Kirov's funeral? I felt as if you thought I was trying to make a choice between you and someone else. I've always loved Russia. The memory of almost everything or anyone I've ever known and loved is there or buried in Russia. But we've left Russia. I've never regretted any of the actions I've taken in life so far." The count took Anna's hand in his then raised it to his lips and kissed it. Stalin's office door swung open. A guard stepped out of the office and stood in front of Anna where she sat alongside her husband.

"Stalin will see you now" he said as Anna left her chair and walked towards the dictator's office. The door opened for her then closed behind her.

Stalin smiled at Anna as he welcomed her into the room but his gaze was grave and sad. "The times are very difficult. The struggle ahead for Russia and its people will be great." Anna was the last ruling Tsar's daughter. He wanted to tell her that she belonged in Russia alongside the people her father once had ruled but the words wouldn't come. Anna sensed Stalin's sentiment and emotion. She understood the dictator's reluctance to allow her to be absent from Russia.

She gazed into Stalin's eyes as she had that day so many years earlier when he'd made her come to Leningrad. Nicholas II was a good man. You are his daughter. I'm saving your husband's life because your husband is a good man too, and because I love you, she'd remembered him saying.

Anna took Stalin's hand gently in own. There were tears in her eyes. She felt torn by sadness and seemed almost indecisive when she said quietly "I love my husband's home in Romania. We hope to return there someday. There is much in Russia I love too. I have both cherished and painful memories of Russia." Then as if looking for a mutual sense of unspoken understanding between them she gazed into Stalin's eyes before finally saying, "We live in uncertain times. If I don't survive this war, promise me that you will have my remains returned to Russia and placed with those of the rest of my family." Stalin was silent for a moment. He didn't want to contemplate the worst but he seemed puzzled by what she'd said to him. He wasn't going to probe or ask for an explanation regarding her request. Instead he replied slowly and deliberately, "You have my word." They then embraced. For a few minutes they just held each other as if they were trying to hold onto the strength and goodness that cemented a lasting alliance of love and loyalty that had been there through all the years of terror and struggle they'd lived through. He knew she had walked through the gate towards her own destiny. They both knew she belonged to Russia. Stalin was determined that someday Anna would return to Russia. He kissed her. It was a farewell kiss. Then with both hands upon her shoulders, he slowly but gently pushed her away from him before quietly saying, "Go to him. He is waiting for you." When Anna left Stalin's office, there were tears in her eyes. She wanted to look back but didn't. She only hoped that circumstances somehow would draw them together again. She didn't bother to put on the coat she had with her. Instead she carried it neatly over her arm as almost in a daze she moved towards her husband.

From a window, Stalin watched her. Carl's head was bowed and his back was turned from her as if he half expected that Anna wouldn't be accompanying him on their new journey. Anna approached him. She spoke softly to him and he turned when she said "He told me you were waiting for me". Carl then took Anna in his arms before burying his face in her lovely loose hair. For a moment he silently held her before they stepped into the waiting car leaving the past and the long journey behind them.

www.ingramcontent.com/pod-product-compliance
Ingram Content Group UK Ltd.
Pitfield, Milton Keynes, MK11 3LW, UK
UKHW040602210726
13854UKWH00008B/1811